"Is there anything better than a GREAT second chance romance with the monsters of the past threatening to destroy everything? **Lakeshore Secrets** *by Shannyn Leah has hit my Hidden Gem pile!..."* **~Dii, Tometender**

"This story is a great story about going home again and family bonds. I can't wait to read the next book In the series..." **~Vicki, The Page Turner**

"Highly entertaining and a complete page-turner. Prior adolescent relationships and family issues combined in a romantic and dramatic story..." **~ Lori, Wee Bit O Whiskey**

"This book is an emotional roller coaster at times. This is truly a great and exciting read. You will not want to put the book down because as usual the Shannyn Leah pulls you into the book from the beginning..." **~ Cathy, Rochelle's Reviews**

"I really enjoyed the chemistry and the secondary characters in this book so I will be reading the rest of what looks to be a fantastic series by Shannyn Leah." **~ Jackie, MI Bookshelf**

D1104601

SHANNYN LEAH

Lakeshore Secrets

SHANNYN LEAH

Lakeshore Secrets

The McAdams Sisters

Book One, Kate McAdams

By The Lake Series

Shannyn Leah

SHANNYN LEAH

For the woman who's always given me encouragement and inspiration to write my stories down, my Momma!

SHANNYN LEAH

Chapter One

KATE MCADAMS' BREATH caught in her chest as she stepped through the automatic doors of The Caliendo Resort.

She was certain this trip would be a landslide of regret, anger and resentment. It was simply a matter of which McAdams would break down first. Out of her entire family, she hadn't considered it would probably be her...until she felt her legs beginning to tremble as she walked through the resort's lobby.

She should have skipped the pencil-line dress and worn dress pants to conceal the tremors.

So much had changed in the last six years that only the building structure of the resort was recognizable. The check-in desk was no longer the central point of the lobby now situated along the far wall tucked under a curved balcony. A new large crystal chandelier hung above a marble-patterned floor. It was brighter, the walls an off white with more lights. So bright, it felt like you were still outside. Change everywhere.

Maybe she would blend in with the change and no one would notice her. Kate wasn't the same little tom-boy climbing up trees without a care in the world. Instead she had to take over her dad's duties when he couldn't even get off the couch. A mess of a thing she had been back then, tromping around in ripped jeans and stained t-shirts, slinging a toolbox in her hands and driving around in his jalopy of a truck to this very resort to sneak around and attend to what her father, Kent should have been undertaking. It had been his job, not hers. But their roles had been reversed when Kate had been forced to grow up in the blink of an eye due to her dad's alcoholic ways.

Her eyes traveled now down the hall that led to the silver ballroom, remembering the day that changed her life forever. Tremors overtook her body again as she remembered the night her mother was rushed out of the resort on a stretcher...the night her mother had died.

Kate shook her head back and came to reality, fluttering her eyelids to keep the tears at bay. She sucked in a deep breath to flush the tingling away and brought her attention back to the front desk.

You can do this.

It would have helped if Derek was standing by her side like she'd originally planned when booking their suite at the resort. But then she hadn't expected to come home and find him sleeping with his secretary...in their bed.

Kate shuddered but didn't know if it was the memory of Derek or from the steps she took closer to the check-in desk.

The girls standing behind the counter were young, maybe early twenties.

As Kate was about to give the bubbly girl behind the counter her name, she thought how the girl's smile should have been relaxing instead of irritating. Kate tried to relax, but then she heard someone calling her.

No. She wasn't ready. She wasn't ready!

She turned to see Izzy Caliendo walking her way.

It couldn't have been worse if it had been Marc Caliendo, Izzy's older brother, himself. Okay, that wasn't true. It would have been far worse if it was Marc calling her...although she was pretty sure he wouldn't call her if he did see her. He would walk away from Kate just like she had been forced to walk away from him six years ago. She felt herself slipping back to that fateful conversation with Marc's father six years ago and the sadness that had consumed her since overwhelmed her again. Walking away from Marc, her best friend, had been the hardest choice she'd ever had to make.

"Oh my gosh!" Izzy squealed as Kate greeted her wearing one of those fake smiles she'd perfected over the years. "I can't believe it's you. That you are *here.*"

Izzy wrapped her arms around Kate and squeezed. Kate's resolve flew out the window. Why had she kept this reservation at the resort? It was clear there were too many memories and reminders here, making this such a terrible idea.

"Hey Izzy," she managed to choke out.

Izzy pulled away, but kept her hands clamped around Kate's arms. For such a small thing, she had a killer grasp.

"Abby didn't tell me you were staying here." Izzy frowned and Kate watched a new and serious side appear on the young blonde's face. "Actually, Abby hasn't told me much. She's stopped responding to my texts and I've gone over there every day—a few times—and she's not answering the door."

Kate felt her motherly instincts kick in at Izzy's news.

Abby was the baby of the McAdams family—and Izzy's best friend. With Abby's twin brother, Avery, touring with his band, Inch Away, and unable to make it to the funeral, Kate was sure Abby would be the one to fall apart first.

Izzy continued. "And when I do see her, she's super quiet. I don't think she's taking Grace's death very well."

Inescapable sadness consumed Kate's body at the mention of her dead gran's name. It pierced through her layers of protective clothing, like the cold, bitter, November chill until it reached deep inside to run its frosty fingers over her sheltered areas.

Pull it together, Kate.

She resumed her fake smile, adding reassurance for her sister's friend. "None of us are taking it well, but we will have each other. We will work through this," she assured Izzy.

"Have you talked to Marc?" And, just like that, Izzy was onto the next subject.

"No. I thought he was working at a resort down south?" *Oh, please let him be at the resort down south.*

Izzy smirked.

Oh no.

She let Kate's arms go. "You don't know?"

Know what? Was he married?

Kate wanted to slap herself upside the head. It didn't matter if he was married. Why was that the first thing to enter her head? She'd almost been married. Just two days ago she'd been engaged to her boss and planning a wedding. It didn't matter if Marc was married. He had moved on regardless.

"Marc came back after Dad died. He took over Dad's position and is working with Uncle Carl running the chain," Izzy said, looking pleased with herself.

Kate's emotions went into overdrive. The mention of Robert Caliendo, Izzy and Marc's father, sent chills through her body. She was fully aware that he was dead. She wouldn't be standing in this resort if he were still alive...she wasn't even sure she'd have come back to Willow Valley if Robert had still been here.

The feelings of dread fought in her stomach with the feelings of excitement and fear.

Marc was back? Marc was back!

How did she not know this? Gran had phoned her at least every other day before she passed and she had never mentioned Marc had come back to town. Odd since Grad had talked about all the other local gossip.

"I didn't know that," Kate admitted.

"Where is your number two?" Izzy asked, glancing around the foyer, taking note through the glass front doors of Kate's parked, and empty, car. "You're booked in the premium suite for two...right?" Izzy's dark questioning eyes looked at Kate.

Kate loosened her jaw before replying. "I'm here alone."

Izzy's round eyes lit up and Kate silently cursed Derek.

Darn him and his cheating ways.

Shouldn't Kate have seen the signs long before? He had left his wife for Kate in the first place...once a cheater, always a cheater.

"Miss McAdams," the receptionist said, handing her a

key and naming off her room number.

"Thank you," Kate said, taking the key. "Well, I'm all set. I better go and get settled and then locate Abby."

At the mention of her best friend's name, Izzy's face turned back to one of the concerned friend. "That's a good idea. Can you tell her to call me or text me?"

Kate hugged Izzy this time. "I will."

"Thanks."

Kate started toward the door. *One Caliendo down and hopefully no more to go.*

Park the car. Get to your room and change, and then off to the meeting at the funeral home...after locating Abby.

"Hey Kate!" Izzy called behind her.

Kate turned.

"Marc's single too." Izzy winked then walked away, leaving Kate unsure how to handle the thrill the simple fact sent through her.

Chapter Two

MARC CALIENDO FLIPPED senselessly through the contract in front of him.

He knew his uncle had already thoroughly read and re-read every last detail, and was satisfied with the outcome, but Marc had insisted. Even if it had been drawn up by their lawyer, wanted to be sure everything was to their benefit. After all, it wasn't just his own money he was investing, but the entire family's money.

But Marc was annoyed that he was too distracted to comprehend any of the content in front of him. He repeatedly flipped from beginning to end without even reading a full sentence.

Argh.

He pushed the papers away, dragging his elbows back across the large antique desk and rubbing his hands over his face.

If only he could wipe away his distractions like the cleaning ladies quick hands worked away at the streaks on his office windows until the glass gleamed crystal clear.

He needed a crystal clear mind to focus today.

Marc reluctantly pulled the papers back with the tips of his fingers, as though they were laced in poison. Taking a deep breath he slowly exhaled, hoping to breathe out all the rattling thoughts swirling around his mind.

Reading was his hobby, always had been, so this should be a breeze.

He flipped to the first page again, bent close to the pages with intention of total concentration.

Let's get through this, he thought, to go play a game of racket instead. Physical exertion was exactly what he needed to quench this anxiety he felt creeping up every time his thoughts drifted to *her*.

He hadn't even made it through one page, when his office door burst open, collapsing his concentration once again.

His youngest sister Isabelle Caliendo, or Izzy as most people called her, waltzed through the door in her carefree butterfly way, content on fluttering from one branch to the next without a worry behind those huge brown eyes of hers.

He was certain this unannounced visit would contain one very inconsequential detail that she considered "end of the world" necessary to share before she would move onto her next whim.

He could only hope she'd make the interruption fast..

"Did you know..." she started, weaving her way slowly across his office, purposely passing by the matching, comfortable leather chairs.

She travelled to his side of the desk instead and plopped her tiny self on top of all his paperwork, crossing her eighties stonewashed clad legs and sending him a questioning stare.

That was his cue to sit back, cross his arms and suffer through all that was about to follow.

"...that Katherine McAdams booked a room here? In this very resort? In a premium suite?" It was a question and statement all in one long, stretched-out breath.

How exhausting it must be to be her, he thought, watching her round and wide eyes stare him down, attempting to interpret his solemn expression.

Good luck.

Unfortunately, she wasn't finished.

"And," she dragged on dramatically. "It's booked for two people. *Two*," she clarified crisply, holding up two of her perfectly manicured fingers in his face for emphasis.

He wanted to grab the two fingers and drag her out of his office. Then he'd proceed to call the locksmith. He was rather tired of his family disrupting him, always unannounced, as though he sat around behind that big office door restlessly waiting for them to pop in for conversations about...*her*. Perhaps a bit harsh, since technically this was the only conversation he'd had about her...today.

Izzy let her long, wavy, dyed-blonde hair fall at her sides as she leaned towards him. "It's probably a man," she whispered, as though the walls eavesdropped on the super undercover secret she was disclosing.

She nodded at Marc, her wide, over-dramatized eyes, only inches away from his. "I think she has a boyfriend."

Of course she has a boyfriend. It might even be a fiancée or a husband...although if it was either of the latter he was sure Abby would have informed Izzy, and Izzy would have already had *that* conversation with him, too.

"Don't you have somewhere you could be?" he asked, not giving her the satisfaction of an answer or reaction. Anything he said or did would certainly get twisted as she proceeded to notify every other family member about this scandalous story.

Her mouth dropped open. "Aren't you embarrassed? I would be embarrassed."

He was sure she embarrassed herself plenty enough on her own without dragging unnecessary embarrassing situations into her life.

"I mean, you don't have anyone!" Izzy sat back, picking up a glass paperweight from his desk and tossing it from hand to hand. "Like, you have Melissa but I can see that's not going anywhere, especially in, like, the next hour." She stared at the ceiling for a moment. "Well, on her part it could happen in the next second. Literally, you could pick up the phone, call her in here, sweep her off her feet like she wants you to and then you would have someone."

Marc remained stoic, but leveled a gaze on her that could not be misconstrued.

She rolled her eyes. "But since that's not happening, you really have no one, and that's just embarrassing. Don't you agree?" She arched her eyebrows waited for his response.

"I don't agree with any of that."

She continued as if she hadn't heard him. "I mean I would hide in here if I was you, like you're doing."

It stumped him that she thought he was hiding the few times he was in his office. He did *work* in here. This resort didn't run itself and, although there were managers in almost all areas of the resort, they all came to him when situations arose. Another reason he couldn't call a locksmith.

"I would remain in this room so you don't run into her and her obviously well-off man...if she's in the premium suite," she continued.

His eyes followed the paperweight in her hands, back

and forth...back and forth.

"And she looks just as gorgeous as ever." That snapped his eyes back to his sister. "Like, Abby texted me some pics. Do you want to see?"

Yes! "No."

She shrugged. "Trust me, you *don't* want to have to look at her and say that you're *single*." She clenched her teeth together and sucked in a breath. "Yikes, that would be embarrassing." She waved her hand in front of him. "See where I'm going with this?"

He really wished he didn't.

"Why *are* you single anyway?"

"Why are you?" he retorted.

"Because I'm young and in my prime. Why would I ever settle down with one person right now?"

At her age, Marc had already planned exactly who he would settle down with. Although that hadn't gone so well for him...so possibly his younger sister had a good point. *Possibly.*

"You're old."

He was only seven years older than her. *A seven year gap qualified him as old?*

"And it seems as though you're still in love with Kate and that's why you won't let anyone else into your heart."

He gripped the arms of his leather chair. Perhaps they should switch positions if she was going to give him a free therapy session.

"Are you emotionally unavailable Marcus?"

"Oh, honestly Isabelle Caliendo, get off your brother's desk and stop mocking him," the next unannounced sibling, Violet, scoffed, as she settled herself across from

Marc in one of the leather chairs.

Her dark blonde hair was pulled into a stylish knot at the back of her head, not one piece of hair astray, complimenting her dark grey skirt and blazer. Sophisticated and poised as always, the perfect looking events planner.

Violet was two years his junior with similarities in regards to how a well-mannered person behaves in public.

"What were you, like, five when she left?" Violet asked.

Izzy turned and shot her older sister a disgusted look. "I wasn't five, *Violet*. What were you like twenty-one?" she asked Marc.

Twenty-three, but he wasn't going to bother correcting her. That was his last year of university, the last year they were supposed to be apart.

"You're acting like it now," Violet said to Izzy.

Izzy rolled her eyes back to her brother. "She was like this the *whole* time you were gone," she quietly whispered, but not so quiet that their sister didn't hear. "Like an old mother hen," she continued, raising her voice as she hopped off the desk and to her feet.

She stopped by Violet and kissed the side of her head. "You do know we already have one of those wondering around here somewhere, right?"

Violet smiled up at her sister. "Why don't you go find Mother and ask her to refresh your manners or, at the very least, teach you about the filter for your mouth? You know, that part of your brain that tells you when to speak and when not to."

Violet made a shoeing motion at her.

"Go, ask Mom to indulge you on how useful it is to

listen to that filter."

It was a playful tease to one another and yet it held a brutal honesty to all of it. Violet was sensible and sometimes a tad overbearing. Izzy was careless and rash.

"I love you big sis." Izzy turned to Marc as she moved to the door. "Oh yeah, by the way, Kate is here and she's alone. No boyfriend, no fiancé, no nothing. Alone and sizzling hot." Izzy shut the door loudly behind her.

Kate was here *now*? *And alone?*

Marc wished Violet hadn't also barged into his office so he would have time to absorb this in private.

Absorb what? She left you, the end. What was left to absorb?

"I don't understand why she doesn't have a job," Marc grumbled, shaking his head and proceeding to flip pages.

Violet understood he worked, and hopefully she would follow Izzy out the door without another word of who had booked a room, and how many people were booked per room, and especially no more talk of McAdams girls. More specifically, Kate McAdams.

"I mean a trip around the world after university and one would think she'd had enough play time," he continued.

"I would say it's her way of grieving the loss of Father, but we all know that's just something we tell our acquaintances, right?" Violet said. "And besides, you just returned from your trip, what five years later?"

"I was employed and earning a living. She runs around like money falls out of trees and work is something to make fun of."

Violet gave him a serious face. "I really believe she

does think money falls out of trees."

He couldn't help but laugh and his sister smiled. Then her serious face reappeared.

"I wanted to pop by to make sure you were okay, since I assumed you'd heard by now. Mom told us, and clearly Izzy couldn't wait to...tease you."

Her choice of word wasn't a term he would use, more like harass or dig for details to gossip. Either way, yes, he'd heard.

He looked up at his sister. "Violet, really? Do you honestly think I'm sitting in my office reflecting about a girl, and she was a girl then, that broke my heart?" He paused. "Years ago?"

Exactly six years ago, but he wasn't going to remind her of that detail.

She shrugged, looking somewhat embarrassed. Violet didn't embarrass easily.

"I don't know. That's why I'm here," she said.

Marc sighed. "Honestly, since I've returned, I haven't had time to think about anything else except running this resort. This week alone I had to fix a double booking in the Courtier Room."

He looked up at her, eyebrows raised, reminding her she'd been the one that had double booked the room.

She narrowed her eyes at him, accepting the blame.

He continued. "The ski hill is asking for extra hands but I have to double check the records and see if it's feasible or if we should just wait until next season. Plus the golf course is adding that new addition by the lake come early spring and the new plans have to be settled before then."

He smiled at her sincerely. "And if I had the time, the

last thing I would be doing is pining. I'm assuming that's what you're assuming I'm doing? That I've been pining for her all these years and I absolutely cannot get her out of my mind and now that she's coming here, probably with a man, I'm scheming of a way to win her back."

A deep red tint crossed Violet's porcelain skin. "Well, when you say it like that, you make it sound ridiculous."

"That's because it is ridiculous."

She grinned. "I guess so."

He nodded, satisfied she believed that load of nonsense. He might not be pining, but Kate was popping into his thoughts more than he liked, which was one time too many.

"Marc do you remember when we were kids playing in the bush that time you found the baby bird that had fallen from its nest? You insisted on taking it home. Remember?"

He remembered.

His sisters hadn't wanted to quit playing. He had been around seven at the time, and all his younger sisters were running around hollering, "Let's go Marc!" But he'd dragged them all home to find his mother. He remembered the exact trail they'd traveled through the large bush to find that tiny bird, all alone on the ground.

"Spark, you named it. You took care of it for a couple days, and when that little bird died you ran to Mom and Dad crying. Dad told you that was part of life."

Robert's exact words had been, *Marcus, stop crying and man up. Things die, that's the harsh reality we live in. If you cry like a baby no one will respect you.* His mother, Eliza had hushed her husband and talked Marc through it.

"And then for days you were moping around lost in

your own world trying to understand why the bird died."

Marc wasn't positive where Violet was going with this, but he understand death now and he had a feeling it had nothing to do with that topic.

How was she going to spin this about Kate?

"Mom took you to the library and into the educational section and you checked out all these books about the body and how it operated and finally when you returned those books it was because you understood why the body died." She paused. "So Marc, I'm not concerned you're pining about Kate. I'm just afraid you haven't got the right answers to let her go."

That was ridiculous. Marc wasn't looking for answers. He wasn't embarrassed like Izzy suggested or interested in anything to with Kate. He wasn't pining away for her or wondering why she left. He was simply angry she kept popping into his mind. Besides, how he felt wasn't any of anyone else's business anyway.

"I'm not a little vulnerable child anymore Violet, so you don't have to worry about me."

"I'm your sister. It's my job to worry." Reluctantly, she stood. "Fine, carry on with, your non-pining, strictly working kind of day."

"Thank you, and how about passing our conversation along to all the Caliendo women, so I can avoid this awkward conversation again."

"It was a little awkward," she admitted. "I should have just let Izzy continue her prying and watched how that played out."

He was thankful she hadn't.

There was a knock on his door, which meant it was

absolutely not any of his family members and was more than likely an actual work situation he'd have to deal with. He didn't mind, in fact, he was relieved.

"Marc?" Melissa's soft voice called through the solid wood door.

"Come in."

She pushed the door open a crack and smiled at him, flashing Violet a friendly smile too.

"There's a problem in the pool room and Kent's not here and nobody's sure who is working for him today. Would you mind going down and seeing what the problem is?"

Kent McAdams...Kate's dad.

He was off for funeral arrangements due to the passing of his mother-in-law...the only thing that would drag Kate back home.

Marc wanted to literally shake that thought out of his head but opted for nodding at Melissa instead, who smiled a little longer than necessary and stayed a little longer than required.

When she finally shut the door, Violet looked at him and said, "Don't marry that one Marc."

Marry? Melissa? Never.

"Emma thinks she's perfect but honestly, between you and me, there's something not quite right about her. I know she's Emma's friend but take my word for it. I have this mother hen intuition."

Violet winked.

"Thank you Violet...for all your concern today regarding my love life, but I think I can manage on my own."

He stood and guided her out of his office.

She grinned at him as she entered the hallway.

"You're really not doing such a hot job by yourself," she whispered to him.

He glared at her. "Honestly? Should I start addressing you as Isabelle?"

She playfully hit his shoulder. "Please don't."

She waved and turned in the opposite direction.

Marc headed towards the pool room.

His love life was fine. There was no need to manage anything. His whole life was fine.

He would read that contract before the two weeks were up and be prepared. He and his uncle Carl would then head north to look at the hotel they were interested in buying. For the next few days all he had to do was concentrate on avoiding any contact with Kate.

How hard could that be?

Chapter Three

KATE HEARD HER phone vibrate as she unpacked her suitcase.

Derek...again.

She glared at the screen. The last thing she needed right now was a stream of texts from a man several provinces away.

Sorry babe. Will see you when you get home.

Was he serious? The only thing he would be seeing was her back walking out of his office after she quit.

Maybe that was a bit drastic, but what was she supposed to do? Continue? She didn't respond to the lying jerk and tossed her phone on the sofa, groaning in frustration.

Another reminder she was doing this all alone booked in, partially unpacked, and staying at the Caliendo Resort. She could have screamed. Quite possibly, in the large three-room suite, no one would have heard her.

She stripped off her clothes with the intention of partaking of a cold shower in the gorgeous marble tile bathroom, hoping it would cool the fire scorching beneath her skin. Instead, she slipped into her swimsuit, a cute little one piece with cut-out sides, and pulled a dress overtop.

A lap or two in the guest pool would be much more effective.

She took the elevator to the second floor where the

pool sat waiting, and made her way past plenty of smiling and laughing guests who were enjoying their visit.

Why wouldn't they be lavishing themselves in the highest rated resort in the area?

The resort was tastefully sectioned off into two wings, one for families and the other for couples and singles, and offered plenty of amenities to attract guests.

Their grand indoor pools, indoor water park, game room, exercise room, three on-site restaurants with buffets, as well as indoor tennis courts, outdoor golf course in the summer and a ski and snowboarding hill in the winter, made this resort *the* place to vacation. For a set rate you could also purchase an all-inclusive week's stay.

When Derek had requested the finest place to stay in the area, Kate could have said she'd researched The Caliendo Resort and discovered it was the top rated, but that would have been a lie. She'd known about the resort without any research.

Kate was staying in the couples/singles wing of the resort, so it was quiet by the pool. No kids screaming and splashing, only elderly couples floating in the shallow end.

She spotted the sauna and abandoned the cold pool water for warmth. A relaxing moment was exactly what she needed to clear her thoughts and push Derek to the back burner so she could strengthen her emotions before she met with her dad and sisters.

The door to the sauna stood wide open, and she pulled it shut behind her, welcoming the warmth that penetrated deep into her skin like a calming embrace on her soul, and easing the needed release of all the worries flagging her tired mind.

"Ma'am, catch that door!" a loud voice startled her and she reached for the door, just as it closed at her fingertips.

She bit her bottom lip.

Uh-oh.

There was more than one reason for the alarm bells that were going off in her head, and they didn't have anything to do with the closed door.

She turned slowly.

The high temperature may have been warming her exterior but the jolting warmth tunneling into the deepest parts of her body like waves of electric shocks was because of the man emerging from the darkness.

Her heart skipped a beat, then another and then another mimicking each step he took closer.

Despite the warmth, her body froze, and the damp mist of the room congested her throat.

Kate watched him wipe a towel across his brow and then his hands before looking up. She could see only a glimmer of frustration in his familiar brown eyes, as he stared past her at the closed door. Calm and collected as always, that was his facade. One might not recognize any frustration at all in those serious eyes, but she knew.

That wasn't all she could see. His expensive pressed slacks grazed the lower half of his body, but it was his upper area that drew her attention. He'd stripped away the plaid button-up collar shirt, which rested on a bench behind him, revealing a muscular torso that captivated her attentiveness. He was older now, and his once tall, skinny body was now filled in like an overripe, juicy apple you couldn't wait to dig your teeth into.

She shook her head. *Where had that come from?*

He'd always been handsome in a refined coy way, not that of a playboy like his older brother.

Marc was timid, although, at first glance, you'd never know. Raised prim and proper, his first impression played the part of the preppy, private school boy, now the man following in the family footsteps. But a guy who lacked any display of true emotions.

"Don't let anyone know the real you" had been his father's constant teaching.

But now, his usually neatly trimmed, dirty blonde locks were a little longer and his face a little harder, giving him a rougher look. He still stood tall, with squared shoulders, holding his head high, as he had been trained.

The young boy she remembered was replaced by a solid, strong man. A tantalizing half-naked man, towering now in front of her, replacing all her pent up worry with emotions she had long forgotten.

Funny, her fear of returning, for the most part, was caused by the anticipation of this very moment. Seeing him now, composed and professional, as he had always been, she scolded herself for ever worrying about running into him. He was, at heart, a kind and rational person after all. She might have betrayed him, but he was too well-mannered and in control of his conduct to ever give her a reason to hide away from him.

His eyes finally fell on her, filled with surprise.

He looked her over, first quickly up and down, then a slow gaze followed, as if trying to decide whether it was her or not.

She didn't move. She didn't talk. She simply watched

his brown eyes conceal his thoughts. He was a perfectionist at the act.

He shook his head. "Of course it would be you. Out of every guest in this resort, why does it not surprise me that *you* would be the one to ignore the warning signs and do whatever the hell *you* want without any notion of the consequences?"

He threw the towel onto one of the benches and turned away from her.

His words instantly snapped her from the daze she'd been in like the closing jaws of a hungry shark and his temper caught her off guard.

"What are you talking about?" she retorted.

He turned back.

"The sign Kate." His voice was harsh with disgust. "The one you so blatantly ignored."

She narrowed her eyes, fury boiling inside of her. What ignorance! She certainly hadn't seen a sign and she informed him of this through clenched teeth.

"Maybe you carelessly missed it." He dismissed, as though this was, without a doubt, her fault. Not that she was exactly sure what they were even talking about.

"Maybe you carelessly forgot to hang it," she countered.

He stared at her hard, and she glared back, mirroring his expression.

"What did the sign say?" she asked, not actually interested, but rather setting up for her next words. "Beware. Jackass alert?" she added.

She watched him suck in a deep breath and answer curtly, "Out of order."

Out of order? Really, that was the problem?

She could easily fix that. "That's fine. I think I need to take a dip to cool down anyways."

She turned to grab the door handle, regretting swiping her visa at the front desk or even before that, typing in their webpage with intention of booking a room. This was the exact disaster she had planned to avoid with Derek by her side. *Damn Derek!*

"The door won't unlock." Marc had certainly lost his cool in his old age. "From the inside."

Kate grabbed the handle anyway, turned, and pushed and pulled like she had the magic touch to pop it open despite his warning. Nothing.

"You locked us in McAdams."

Kate closed her eyes.

Why hadn't she jumped into the pool, done her laps and went back to her room like she'd planned?

"And that sign you didn't see, is directly in front of you." *Was his tone smug? How...Caliendo of him.*

Without glancing at the white paper in her peripheral view and satisfying his triumph, she opted to turn and face him, ready to dish out the same smug attitude back to him.

Eliminating all emotion from her face, Kate unzipped her dress and let it fall around her feet.

She solemnly stared at him, staring at her, as she stepped out of the bunched up material, and then bent down to pick it up.

Whatever his thoughts were about her minor striptease, he snapped back into standard Marc mode: unreadable.

"I guess I might as well enjoy the heat then," she said,

sprawling out on a wooden bench, and propping her back against the bench. She presumed it would be about twenty minutes before maintenance found their way to fix the door handle, precisely the amount of time she had planned on spending in the sauna anyway. She wished she hadn't left her phone tossed on the chair like a useless electronic, because right now it would have served useful.

Marc grumbled something incoherently, but her back faced him, intentionally.

Relaxation would be a fleeting if his naked, muscular upper body continued to taunt her eyes.

She focused instead on forgetting the reality beyond these walls: the heartbroken sisters she would be meeting at the funeral home in a few short hours. She shamelessly hadn't been thinking about them at all, until she purposely tried to remember why she had decided to pop into the sauna in the first place. Now, all she could think about was *who* was with her in the sauna, and how amazing he looked.

She breathed deeply. Through the humid fog, she could smell him, his designer cologne mixing with the thick sauna air.

Focus, breathe, focus. Stop breathing his smell, stop focusing on him.

But every bang and clang coming from his direction piqued her curiosity. She was going to be exhausted, instead of relaxed, by the time twenty minutes ticked by.

Kate glanced over her shoulder, and saw him hovering on his haunches by the control panel, working away, and acting like he actually knew what he was doing.

She almost laughed out loud.

Unless he had gained some handy skills in the past

years, other than picking up weights, this was going to be a disaster.

Rolling her eyes, she slid from the bench, her bare feet hitting the warm, damp floor and settled down on the bench beside him.

"It's warmer in here than usual," she observed.

She crossed her legs and leaned her elbow against her knee, resting her chin on the backside of her hand.

"I think we should turn the dial down a notch or two," she suggested, watching his body stiffen.

This would teach him to think he could talk to her like a clueless child.

"Would we do that here?" She played dumb, pointing to the control panel.

He turned to look at her with his serious eyes.

"You broke it, didn't you?" she asked.

His lips thinned. "No."

"But you can't fix it either."

No big surprise. He wasn't a handy man...well not in that aspect anyway.

"Maintenance is on their way."

By then they would be a melted puddle of goop.

"Oh move over." She didn't give him a chance to object squeezing down alongside him, the sides of their bare skin sliding like dew down a leaf after a rainfall.

The distraction gave her the opportunity to seize the screwdriver from his hand. A maintenance man's daughter knew how to fix a knob or wire.

Suddenly, the heat of the spa was nothing in comparison to the heat of his body, like the touch of fire, against her skin.

He grabbed the screwdriver back. "You're not on my payroll."

"So, you're exactly where your father wanted you to be." She meant the comment to sting.

He was obviously paying the bills, running the resort, and doing exactly what he never wanted to do.

Kate reached for the tool, but Marc pulled it further from her grasp and glared at her.

"That man never dictated my actions," he clarified firmly, fire burning behind his eyes.

He really had gotten sloppy with his emotions, she thought. His father would be rolling over in his grave with disapproval.

Kate knew his words were true, though, and wished she could declare the same with such passion.

"Just give me the screwdriver, Marc."

"I got this."

"No, you don't. You're going to end up electrocuting yourself or worse, *me*."

She reached again, and irritatingly he lifted it higher. His arms were like magnificent pillars, never ending and built to last against time.

Ugh, stop noticing him that way. He can hardly stand you, and you're half naked.

Stepping up from her knees, she steadied herself on the ground and reached for the tool again, only this time with a little more bounce in her reach.

Her foot slipped on the damp floor sending her falling forward...directly toward Marc.

It all happened so fast.

His arm caught her waist as their flesh met in the

center, throwing him off balance and sending them both backwards in his direction.

Kate screamed.

Marc cursed, but managed to steady them with his other hand slapping against the hard wood and propping them up.

When they stopped toppling, Kate slowly exhaled the breath she had been holding and rested her forehead against his shoulder.

"Are you alright?" he whispered.

It was the first time she had heard the real Marc, or at least the Marc she remembered.

Her heart was pounding from the tumble, and was increasing rapidly as she became aware of their landed position, twisted and turned like a crashed kite on a windy day.

One of her arms wrapped tightly around his neck, when there had been nowhere else to grab. Her legs had landed, knees on the ground, on either side of his solid thigh while his knee was raised, pushing her directly against his whole body. Under her free hand, she felt the solid wall of his muscles and the steady beat of his heart.

Damn it. She felt everything.

"I'm okay," she breathed against his skin.

Every feeling she'd ever known for him was fully dominating her body like an unwanted wave of sickness.

Kate lifted her head, pressing her free hand harder against his chest to steady her.

"Are you okay?" she asked.

Marc nodded slowly as their eyes locked. She found that his anger had fallen with them. Now his hunger reflected her own.

His eyes traveled to her lips and, against better judgment, hers fell to his.

She couldn't count the times their lips had touched or how many times she'd moved towards him or him towards her.

This couldn't happen now.

But, oh how she wanted it to.

Against her better judgement, she felt her seductive hands moving up his chest. She heard his quick intake of air as his chest rose and fell against her hand. Not a second later and his hand was moving to the side of her face.

Stop this now.

She bit her lower lip, a reaction to his gentle touch as his thumb tracing her jaw line, stopping just below her lips.

Kiss me now. No don't...yes do.

Her tongue wetted her dry lips just as Marc's mouth came crashing down on hers. All the years absent between them and he still tasted delicious and she wanted to flavor so much more.

Together, they rose to their knees, their bodies moulding as one. Marc was gentle, as he'd always been. His hands roamed her body, but with a familiar tenderly respect for her. But his harder kisses held an underlying of want and desire that matched her own. Her mind might have been screaming this was a bad idea, but her body was demonstrating how perfect they were together. But they weren't perfect together. They weren't even together. They were nothing and if they followed through with where this was leading, it would only add more difficulty to their already complicated future.

Kate pulled away from Marc's lips and said, "I scraped my knee." And just like that, like the popping of a balloon, she broke the enchanting ambience encircling them, purposely returning them to a reality where he couldn't stand her.

At this point, it was better he hate her, then to have hot, wild, passionate sex on the floor of the sauna. *Wasn't it?*

Marc's eyes fluttered back to hers for a brief second, sharing the confusion that bewildered her, before pulling away.

Wise decision.

She had to fight the urge to wrap her arms back around his neck and connect their bodies again.

Kate closed her eyes, taking a deep breath to maintain her dignity, although she was sure they were past that point.

She hadn't paid attention to what Marc was doing, mostly because she was too busy noticing every warm spot his touch left on her skin, until she felt him lift her leg, caress her knee and chuckle.

"Hardly a scratch," he said. "You can fix a switch like no other, but whimper about a tiny scratch."

She could handle a tiny scratch like no other...but he already knew that.

Marc sat back on his feet and handed her the screwdriver in defeat.

Kate's hand trembled as she took it from his and she knew he'd noticed.

But had his hand trembled too?

She turned away from him, persistent at the task at hand and trying hard not to think about what her back would feel like on this damp floor instead of her knee, had she not mentioned her scratch.

After she fixed this mechanical issue, she didn't plan on waiting in here any longer for maintenance. She was going to walk straight over to the knob and pop that handle right open and get the hell out of here.

This was the opposite of the relaxing moment she had envisioned.

Chapter Four

MARC STRIPPED OFF his clothes, abandoning them wherever they landed, from the front door all the way to the bathroom.

He reached directly for the chrome shower handle, allowing the water no time to warm, before standing beneath the streams of icy water slapping against his body.

The drastic change in temperature, from the hot sauna to the cold shower, startled his body, but he leaned his flat palms against the tiled wall and welcomed the onslaught of water cascading over his head. He welcomed this punishment; he deserved every minute following that little episode.

His thoughts had been a jumbled mess in that hot sauna, but it wasn't long before his thoughts now cleared.

Thank goodness!

After maintenance had finally arrived, he'd anticipated a quick walk back to his suite to clear his head.

With Kate's half-naked body seared into his memory, replaying repeatedly like an old movie, there hadn't been room for any other thoughts.

What the hell had happened in that sauna?

He was livid that the betrayal in Kate's eyes hadn't been enough to quench the desire that had built up in his body.

The anger that had consumed the last six years of his life, had led him to believe such emotions and desires were labeled hazardous, and unsafe. Yet, a six-minute greeting, after six years apart, had dispersed all caution like the heated steam of the sauna, like fog stealing the night.

He would have lifted her onto the bench in that sauna and stripped them both down naked, had she not spoken, smashing the aura of desire between them.

He would have laid her down on that floor and...

Marc rubbed his hands across his face now in aggravation, then lathered up his body with his masculine-scented wash that began erasing the traces of Kate's warm vanilla scent.

Her hot, warm, soft body pressed against his.

This shower was not as helpful as he'd originally contemplated, as his mind dragged her sexy, body into the shower with him. He would rather be lathering her tender skin beneath his hands than his own.

And Izzy had been right, Kate was definitely gorgeous. She'd grown into a curvaceous woman and every new curve attracted him more than the last.

Marc rinsed off, wrapped a towel around his waist and made his way to the kitchen for a cold beer.

A light rap on the back door pulled him from his goal.

His petite mother greeted him as she entered with a light-hearted smile, glancing down at the towel wrapped around his waist. "A bath in the middle of the day, Marcus?" she questioned.

He nodded.

She had no idea.

"Give me a second to grab some pants."

When he returned wearing slacks and a t-shirt, he found his mother pulling a kettle he didn't even know he had out of the cupboard. Two clear mugs sat on the counter with tea bags awaiting the boiling liquid and his beer was nowhere to be seen.

His mother's theory was that tea could heal or relax anyone. She was wrong in this case. Only beer would do the trick this time.

She smiled up at him. "I stopped by your office but you weren't there."

Marc sat on one of the stools and quickly told her about the sauna troubles, omitting Kate's presence entirely.

"I had a nice lunch with the girls this afternoon," she began.

He had intentionally avoided that gossipy social event.

"The visitation for Grace is tomorrow," his mother continued quietly.

Eliza moved across the room and stood on the opposite side of the counter facing him, her arms resting softly folded across her rose-colored chiffon blouse. She was always dressed fashionably chic and today was no exception. Her blouse was tucked into high-waist black pants that flared into wide legs just above black heels. A strand of large pearls graced her neck.

"I would appreciate it, Marcus, if you would drive us to the evening service."

He would rather not, especially after his altercation with Kate, not to mention their awkward collision.

He would be surprised if Kate ever wanted to see him again. It was an odd thought, since she had left him six years ago and clearly hadn't wanted to see him again.

If his mother learned about the altercation in the sauna with Kate she would be mortified by the elevated tones and unkind words he had spoken to Kate.

Marc could foresee his mother's round, disappointed eyes scolding him while shaking her short bobbed gray hair and, none too subtly, requiring an apology.

Guilt suddenly burdened him for his behavior during Kate's grieving.

What had he been thinking?

Kate was here for her grandmother's funeral and he had jumped down her throat over missing a sign.

His mother continued, "Izzy said Abby is an absolute mess. That poor girl was so very close to Grace after Kate left."

Marc forced himself to continue breathing regularly but didn't like the way his mother was watching him so closely.

Was she fishing? Did she know what had occurred in the sauna? How could she?

Or was she just concerned because Kate had broken his young heart? If that was the case, why was she suggesting he take them to the visitations? *Why were all these questions flooding his head over one tiny sentence?*

"And now Grace is gone and Abby is beside herself, that poor soul," Eliza said, obviously not having any idea of the conflict going on in Marc's head.

After Kate left, Marc hadn't lived at home so he never noticed what was happening with her family.

His father had brushed off Marc's broken heart as a young meaningless love. His father thought it was too early in Marc's life to know about real love.

The thought now intrigued Marc. Back then he hadn't experienced the same heart-wrenching emotion that he just had upstairs with the same wild brunette. So maybe his father had been right.

Schooling had been his parent's, or rather his dad's, top priority for him. After Marc finished school, he was expected to return to the resort, but Marc opted to stay as far away as he could instead.

He'd mastered business management and established a job down south, managing a resort and distracting himself with sun, bikinis, and unlimited fresh fruit.

His mother's words continued to interrupt his thoughts. "Izzy and I will be attending the funeral."

The funeral? Was he supposed to attend the funeral?

He certainly hadn't planned on it.

"It's so sad. I remember when Annabelle passed away and how hard it was on those girls."

Marc remembered, too, probably more than his mother.

He had been there that night. When he and Kate had returned from a secret ice cream run, they'd turned the corner, laughing and carefree, and holding hands for the first time, to find a slew of medics taking Kate's mother away on a stretcher.

That moment had changed everything.

Eliza was still talking and Marc caught parts here and there while his mind continued reverting to the past.

"...poor Kate being tossed into an early motherhood at such a young, *young* age. All the adults in her life simply quit. But not Kate."

Why were they talking about Kate now?

The guilt of his behavior multiplied with his mother's every word...she seemed to be full of lots to say.

"And now, another adult in her life...gone."

Marc decided he owed Kate an apology. He might have some pent up anger towards her, clearly, but that was no excuse to drag it up during this difficult time in her life.

"So, I was hoping you would join me at the visitation and show these women our support," Eliza finished with a half smile and waiting eyes.

He wouldn't have been able to say no to his mother anyway and now, with the multitude of remorse for his actions, he had to attend.

No matter what transpired between he and Kate six years ago, he was a grown man who had acted today like a broken, hurt teenager and there was no excuse for those actions.

"What time?" he asked.

Eliza clasped her hands together in delight. "Wonderful Marcus."

Chapter Five

KATE WAS THANKFUL to escape the walls of the Caliendo Resort. Even now, as a guest, instead of the maintenance man's daughter, there was a condemning atmosphere. Like a twister, it sucked up her rationality then discarded it, broken, on the ground.

What was she thinking playing with fire like that in there?

She breathed in the crisp, tranquil air now before making her way to her car. As she drove through Willow Valley, the popular tourist cottage town where she had been born and raised, she admired the small, pride-filled businesses flanking the main strip. The road ran parallel to the lake, and alongside a long, wooden boardwalk, inviting visitors off the road and onto public benches and tables.

Nestled into areas on the sandy beach, sat ice cream stands, yogurt shops and food huts, all currently closed for the season.

When the quaint, old-fashioned bakery came into view, Kate pulled her rental into one of the slanted, parking spots.

She needed a strong boost of java to get through the rest of the afternoon. She also intended to take a tray of coffees to meet her sisters and dad at the funeral home.

Facing the beach, she stared at the highlight of her childhood: the large sandy shoreline flanking the long sparkling lake, which was now currently covered in a blanket of white snow.

Folks journeyed from all over the province for holiday escapes to enjoy this view.

However, the McAdams, had always enjoyed only a short, fifteen-minute walk from home or a quick jaunt from Gran's place to bask in the splendor of the lake.

The landscape was beautiful even on this cold November afternoon. A light snow danced in the air to the sound of the outdoor speakers tuned into the local radio station and tall greases planted by the town teased the falling snow between the boardwalks.

Much more beautiful than she'd remembered.

Home sweet home.

She climbed out of the car, the wind whipping against her face and quickly crossed the road, pushing open the old wooden and glass door.

The captivating aroma of freshly baked bread lured her tummy and the glass cake displays brought back memories of being served delicious slices of Gran's famous pies. Although she didn't expect a slice now, the familiar, warm feeling filled her body regardless.

Mrs. Calvert spotted her right away and greeted her with hands on her round hip. "Well, look how gorgeous you are," she said. "I mean I have seen pictures, but honey, they did you no justice. What a beautiful woman you have become Miss Katherine McAdams. Here sit, sit."

The older lady motioned to the stools lining the lengthy antique counter.

"Have a coffee."

It wasn't a question. Mrs. Calvert flipped a mug onto the counter and filled it before Kate had moved a muscle.

She thanked the older lady, warming her cold hands around the mug. There had been no problem keeping warm at the resort, she thought, but quickly nudged the notion away.

Mrs. Calvert reminded Kate of Gran. They both carried a spark for life and nothing had slowed either of them down, especially not their age. Kate knew that their bond had grown after Mrs. Calvert's daughter and granddaughter died almost two years ago in a car crash—the unfortunate result of a drunk driver. It had been a rare, ill-fated bond, but had helped each older woman to push onward.

Mrs. Calvert finished some business at the end of the counter with two younger girls and then settled herself across from Kate, her arms folded and her elbows leaning on the counter.

"How are you doing sweetheart?" she asked sincerely.

Kate smiled at her. "I'm okay."

It wasn't a lie. She was as okay as she was going to be under the circumstances.

Mrs. Calvert cast her a warm smile. "Gran used to brag about you, little gal," she continued. "She was so very proud of what you have become and what you have accomplished. She would return from her trips to visit you and babble on and on telling all kinds of stories. She looked forward to every Christmas, when your family would all stay at Peyton's for a week. That was her favorite time of the year." Her voice quieted to a whisper as though Gran might walk through the door and catch her giving away her little secrets. "Because she would always sneak another day or two with you girls and sometimes a week."

The old woman suddenly laughed out loud.

"She thought she was being so smart, tricking you girls into more quality time."

Slowly shaking her head, her eyes travelled to a blank space off in the distance, obviously remembering her own memories of her dear friend.

Kate let her be, enjoying the way Gran had touched this woman's heart. She waited patiently until Mrs. Calvert's focus returned and she remembered she was sitting across from Kate. The older woman batted away some gathering tears.

Kate reached across the counter and covered the warm, aging hand with her own.

"She loved you, too, Mrs. Calvert. She told me many stories about you two and your yoga, bicycle rides and karate classes."

A smile crossed Mrs. Calvert's lips and she opened her mouth to reply, when a side door opened and a rough looking biker kind of guy entered. He headed straight towards them on the opposite side of the counter as Kate.

He wore denim and a leather jacket opened over a black sweater. His long tousled dark hair matched the trimmed beard along his jaw line. His eyes looked murky, haunted, mean and challenging.

"What's wrong?" Mrs. Calvert asked him.

The man sent Kate a quick, thin-lined, but fake, smile, loosening his rough exterior, before taking one of Mrs. Calvert's arms and leaning in to whisper in her ear.

Kate looked away, sensing this was none of her business, but she couldn't help overhear Abby's name in the whispers. She noticed a grim look across the older lady's face, enhancing the lines of age and then heard a little gasp.

Panic gripped Kate.

"I'll stay here," he offered, as he finally pulled away.

"What's going on?" Kate asked, beginning to stand.

Fear of what could possibly be going on with Abby squeezed her heart like a vice grip.

The dark eyed man didn't offer an explanation, but sent her a fleeting and clear warning message with his eyes: *This is none of your business.*

Kate ignored him. "Did something happen to Abby?" she asked watching Mrs. Calvert tearing off her apron and abandoning it on the counter.

"Come on Kate, I'll explain on the way," she said. "Riley this is Abby's sister. Kate this is Riley O'Conner. He works for me."

Mr. Brown Eyes, that's what she decided to call him, stared at her with a little more warmth now, sensing that it was indeed her business.

But there was no time for niceties, Mrs Calvery was off and Kate had to take quick strides to keep up.

As they reached the side door Riley had entered, Kate considered him. His protective glances in Kate's direction indicated he must have a trace of affection for Abby. Although Kate had certainly not been informed of any love interest by her sister. She made a mental note to address that issue later.

For now, her first intuition about this trip was about come to fruition.

They entered a small, gloomy hall with a staircase. Kate figured they must lead to the second floor—probably

Mrs. Calvert's living quarters.

Mrs. Calvert grabbed a winter coat from a hook before pushing another door open and stepping into the alley.

"Abby's not taking your grandmother's death very well," she said.

Who was?

"I mean she's *really* not taking it well," Mrs Calvert clarified, as though reading Kate's thoughts. "And I'm not sure what's happened now."

Their footsteps left a trail in the light dusting of snow that had fallen. The alleyway opened out into parking spaces for the business owners and employees of the commercial buildings. Behind the parking spots were a row of trees concealing the houses behind...more specifically the house Kate hadn't wanted to go. Not right away anyway.

Past the trees lined in a row and a fence was the house Kate hadn't wanted to go. Not right away anyway.

Stopping at a little space tucked between the trees, Mrs Calvert pushed open an old wrought iron gate and Gran's backyard opened in front of them.

The small house resembled a little red brick cottage from a fairy tale storybook.

Sitting on the back porch attached to the sunroom was her little sister, looking like a tiny, lost doll.

Abby only wore a bright neon pink sweater, the hood pulled over her brown roots to the blonde ombre ends, and a pair of black tights.

She sat hunched over, holding her head in her hands, her elbows resting on her legs just above her cut and bleeding knees.

Kate's hesitance to go by that gate vanished at the

sight of her forlorn sister. She ran to her, instincts from the past rising to the surface and flushing away all her resistance.

"Abby!" she called. She fell to her knees to examine her sister's wounds. "What happened?"

Her sister looked up slowly.

"Kate?" She sounded surprised and confused all bundled together.

"Yes sweetie, it's me." Kate brushed her hand over Abby's forehead, pushing wet hair away from her skin. "What happened to your legs?"

Abby's eyes slowly looked down at her injured legs. Her eyebrows gathered in confusion, and then she shrugged slightly and looked back at Kate.

"Gran died," she said flatly.

Kate touched her arm. "I know sweetie."

"I mean she just died. I just came home and she was dead. Like dead and no one was there. You weren't there, I wasn't there, Sydney wasn't there, Avery wasn't there, and Peyton wasn't there and Gran just died."

Kate's heart sunk.

"I'm here now."

Mrs. Calvert caught up to them. "Do you need to see a doctor Abby?"

"You're here now?" Abby said, ignoring Mrs Calvert's concerns. "Everyone's here *now* and then you'll all be gone again."

Kate looked up at Mrs. Calvert. "We should take her to the hospital."

Abby jerked away from her suddenly, then stood, looking like a scared little child and not the twenty-three year old she was.

"No, I'm not going there." Abby's voice trembled.

"We want to help," Kate said reaching for her.

"I just fell," Abby explained. "I'm not going back to that place. Ever."

Kate stood too. "Let us clean you up then honey," Mrs Calvert said. As she climbed the stairs quickly and grabbed Abby's arm. "Come on, let's get those cuts tended to," she said, leading her into Gran's house.

Kate followed behind, dialing other her sister's number on her cell. When Peyton's voice mail answered, she hung up and dialed Sydney instead, who picked up on the first ring. Kate quickly explained Abby's situation and suggested meeting at Gran's.

Sydney promised to send their father over right away after trying to reach Peyton again. Kate hung up and braced herself for the full McAdams treatment.

***

KATE'S DAD HAD left Sydney at the funeral home in order to tend to his youngest daughter.

Kate felt guilty for leisurely taking her time in town when so much work for Gran's funeral still had to be done.

Dread filled her heart, knowing Abby battled demons behind the emotional walls she built long ago. Would those walls crash down around her now that Gran was gone?

"Hi sweetheart," her father said pulling Kate into a long hard hug after he set two bags of take-out on the counter.

"Hi Daddy."

She squeezed back. "How are you doing?" She

readied her watchful eyes to catch any little sign of alcohol or indication of lapse. Years of battling with him to leave the bottle alone had taught her what to look for.

"I'm doing alright." He leaned against the counter, crossing his legs and his arms.

He was average height, but his face had aged quicker than the numbers on his birth certificate. The years spent drinking had caught up to him, like the beginning of a wilting flower.

But he seemed to be sober. She prayed he could make it through another serious loss.

His eyes weren't darting...good sign. His body wasn't jittery...another good sign.

"How's Abby?" His concern seemed sincere, not the usual game he'd played so many times as a distraction from his true addictions.

Kate breathed a sigh of relief and shrugged.

"I don't know. She's an emotional mess, that's for sure. But Mrs. Calvert got her knees cleaned up and she went to bed early."

Kate motioned down the hall and explained how Abby was running and fell, scraping her leg.

However, her minor physical injuries weren't what bothered Kate or Mrs. Calvert the most. It was the distance Abby was putting between herself and others, shutting them out like the black curtain pulled across the window in her room, blocking the suns access. Abby hadn't spoken another word to Kate since those moments on the porch.

"In the morning we'll sit down and talk to her," Kate said.

Her father nodded and said, "How are you doing?"

"I'm fine."

It was a lie, like he had just lied about how he was doing. They were all sad putting up faux facade to each other in order to avoid the truth, to avoid the pain.

"First time back in a very long time Kate," he observed with the voice of a concerned father. So many years when she'd needed him to be concerned, but he'd consoled himself in a bottle of liquor instead. Now that she was an adult, she didn't need his concern, although she wouldn't push it away either.

She shrugged. "It's no big deal, Dad." *It's a huge a deal!*

"Peyton mentioned you're staying at the Caliendo Resort?"

Kate nodded, shrugging it off like it meant nothing too, keeping her facial expressions neutral.

She and Marc were grown adults after all. They could obviously run into one another without shouting or winding up embraced awkwardly on the floor of a sauna...*weren't they?*

Kate blamed Marc.

He started it in that sauna with his saucy tongue. His unusually saucy tongue had her mouth now tingling.

"You could have stayed with me," her father said, bringing her out of her reverie about Marc.

Originally, she'd intended on introducing Derek to her family and Derek wouldn't have stayed in her father's house. She wasn't about to bring his name up now and go into all those details

She had put off introducing him to her family for a while. It was like her mind exploded at the thought of trying to explain their relationship, but it was probably best now because now they were nothing. They were over and done with and she was glad her family hadn't known about him.

"Peyton was staying with you and I didn't want to crowd the house," she told her dad instead.

He nodded slowly.

He probably thought there was a much deeper reason for her staying at the resort. Like Marc reasons.

What did her father think was going to happen exactly?

Because she was pretty sure he could never imagine the trip, slap, and fall that had landed them together almost lip locked in a hot steamy sauna.

Kate didn't think it wise to go down this road with her father...or with any of her family members for that matter.

Luckily, the door burst open just then and her twin, with matching brown curls layered above her shoulders and highlighted in platinum blonde, ran straight in for a hug.

"Oh I missed you!" Peyton cried, her arms wrapping tightly around her shoulders, in an overly extended, I'm-never-letting-go-of-you, bear hug. Kate squeezed back.

"Share." Sydney, only a year younger, pushed Peyton off and scooped in for her own hug. "I love having you home," she whispered. "I missed you so much."

Sydney had their father's wavy, light blonde hair and light eyes, completely the opposite of all the twins.

"I missed you too, Syd."

After hugs were completed, Kate gave them the run down on Abby as they settled around the table and pulled open the take-out bags, popping the lids off and digging into Chinese food.

Sydney's brows maintained a furrowed position as she listened to Kate's recounting. She looked mortified that she had missed the signs of their youngest sister's breakdown.

"This has all happened so quickly. First, we were at the hospital and Abby seemed fine," Sydney said, glancing at their dad who nodded in agreement. "I mean obviously not fine, but under the circumstances..." she paused, re-thinking the situation. "Maybe she was in shock," she offered as an explanation. "I don't know. She wouldn't come home with me or Dad and said she was tired. Then I was making funeral arrangements and calling all of you and I just didn't notice."

Sydney looked down at her trembling hands holding the chop sticks.

Kate touched her arm in support. "No one's blaming you Syd. We definitely couldn't foresee Abby's actions. But we should all talk to her in the morning."

Everyone agreed, because if this was any indication, Abby was heading down the road of disaster.

"Why don't you tell us about all the arrangements?" Kate said to Sydney. "Since none of us were able to make it."

Kate glared at Peyton and she innocently shrugged.

What had kept her away?

Sydney listed off the times and dates for the visitation, the service and the brunch afterwards.

Then they easily moved away from the subject of death and started contributing a little part of their current lives to lighten the mood.

Sydney bragged about her daughter, Haylee, being an "A" student in school.

Peyton beamed about the rise in her clientele and

how, if she ever decided to open a business in her house, she would now have a fantastic following to support her.

Kent offered up some small town gossip and all the girls looked surprised that he would even know these sorts of things. He wasn't a gossiper, nor had he ever known much about the lives of the locals in town. Even when Kate's mother had been alive, Kent had been a family man and not a rumourmonger.

Kate contributed her excitement on her new condo, but left out the part where Derek had been planning on moving in and was now definitely not. She didn't want to talk about a heart breaking time in her life, but she found herself angrier for not seeing the signs and wished she could share it with her sisters. Or had she seen the signs, but simply ignored them...maybe because she had never really cared. Had she really loved Derek? Had she really pictured a life with him?

Those were easy questions, especially when Marc's beautiful image was now burned back into her head.

Kate had spent six years trying to eliminate that image and now it was back...but now even more gorgeous and with a little spunk.

Why was that intriguing?

An hour later, their exhausted father announced he was heading home. "I'm going to spend the night here," Peyton told him, declining a ride home. Kent made goodbye rounds, giving hugs to each of his girls before leaving. The sisters casually waved and watched him leave from the porch.

Then, like they'd been doing their whole life, Peyton turned the lock on the door, Kate grabbed wine glasses from the cupboard, and Sydney dug into the cleaning cupboard to pull out a bottle of hidden red wine.

They collapsed on the white wicker furniture in the heated sun room.

Living through their dad's drinking addiction they'd vowed to never take a sip of alcohol with him present and supported his decision to quit. Deep down they all silently feared that he might slip.

"What is that delicious smell?" Peyton asked.

The sun room smelled of lavender, citrus, vanilla and so many more alluring smells teasing their senses like a field of wild flowers.

Sydney stood.

"Do you want to know a secret?" she teased, wiggling her hips across the room.

The sisters laughed.

Sydney put her finger over her lips, silently hushing them before reaching towards the large wooden doors and opening the mammoth of an antique pine cupboard.

The aroma intensified. Inside were rows of handmade soaps.

The curious twins, ventured over, mimicking Sydney's walk.

The soaps were wrapped in twine and adorned with little handmade, descriptive listings, with all of the properties of the essential oils listed on the backside.

"What is this?" Kate asked.

It couldn't very well be Gran's personal collection of soap since there were multiple rows of the exact same one.

"Abby started making these for her and Gran. Gran suggested when her friends started wanting them, that they sell them," Sydney explained.

Kate picked up a shea butter bar and smelled it. It was wonderful.

"These are amazing. Abby made them?" Kate was surprised.

Sydney nodded. "This is her third batch and they started taking orders and delivering to friends."

Kate was impressed. "That is wonderful. Is she enjoying it?"

Kate would love to see Abby do anything other than waitressing in Jake's bar. When Kate expressed her concerns to Gran about Abby's lack of desire to acquire a career and grow up, Gran had promised Kate that Abby would find what she loved even if she had to work at Jake's bar on her way to success.

Kate wondered if this was Abby's calling.

Sydney nodded. "This is amazing soap. I have to admit that I was skeptical the first time I used it, but amazed at how soft and moisturizing it is. It's made with all natural products. No chemicals or additives are put into the soap. When you're finished, your skin feels smoother and younger."

Kate gave her a slanted grin. "You could be the spokesperson for this product."

"You're the advertising designer, maybe you should make her up some posters and flyers to help her advertise," Sydney told Kate.

"Maybe I will."

Sydney pulled a paper bag out of the cupboard and handed it to Kate before she resumed her position on the couch. "Just don't forget to buy a few bars of soap before you leave," she said. "It would mean the world to Abby."

Of course she would...if she was leaving. *Not leaving? Where did that come from?* Of course she was leaving.

Kate's life was in the city where her career sat on hold while she figured out how she could face Derek day after day. Her condo was there, empty and alone...Kate wasn't sure she wanted to go back to that empty condo. But what would she do here?

Kate couldn't help thinking about Marc. He hated her. Or so he had hated her, then after they'd slipped, he'd loosened up and maybe...just maybe he didn't hate her so much.

Kate, you can't go back to him. Too many secrets. So many lies.

The six years of separation didn't fix what had happened. And she could never reveal to Marc the real reason for her departure from Willow Valley.

Kate shut the cupboard doors like they concealed her heart and remembered why she couldn't allow the true feelings they held to reveal themselves. Not to Marc...not even to herself. It was too hard.

Focus on the present. Focus on Abby.

Abby. What were they going to do with Abby?

Chapter Six

MARC DROPPED HIS mother and sisters off at the glass double doors of the funeral home, before driving he and his uncle to a parking space in the back.

"I'm proud of you Marcus, for putting aside your feelings regarding Katherine and attending tonight," his uncle said, as their quick strides took them across the wind whipping evening. The sun settled earlier now and was beginning to dip behind the lake, and like his feelings towards Kate, shadowed them in darkness.

He shrugged.

"You take it lightly but it's difficult to get over betrayal," he continued. "No matter the people involved, or the volume of the betrayal." He spoke as if reliving the experience. It was a betrayal linked to the brothers no doubt.

His Uncle Carl spoke with consideration in contrast to Marc's father's unsympathetic, and generally selfish, nature. It was hard to believe complete opposites shared the same bloodline. Since the loss of his brother, his uncle had strived to bond with his nephew. A healing process, Marc believed.

It was a nice change from having to disguise his feelings and thoughts as if at a masquerade ball. He'd always adorned a mask with his father, never revealing what he felt and, under no circumstances, ever requesting his father's opinion. It was him and his mother alone. Until now, and even after a lifetime of trusting his uncle, Marc couldn't help but be cautious. He felt that little mask was still dangling whenever he conversed with his uncle, ready to be slapped on at a moment's notice. His father could take credit for his caution after heeding Marc this warning: *Your Uncle Carl is not who he seems and it is best you figure the truth out after I'm gone. Don't hate me for keeping it from you or those involved Marcus, your heart is better than that.*

Marc wasn't sure what that meant but wondered if all the strange up and downs with his uncle were tied to his father's warning.

His father had changed in his last months of life. It had been an aggressive cancer that had taken him down quickly like no human could. And Marc found a lot of his father's ramblings at the end to be sincere, and left him taking extra precautions he never had with his uncle in a time when he was trying to get closer to Marc. He didn't know whether to believe his father or the strong relationship he had always had with his uncle.

It was all exhausting.

However, if his uncle uncovered the events that had transpired in the sauna, he might scrutinize his nephew differently. How Marc had initiated the exact lack of self-control his uncle was presuming he carried.

"Let's see how this plays out," he said patting his uncle's shoulders.

Inside, they found the Caliendo women scattered between the three rooms opened for visitation. Situated in an old Victorian home that had long since been transformed into one of the two funeral homes in town, the grand foyer displayed a large winding staircase located at the heart of the house. The main areas on each side were open and wrapped around behind the staircase where another room connected the three in a half moon. It was casual visitation, with no line up to wait in to pass your condolences, but instead an open gathering in which to show your respect.

His uncle was quick to a find a group of old acquaintances to pass his time. Marc didn't mind. He hadn't turned up solely to please his mother, he was on a search for a proper apology to Kate.

The rooms were separated by large columns or French doors propped open with cast urns filled with cascading flowers. Each room was crowded. He recognized plenty of business owners likely stopping by on their way home before supper.

He wasn't able to simply walk around and zero in on Kate. He was a Caliendo, and accompanying the name, was the expected communication of many. People wouldn't allow him to pass without a greeting. Some inquired about the resort, others about his family while others wanted to share a piece of their business or family. He was getting used to the friendly banter, since that was a big part of his job at the resort: making sure the guests were always satisfied.

He spotted Izzy hanging out with Emma and found it rather odd she hadn't scoped out Abby.

As he walked into the second room, he stopped by Grace McAdams's casket. Flowers brightened up her area for the locally adored woman, and he silently paid his respects.

Through the second set of French doors, he finally spotted Kate. She was off to the side of the room, rearranging coffee mugs and napkins at a small beverage and snack table —alone. There were less people gathered than in the last room, as though they had not quite made it that far yet. He nodded at guests, quick and brisk, brushing them off, heading directly towards Kate.

As he approached the table, she took no notice, her eyes lost in her own deep thoughts. He had the opportunity to notice her shimmering long-sleeved, fitted black dress with a delicately crocheted neckline. He preferred her curls loose and wild, but they were pulled up and around the back of her head, sleek and professional...nothing like they had been in that sauna. *Get the thoughts of the sauna out of your head!*

He picked up a mug casually and set it in her row. "I can't stand it when the cups aren't sorted at such events," he teased.

She looked up, confused at first, then when she found his eyes, hers lightened and her cheeks stained from embarrassment.

"Busted," she said, setting two mugs back on the table. Her hands clasped together as though they couldn't stay apart. He could hold them apart. *Enough.*

A couple came to the table for coffee and he touched the small of her back, guiding her away for private moment. "I wanted to give my condolences for Grace."

"Thank you."

"I also wanted to apologize for the way I spoke to you yesterday."

She smiled up at him. "It should be me apologizing," she said. "I offended you about your father and it was inconsiderate with his passing not that long ago."

He hadn't even considered that. Maybe it would have saved him the drive here as though an eye for an eye solution was mature. "I guess we both said things we didn't mean."

She smiled shyly. "I suppose we did."

Awkwardness, that had never interrupted them before surrounded them both now.

"How's your knee?" he asked.

She half smiled again. "I think I will survive."

Another wave of awkwardness.

"Marc, since you're here, I think we should clarify that what happened yesterday, um, after the fighting, you know." She looked flustered. "Anyway, that can't happen again."

He definitely agreed with her one hundred percent and then some. "I wasn't looking for anything here."

"Of course you weren't," she said giving her head a little shake. "You probably have a girlfriend, or fiancée. There's no ring on your finger so I know there's no wife and if there was a wife I'm sure Gran would have told me and..."

She was rambling. It was very unlike her. He touched her hand to silence her. "I do not have any of the above." That wasn't as embarrassing as Izzy had said it would be.

Her head whipped up. "I wasn't meaning to pry, I..." She took a deep breath and smiled. "I actually hate this, being here."

"Back in Willow Valley?"

She shook her head. "No, not at all. I like being back here." He wondered why she hadn't come back before now. "It's *here*." She glanced at Grace's casket and he knew where her thoughts had been when he'd arrived. She'd been thinking about her mother, Annabelle. Suddenly, he was lost with her, the name bringing back a slew of memories and emotions. He forgot she had left him broken hearted and he found himself simply standing beside his best friend, whose eyes he couldn't stomach to see filled with so much grief. It was like they were back in time and her mother was in the coffin instead of Gran. After all the years of her being there for him while he was growing up, that had been his turn to be the strong person she needed him to be.

Without thinking, he wrapped his hand around hers. Her fingers trembled but didn't pull away. "Come on," he whispered. She didn't argue and let him lead her through one of the back doors, just as they had done on that sunny day she buried her mother. They ended up down a hall and in the staff kitchen. Two older, grey-haired ladies smiled at them as they entered.

"Marc, what are you doing?" she asked, sending them an apologetic and slightly embarrassed smile.

"Do you ladies know if you might have some ice cream in that freezer?" He felt her hand tighten around his. He couldn't tell if she was excited or mortified. The young Kate would have been thrilled, the older Kate...he didn't know at all.

The shorter, more round lady stopped what she was working on, flashed them a friendly smile and said, "I think we do." She bustled her way around the kitchen, fetching ice cream out of the freezer and bowls from the cupboard. She glanced at them. "One bowl or two?"

"One is fine," he answered. She handed them one bowl of heaping vanilla ice cream with two spoons, then went back to her work, casually, as though this was a common occurrence, which he was sure it wasn't.

There was another staircase in the back hall between the kitchen and visitation room and they stopped to sit.

"I can't believe you did that," she said, passing him a

spoon, a shocked grin spread across her face. He didn't have the same passion for ice cream as she did, but he took a spoonful.

"I wanted ice cream," he said.

She laughed. "I don't really believe you."

He winked at her. "I guess you will never know."

She ate her ice cream. He could see the weight of her grief lift a little bit and the weight of his conscience lifted along, floating into the air like petals escaping their stem.

"Why are you being so nice to me?" Her voice was grave.

"Why wouldn't I?"

"You know why."

He rested his elbows on his knees and gazed down at the side of her soft face. "You were my friend Kate, long before you were my girl. I wish you would have remembered that before you left."

Her eyes lifted to his, so beautiful yet so full of sadness. "I never forgot," she said and they stared at each other for a long, silent moment before going back to the ice cream. He chuckled to himself watching her devour the cold mountain. Some things never changed.

"Do you remember the first time we met?" she asked.

How could he forget, she took his brother, who had towered over her in height and age, to his knees without a doubt in her mind that she couldn't. Marc had always been smaller than Corbin, his brother, even if there had only been four years between them. But Corbin had also been a bully and Marc had been an easy target.

That day, the two brothers had been waiting for their dad to finish in the office for supper. Marc had been reading a book and Corbin had been kicking the toe of his shoe on the floor board when he decided he wanted Marc's book and had snatched it from him. Of course, Corbin never did anything shoddy, and he began ripping pages out of the book and flagging them in front of Marc before crinkling and throwing them at his feet.

Marc had asked for it back, politely, which in turn had made Corbin laugh and continue tearing. Marc had just stared in horror as his brother had defaced the book he hadn't finished, unable to work up the courage to get it back. That was when Kate had rounded the corner of the resort and intervened, dropping her hands on her hips and giving Corbin a straightforward warning. He laughed at her just like he had laughed at Marc and she took him to his knees, making him cry like a baby.

"I do," Marc said now.

She laughed. "You were so scrawny, like this skinny, geeky ten-year-old." She laughed. "You had thin rimmed round glasses, like Harry Potter."

"I thought we were done with the insults."

She smiled.

He thought back. "You were this wild spark with such determination."

She smirked at him. "I'm sure I looked like a wild, unkempt brat," she said. "Remember my hair?" She put her hands beside her hair making a full motion. "I bet my jeans had been ripped."

He nodded. "Yes, they were ripped."

"Probably oil on my face."

"Dirt down your shirt."

She laughed. "I don't understand how we just clicked.

You know."

He nudged her side lightly with his elbow. "You were my hero, didn't you know?"

"I don't think that's an accurate title."

"My brother never bothered me again after that day." Of course he had only lived four years longer before the car crash had taken his life. The two brothers had been so different. Marc enjoyed books, Corbin liked television. Marc was calm like a warm breeze, collected with poise; Corbin was a wild bullet ready to thrash ahead without warning.

"I'm surprised your mom invited me back," she said. "Is she here?"

He nodded. "I was her favorite child and she couldn't say no to me."

Kate laughed. "Oh stop it. Your mom didn't play favorites. She probably thought you could use a bodyguard."

"That must have been it. You're awfully full of yourself."

"Well, I was your hero."

He laughed and she laughed in return.

"I should probably get back," she said. They stood. "Wait, did you come with Izzy?"

He nodded.

She smiled in relief. "Thank you for the ice cream...the distraction." She handed him the bowl. "Abby has disappeared since this morning but I bet your sister can pinpoint exactly where she is."

She began to walk away but turned and grabbed his arm gently, each finger marking his skin. "I'm sorry about your dad. No matter what he was to anyone, he was your dad." He was an ass to everyone, but she knew that. "And," she paused taking a deep breath. "I'm sorry Marc."

"For what?"

Her eyes didn't budge from his. "You know for what."

He nodded his understanding, he wasn't sure that he accepted it, but he heard it.

Chapter Seven

KATE DRAGGED ABBY through the resort's automatic double doors by encircling her own arm through Abby's and leading the way in a much faster pace than her rebelling sister's short steps across the parking lot had been. She thought it much classier than the alternative dragging her by the sleeve of her jacket. Although Kate wouldn't call what Abby was wearing in this cold weather, a jacket. It was more like a knitted windbreaker. But she had to pick her battles and her sister's attire wasn't among the ones worth fighting for at this moment.

After a tiresome daylong game of hide and seek, Izzy had broken down at the visitation and told Kate where to find Abby, at Mrs Calvert's, hiding away in that Mr. Brown Eyes, biker man's apartment above the bakery.

He looked like a whole lot of trouble that Kate did not want her sister engaged with. Tattoos down his thickly built arms, holes where piercings had obviously once adorned his rugged and dangerous looking face and the leather jacket he wore only added to the mysterious uncertainty she felt about him. Even though he was connected with Mrs. Calvert, Kate was convinced he must have done something bad....at some point in his life. No one like *that* just started working in a bakery. Maybe he was a fantastic chef or something, but his eyes spoke of a dark past and Kate didn't want that for Abby.

Especially not right now when Abby's thoughts were scattered...much like her attendance.

They crossed the lobby, Kate's heels clapping as Abby's boots scraped across the marble floor like those of a pouting child.

What different lives they lived, thought Kate. When Kate had been Abby's age she'd moved away from home, went to school, and had started interning at an advertising company. Abby was schooled, thanks to the money Kate had set aside for her, but spent her nights working at Jake's bar and apparently dabbling in soap making. *How serious was soap making as a career?*

The extraordinary glass crystal chandelier above them cast beams of light across Abby's tear-stained face. Her pale face today was quite the opposite of her normally dark eyeliner cat eyes and deep blush that accented her high cheekbones. She was probably more exhausted and worn out from creatively hiding from her sisters for the past couple days than actually dealing with the grief of Gran's death.

They turned in the opposite direction of the check in desk, where a set of young ears were ready to listen as her sister murmured, "I don't understand why you even care."

Was she serious? Everything Kate had given up was for her, Abby, her other siblings, and their father! *Did they think that their trust funds for college had just appeared out of thin air!*

"Oh enough," Kate snapped, immediately allowing guilt to wash through her body, like a wild wave slamming against the sandy beach shore. Abby was hurting. "You know I care," she said more softly, directing her around the corner towards the elevators.

"You have a funny way of showing it...moving across the country."

When they arrived at the mirrored elevators, Kate pressed the button furiously, letting go of her sister's arm. If she ran, Kate was mentally prepared to chase her down the long halls in her heels, and was prepared to tackle her to the ground, even in her tightly fitted dress.

"This was important today Abby, and you were expected to be there and you snuck away. You didn't even let any of us know where you were, or that you were okay." If she couldn't handle attending the visitations, she should have told them, not hidden unaccounted for all day long!

Abby leaned against the wall and crossed her arms to match her ankles. "So, let me get this straight. You would like me to check in with you, for the few days that you're here, and when you leave, we can continue our normal lives with no contact. Is that right?"

They texted each other every day! All their sisters did, but this sister was just being abnormally frustrating.

It's because she is hurting.

"I would rather you talk to me instead of pushing me away with insults."

"I would rather not talk at all."

That would probably be wise, at least until they got to her room, where the walls weren't listening. "Finally, we agree on something."

"Whatever's easiest for you. It's kinda like running away."

Argh! She was relentless!

"Or sleeping with your married boss."

"Abby!" she cried horrified.

Kate's appalled squeal was interrupted by another obnoxious sound—that of Isabelle Caliendo, tromping toward them.

From the not so innocent grin her sister flashed Izzy, it left no doubt in Kate's mind that the texting madness Abby exhibited the whole ride here had been these two preparing a getaway plan.

The friends embraced in a long, overly exaggerated hug, meshing together their similar outfits consisting of tights and long chiffon blouses like twisting sheets hung along a clothes line on a windy day.

"Hey, fancy running into you here," Izzy said, pulling away and squeezing her friend's arms.

Fancy? What young adult used such terminology, unless rehearsed, and was that a wink she caught from Izzy? No doubt. Little brats, she thought, forcing a half smile. Kate was exhausted but now found herself preparing for another fight.

"Abby, why don't you come to dinner?" Izzy suggested. "With me and the family," she added.

Kate crossed her arms skeptically as she watched the women's getaway plan unfold. Dinner? She didn't buy that for one second.

The elevator doors opened and Kate tugged her sister inside with Izzy chatting away and joining them. She couldn't very well forbid the blonde from entering the elevator, since her family owned it, but the thought did cross her mind.

Abby was agreeing to Izzy's plans as the door shut while Kate was mentally strategized a game plan of her own to prevent losing sight of her sister. She feared she'd lose the opportunity to speak to her before the funeral. And, they absolutely had to speak before that funeral, so Abby didn't have a breakdown there.

A hand slipped between the closing doors and a deep voice asked them to hold the elevator. Kate pressed the open button as Marc slipped inside and the doors slid together behind him. The small elevator felt like her tiny childhood closet as his tall, thick body and the yummy smell of his cologne invaded every inch of air.

He looked taken aback at the sight of all the girls inside. No, probably just her. He had been nice to her at the funeral home, not an hour earlier, out of respect for her loss, but it didn't automatically put them into the friends category.

"Good evening."

Izzy quickly latched onto her brother's arm and filled him in on the generous invitation, aka the "secret escape plan."

Kate thanked her, but declined saying, "We're just going to retire to our room for the night and order room service." Maybe with Marc's presence she should be able to thwart the girl's game plan and get Abby all to herself.

"Don't be silly," Izzy said. "We're eating at the pub and the food is way better than ordering in." She made a face as if to suggest that the take-out in this five-star resort was appalling. "You can come too, Kate."

"Oh, I can't intrude."

"Yes you can. It's been too long since we've seen you. Everyone would be so excited! I mean you used to always be around." She only knew half the truth of that. The later years when Izzy would have remembered Kate, she was usually there to find her father, sober him up, help him finish his duties and then only have a few minutes to sneak with Marc before she had to go home and take care of her siblings.

"That was a long time ago," said her youngest, unappreciative sibling.

Kate ignored Abby. She wasn't about to display their dirty garbage for Marc to witness. "We really can't..."

"Don't speak for me," Abby interrupted. "I'm going."
Stubborn little spark.

Kate held her breath for a second, forcing herself not to show the exasperation she was feeling from her toes all the way up to her clenched hands—hands that were fighting against lashing out at her sister and shaking some sense into her.

"Marc, convince Kate to join us," Izzy whined, tugging his arm and laying her head on his shoulder to stare up at him with big, round puppy dog eyes, dramatically making her point.

Kate was sure he would agree they had already spent more than enough time together.

Marc smiled at Kate. "She doesn't need my convincing but you're more than welcome to join us. It might be a nice distraction for you two."

Kate had never allowed herself to dream he would ever be so forgiving and welcoming. Then again, she had never allowed herself to dream of ever stepping foot back in this resort in the first place.

Izzy jumped away from her brother clapping her hands in delight. "A wonderful distraction, so it's settled."

Izzy was a firecracker. Kate was thankful her own little sister paled in comparison to this gusto of a blonde. Well, brunette sporting blonde bleached hair with definitely a few layers of hair extensions.

Before Kate knew it, she had agreed to supper and they were entering the loud pub. The restaurant was packed with a lively bunch of people—their voices clashing with the music flowing from the speakers. It was a bar and grill style eatery with flat screens on the barn board walls displaying different sports games. A bar room with pub tables and stools, sat to the side of a maze of separate booths and open tables.

Izzy pulled Abby in front leading the way to their table in a speedy fashion, which left Kate to walk beside Marc.

The walkways were snug with guests pushing their seats into the aisles as they ate and drank, enjoying their retreat getaway. Forcing Marc and Kate to walk front to back...and too close for Kate's comfort.

"I'm sorry we're intruding on your family," she said to Marc as he paused to let her go first between two chairs.

"We will call it even after I enjoy watching you squirm."

She turned suddenly, taken aback by his teasing words. "Why would I squirm?"

His body collided against hers...again. She flushed and quickly apologized.

He grinned. "If I didn't know better, and I suspect I do," he clarified, taking a deep breath against her body, his warmth sneaking through her clothes and tickling her skin. "I would think you are trying to seduce me."

She rolled her eyes and shook her head at the same time. "If I was trying to seduce you, there wouldn't be any question in your mind." She turned not giving him a chance for a comeback. *Why had she turned in the first place?*

She didn't press the issue further as they arrived at the Caliendo table, where everyone was already engaged in laughter and conversation. As she scanned the table, meeting the eyes of surprised family members, she discovered why he was convinced she would squirm.

In addition to his sister Violet's children, there were the usual Caliendos. Of course, Marc's deceased father was replaced with Marc's Uncle Carl. He had always been very nice compared to Marc's father. He was quiet and didn't stare down at you, with condemning eyes, merely because you didn't come from a family of wealth.

His mother, Eliza, sat across the table showing little signs of aging, her blue eyes widened in pleasure at Kate's presence. "Oh how lovely, Katherine McAdams, come and sit." She swept her hand across the long table at the empty chair in front of her, then thought better and stood up. "Let me get another hug first."

She came rushing around the table as Izzy dragged Abby to the far, opposite side. Eliza pulled Kate into an extended hug, whispering her condolences again. They had already done this at the funeral home. "We have missed you around here," she said pulling away and examining her tamed curls all the way down to her designer heels. "You are beautiful. Isn't she beautiful Marcus?" It wasn't rhetorical. Kate looked up at Marc standing beside her and waited for his answer.

He didn't even flinch. "Yes, beautiful."

Kate swallowed hard.

Eliza moved to Marc and gave him a hug. "Not sure what happened to this one," she teased.

"Thanks Mother."

Eliza laughed and kissed one cheek and patted the other. "Sit, sit, sit you two."

On the opposite side of the table, across from where Marc had pulled out an empty chair for her to sit, was Marc's entertainment. Melissa Carter forced her own surprised and judging smile at Kate. They shared a true hate/hate relationship. Kate sensed things had not changed.

Kate suddenly wondered if Melissa and Marc were an item. No. He'd made it clear earlier in the evening that there was no woman in his life. Not that it mattered who he dated. But Melissa? She had been such a nuisance back in the day. A very good friend of Marc's sister Emma, who was now seated between her and Eliza. Neither of them had been on Kate's list of friends and she was sure Emma had been biased towards Kate because of her relationship with Melissa. They both came from wealth and their clique didn't include Kate. Or so they'd pointed out on many occasions.

"Let the games begin," Marc whispered in her ear before sitting beside Melissa, a mischievous grin on his face.

Mature, she thought. Did he really think she would fall into old habits during this short, hopefully short, dinner?

"It's nice of you to join us," Carl said. He had always been nice to the staff, Kate's father included, and treated Marc, his sisters and mother with a respect Mr. Caliendo had never. She wondered how Mr. Caliendo lacked everything humane when his brother had so clearly acquired it.

"It was nice to be invited." *Oh, what a lie.*

"Your grandmother was an amazing lady and not a bad pie baker either," he teased with a wink. "Her pies will be missed here."

She smiled at him. "Thank you."

"How long are you in town for?"

"I leave Friday." *As long as everything was settled by then,* but she didn't add that part.

The table engaged in some small talk before dinner was served. A few more questions were directed at Kate, but all in all, everyone was surprisingly respectful of her privacy. They didn't pry or seem angry that she had left Marc all those years ago. She hadn't been sure what to expect, but even if she had, this reception was most delightful.

Right after dinner, a delicious plate of Salisbury steak, mashed potato and vegetable with a fancy roll on the side, Izzy and Abby excused themselves. Izzy kissed her mom's cheek and talked the whole way around the table, not allowing another person the opportunity to get a word in, until they were lost in the crowd.

Were they kidding? Kate's insides boiled like a witch's brew and she wished she could curse her sister straight up to her suite. Since that wasn't realistic, she forced a friendly smile, and rose from her chair. "Excuse me for a quick second."

She caught Marc's concerned look but didn't have time to explain, nor did she want to with a table full of his family around them.

She stormed out of the pub and cried out to her sister as she made her way down the hall.

"Abby!"

Surprisingly, her sister stopped and turned, even against Izzy's pulling hand. Abby met Kate halfway, leaving Izzy to find an employee to pass her time in a flirtatious manner that had Kate inwardly shaking her head.

"Where are you going?"

"Kate, I just need some space."

"From me? From your family?"

"It's not about you." She rolled her eyes. "Okay, it's a little about you."

"Abby..."

Abby cut her off by pulling her into an unexpected hug. "Top floor, room 237. I will see you later tonight. I promise."

And just like that she was down the hall and had disappeared with her friend. Kate realized Izzy had been there for Abby more than she had the last few years. Kate had abandoned her, no matter her reasoning at the time, and now she wondered what it would have been like if she had stayed. What might have been if she had just stood up and faced things head on. She would have crashed, that's what would have happened. She would have had her life ripped out from under her and everyone she loved would have been in jeopardy.

Abby was probably better off with that crazy Caliendo after all.

Chapter Eight

MARC WANTED TO chase Kate out of the pub as she had chased her sister. It was obvious she was having a family dilemma with Abby, and Izzy was squeezing in where it wasn't her business. What else was new?

He knew how it would look to everyone deep in conversation about the Snowflake Ball, if he excused himself in search of her. They were all well aware Kate brought out something in him that stole his rationality. It was why they had all chased him around the resort the day before. If he went after her now, he would also look like the love-struck, heartbroken, emotionally unattached fool they all hoped he wasn't.

He weighed his options, dancing around in his head. He didn't care when they thought. Not when it came to Kate. He threw down the napkin he hadn't realized he'd been twisting in his hands beside his plate. He knew exactly what it was like to have a whirl-wind sister and felt a twinge of responsibility since it was his sister causing the conflict. How could no one else see that? That was the reason he fed the logical part of his brain, even though deep down he knew it was more. It was always more with her.

A hand rested on his shoulder keeping him grounded as he was about to stand. "I'll go check," Violet's soft voice whispered to him. "She left her jacket and purse," she pointed out, squeezing his shoulder reassuringly before removing her hand and merging into the crowded pub.

He felt his shoulders relax, glad someone was going to check on her, and pushing away the disappointment that it wasn't him.

"Where is she off to?" Melissa asked, nudging his side lightly.

"Checking on Izzy," he lied. "Probably followed by a lecture on her early departure," he added and Melissa chuckled before diving right back into the conversation she had been having with the rest of his family.

Marc tried to focus on the conversation at hand, but felt less than interested. It wasn't until he spotted Violet and Kate laughing and smiling their way back through the tables that he felt better.

He was ready to excuse himself on that notion. This protective desire he felt could only lead to trouble. But that was what friends did, they protected each other. Right?

"Is everything alright?" his mother asked when they returned. He was glad she had asked as the words were on the tip of his tongue.

Kate nodded. "Yes, thank you."

Kate settled back in her seat and his uncle whispered something to her, bringing about a true rumble of laughter from Kate. Marc was jealous it was his uncle on the receiving end of her beautiful laughter and not him.

Then Melissa interjected. "Kate, did you come alone?" The table conversation came to an abrupt halt, and the silence was suddenly deafening. They only sounds still remaining were Violet's kids, Sophia and Parker, who had no interest as they continued amongst themselves, not realizing the air had shifted around them. Melissa made sure everyone else was focused on Kate.

Marc watched Kate's face alter as she switched gears from the enjoyable conversation with his uncle to Melissa and her meddling ways. He noted the ever so slightly tightening of her jaw and raise of her eyebrows. He was sure no one else, except him, recognized it as her protective face.

Inwardly he cursed Melissa, but knew he was curious, too. Even though he hadn't dared ask it himself.

She smiled for the rest of the table, certainly not for Melissa and answered in a surprising cool manner, "Yes, I did." This was a new side of Kate, he thought, able to mask her dismayed face.

Melissa smiled back, she was first-class at disguising her true feelings. He'd noticed since he returned home that Melissa portrayed the pretense of a woman madly in love with him, but he sensed something was off...just as his sister had warned. He couldn't put his finger on it. But these two gals here, he knew exactly where their relationship stood by the hatred sizzling between them like an electric charge ready to split.

"There is no special someone in your life? Boyfriend? Fiancé? Husband?" Melissa continued to pry.

A gracious smile found Kate's lips, in contrast to the surprised look of the rest of his family.

Kate replied, "He certainly wouldn't have missed my grandmother's funeral, if there was."

There was no one in Kate's life, good to know. *Why was that good to know?* What was he thinking was going to happen here?

He barely had time to scold himself before Melissa

stepped overboard and said, "Oh, that's too bad."

Kate's eyes widened as Melissa casually, and contently, turned back to her meal. If she had really thought Kate was going to let that comment slide, she was forgetting the young Kate, unless she had changed over the years. Evidently, Melissa had not.

"I don't see a ring on your finger Melissa. No someone special for you either?" Kate threw the words back at her, making full eye contact with Melissa.

Marc wondered if the others around the table could see what was conspiring in front of them—a cat fight in the making.

Melissa smiled back. "There's always been someone special in my life," she replied. And, that was exactly the talk that had always resulted in these two sparring. He didn't like that Melissa threw comments like that so casually around. Comments obviously about him. Comments that he knew his family, especially his mother, would analyze.

"That's wonderful," Kate said, her tone not gracious, not condemning like he knew she felt. Her gaze settled on Marc. He put a mouthful of potatoes in his mouth to cover the grin and giving him a reason not to get involved.

"So Marc, did you ever get that sauna lock fixed?" Kate asked, her voice full of fake curiosity. So much that it almost made him laugh. Then, the images of that distracted him. When the image of her half-naked body pressed against his flashed into his mind like a bolt of lightning, he nearly spit out his potatoes.

A classic Kate move. Maybe not as blunt as the feisty brunette had once been, but none the less it got the point across and he saw exactly where this was going. But he didn't mind.

He grabbed his beer and washed the potatoes down before nodding and saying, "I probably did a number on it with that screwdriver."

"You were in the sauna?" Eliza inquired. "With Marc?" she added, obviously curious as to why he hadn't mentioned it yesterday. She shot him a questioning look as Kate sent him a teasing smirk.

Now the stares of the others returned to Kate and she smiled sincerely. "It was quite the coincidence. When I arrived here yesterday I thought, what better way to relax than a steaming hot sauna?" She shrugged. "So I headed down and it was extremely hot in there, it hit me right through the doors and Marc said," she glanced over at Marc. "What was it you said I did?" she asked innocently, pretending hard to figure it out.

This was going to get a rise out of his mother for weeks. "Blatantly ignored the sign," he filled in the blank.

Gasps turned to laughter around the table. She'd always been able to make a table laugh. It normally had been her sisters, instead on those long parentless nights. They'd all sulk around until and Kate would convert their frowns into smiles full of laughter.

She clapped her hands together now dramatically and nodded. "YES! That was it!"

"Marcus, you did not," His mother asked, a smirk on her lips.

"He did," Kate insisted. "All because I missed the tiny little 'out of order' sign," She parted her thumb and pointer finger an inch to indicate how small the sign had been. "Which he politely pointed out to me after I locked us in!"

Curious eyes arose again around the table like kindergarten children being read a story book.

"You were locked in the sauna?" his six-year old nephew called from the other end of the table. "I'm not even allowed in there. How long were you locked in? Were you hot?"

"It was steaming hot," Mark added. Steaming with hot, bare skin everywhere. "The thermostat was broken."

Kate laughed. "Can you all imagine my surprise, finding Marc in there wearing his expensive slacks, shirtless, dripping sweat and holding a screwdriver." Her gaze locked with his eyes for a moment and they were back in that steamy room together, staring at one another with lustful eyes. She turned away. "Because, as we all know, he's not really as handy as he thinks he is." She smiled at him enjoying the story just as much as everyone else.

Another round of laughter made its way around the table.

"Hey," he interjected. "I'm the one who changed the door handle."

"I could do that in my sleep." Kate dismissed, waving her hand at him. "So anyway, I let him at it for a little bit but when I couldn't stand the heat anymore I bumped him out of the way..." She looked at him with a mischievous grin. "Literally, I set him on his..." she glanced down the table at the kids listening, "...rear end."

More laughter erupted and she winked at him, purposely omitting what had really happened in the steam.

"And not alone," he added. "She came tumbling down with me."

Kate's eyes widened and her cheeks flushed. Melissa coughed and his family gasped. Then Kate laughed and the rest couldn't help themselves.

"And then I fixed the thermostat before popping the door knob open," she retorted.

That wasn't exactly the details he remembered.

"Hey," Violet interjected. "You told us you'd fixed the thermostat."

Technically, he'd said it was fixed and didn't include the specifics, purposely trying to avoid the cat and mouse game he was sure to have with each pair of those curious eyes.

Kate laughed. "If passing me a screwdriver is fixing it," she said.

"At least we had one McAdams to save our day," his mother praised.

Round one. Kate's win. He enjoyed the true smile he saw on her face. This might actually work to his benefit, deterring Melissa from engaging in flirtation and Emma from always trying to set them up. The only downside was that in a few days she would be gone. Again.

The table resumed the Snowflake Ball conversation after supper and their glasses were all re-filled. Kate declined more wine and politely excused herself before the rest, with courteous appreciation for the invitation to their meal and insisted on paying for her and Abby's uneaten portion. But his mother wouldn't hear of it.

"Don't be shy Kate. Next time you're in town drop by and say hello," Eliza encouraged. "Maybe we will see you again before you go."

"That would be nice. Thank you again."

He rose with Kate and offered to walk her out, he would have argued talk of snow, icicles and fondant shaped snowflake cupcakes were the basis of his quick departure, but on one would have believed it anyway.

It was Kate.

He felt like this was his opportunity to ask the question frequently popping into his mind. He needed the answer. He needed some closure so he could move on. He hadn't realized the extent of nagging the question had implied over the years until he was in such close proximately to get the answer. He needed to know just like Violet had said he did. Marc hated it when she was right and he certainly didn't look at her before following behind Kate.

Kate chuckled on their way down the hall.

"What?" he asked.

She shook her head, looking up at him. "I'm so sorry if that was inappropriate but that girl prickles me in a way I can't explain," she laughed, grabbing his arm. "She turns me back in time to a crazy love struck teenager." As the words came out, her eyes snapped up to his and she quickly retracted her hand. "Sorry."

He shrugged. "She kind of asked for it."

Kate laughed. "She totally did, didn't she?" She shook her head. "Thanks for supper. It was a nice distraction, but now I have to wait impatiently for my sister." She looked up at him. "That girl is driving me nuts."

He knew exactly what she was talking about. "I can relate."

She nodded. They stopped at the elevator just as it opened and Kate thanked him again before stepping in. He wasn't done yet, so he stepped in with her.

She looked him over suspiciously. "Directly to my door, that's service," she teased.

He smiled. "It's not that unselfish," he said as each floor they passed sounded a little beep.

When the doors opened, he walked her to her door. She got out her card and looked up at him. "I'm not asking you in."

She had already made that clear. But it wasn't her lips he was after, well...it wasn't entirely off the radar either. He leaned his side against the doorframe hovering above her so close her vanilla scent wafted around him...again. "I want you to ask me in."

She stared up at him with pleading eyes. "Marcus," she whispered.

He leaned his arm above the door frame to shelter them. If this was as far as they went he had to ask now.

"Why did you leave me?"

There it was, the question that had plagued him all these years. He had learned to live with it, but now, with her only inches away, he wanted the truth.

Her eyes filled with pain, but she didn't budge. "My mom had left money to all of us in a trust fund for college. My dad didn't tell any of us and one day, when I was cleaning, I found the papers. I had to go Marc and see what else was out there. I had to go to school and start a career. And when I got there, I realized..." She paused, sucking in a hard breath. "I didn't want to come back."

Her eyes apologized for the harsh truth and stung his heart like a bee sting, quick and immediate. This was what he wanted. As painful as it was, the truth would help him to move on with his life, move on without her.

He wasn't about to continue standing there and make a complete ass by inquiring about a love that had obviously been so one-sided. He nodded his understanding and held out his hand. "Friends?"

She half smiled and accepted his hand. "Always."

Chapter Nine

KATE WAS UP before five and texting her sisters, minus the youngest who hadn't bothered to locate room 237 the night before and, again, hadn't bothered sending a text saying she was alright either.

They decided to meet at Gran's before Abby could escape them. Peyton had heard her come in here the night before. After making a strong pot of coffee, they all silently nibbled on some baked goods from Mrs. Calvert's as Abby slept just down the hall. They all wore their black dresses: Kate a full-length, fitted wool dress, Sydney a lace covered dress that fell just below her knees, and Peyton in a chiffon dress with a string waist. They all wore waterproof makeup.

The room was hushed but filled with anticipation and anxiety. They all knew, like the seconds before the rising of the curtain in a theater, that there would be a show once Abby appeared. She finally stumbled into the kitchen, hung-over. How lovely.

"Morning," the sisters greeted in her unison, smiles on their faces. It was unfortunate how those smiles would depart in a few hours as they buried Gran.

Abby paused in the doorway, her eyes swollen and bloodshot, her rock star-looking hair frizzed in every which direction. She was missing her pants, wearing only an oversized t-shirt. "What are you all doing here?" she asked, rubbing her eyes.

Peyton set down her coffee. "We're here to rage," she announced proudly.

Kate grinned against her better judgement.

Abby stared at them dumbfounded.

"I'm pissed I never opened my own business," Peyton sais, announcing the same regret she had confided in them over and over again.

Abby's face squished together. "Huh?"

"I'm pissed I missed all my teenage years because I got preggo at sixteen," Sydney said. "Although I love Haylee and wouldn't trade her for anything," she clarified quickly.

Peyton slanted a look in her direction. "Isn't that like cheating? You can't add a positive to a negative or it equals out. You could look at it that way or you could look at it as though the positive wouldn't have happened without the negative."

"I think we'll let that slide because we all love Haylee," Kate interjected. "But how about last time, cause technically that's not raging, it's rationalizing."

The sisters nodded, agreeing.

Abby was still lost. "What's going on?"

"I'm pissed that I slept with my married boss," Kate continued. *More pissed the jerk couldn't make it to her grandmother's funeral.*

"I'm pissed I didn't sleep with my married boss," Peyton said, then gasped. "Oh Sydney you say it, tell us you're pissed you slept with Jake and then rationalize because you're actually happy you did."

"I didn't sleep with Jake."

"You should." Peyton winked at her sister.

Sydney took a deep breath, clearly annoyed with her sister. "I'm not going to and you're going way off topic. Why don't we bring up the man's voice on the phone yesterday when you were *supposed* to be at the funeral home helping me with arrangements?"

Hmm...so that's where Peyton had been.

"Who was that you were entertaining?" Sydney asked. "And where were you and what were you doing?" Her accusing eyebrows raised, turning the attention away from herself.

"Oh please, it was probably the radio." Peyton waved a dismissive hand at her.

"Oh please, I don't buy it," Sydney said.

Kate whistled, and they all looked at Abby. "Your turn," Kate said.

Abby's sleepy eyes darted from one sister to the next. "You three are crazy."

"Come on Abby, rage it out," Kate encouraged.

"I'm pissed you drank all my coffee." Her tone was mild followed by a yawn and as she stretched her arms high above her head.

"Oh don't worry, there's a cup for you," Sydney quickly poured a cup and handed it to her. "You look like you need this."

"That's rude," Abby said, but smiled as she inhaled the aroma.

This was going nowhere. "I'm pissed mom died," Kate said and watched all her sister's faces drop. It was time they faced this head on...together. Again. Just like when they were children. "I'm pissed Gran died."

"Why are you doing this?" Abby asked dismayed. "It

won't bring her back. It won't bring Gran back."

"Say it," Kate encouraged.

"No."

"Don't you hide away and blame the world Abigail McAdams. This stuff happens and there's nothing we can do about it except be pissed, support each other, accept it and move on."

Abby set her coffee on the counter beside her. "What do you want me to do? Move away like you? Is that moving on enough?"

"Abby's pissed Kate moved away," Peyton said.

"I'm pissed I moved away." She really was and they had no idea how much.

"Then you shouldn't have!" Abby yelled.

Kate softened her tone. This was one touchy topic for her. "But I can't change it now Abby. And if this bothered you so much, why are you just now telling me?"

Abby's upper lip trembled against the angry facade she was withholding. "Because my third mother just died and I'm pissed my second one left me here after my first one died and now I'm all alone." Tears welled in her eyes. "I left Gran alone that night and didn't come home until morning and you know why?"

The girls shrugged.

"Because I was off drinking...like Dad. And last night..." She glared at Kate. "When you left, I took my first sip of alcohol and two years later woke up just like this: a horrible hangover. I'm going to likely vomit in the funeral home...I'm a drunk. And now you two will be gone and Sydney will be dealing with her other life and I'll be alone with Dad. Just like when you left the first time. I'm a drunk, just like Dad. And this time I won't have Gran to come pick me up and put me back together."

Kate hadn't seen that coming.

"I'm pissed Dad was a drunk..." Peyton said in a low tone. Kate sent her a glare and shook her head.

"Abby sit down." Kate pulled a chair out and waited for her sister to collapse into it like a raggedy doll. "Are you an alcoholic?"

Her tone was serious for show, but she already knew the answer. None of them were the young, lost kids of their youth. Even Abby, although the youngest, was still past those surging, teenage hormones.

"I drink. I get drunk."

Kate raised her eyebrow. "You know the difference."

"It's in our genes," she said. "Dad's doomed us all."

"Abby..."

"Well, I'm scared I'm going to end up like him."

Kate rubbed Abby's bare arm. "I know you won't. Gran certainly didn't think you would and you will always have the three of us, plus Avery. We are your family and it doesn't matter how far away we are, we are only a phone call away. We love you kid."

Tears streamed down Abby's face, staining her white t-shirt.

"And Abby, you couldn't have helped Gran. Even if you had been here, she died in her sleep. You would have never known sleeping in the room next to her," Sydney explained. "And she would never want you to blame yourself. Ever."

Kate grabbed some tissues from the box on the table and passed them to Abby. She blew her nose overly loud like a foghorn. That was going to be attractive in the quiet funeral home.

The girls all laughed.

"What?" she said as though she hadn't heard. When none of the sisters responded, she changed subjects. "Why didn't you say you're pissed you had to raise us?" she asked Kate, wiping away at her face. "The first opportunity you got you left." Her anger was less now but her sadness remained.

"I'm not angry that I had to raise you and Avery. I'm sad Mom died. I'm sad Dad drank. I'm sad Gran was so sad, but I loved all of you. I'm pissed I left you." Kate paused to gather her thoughts. She didn't want to hurt Abby again. "I never should have because you were only fifteen but all of a sudden I had the opportunity to get a career and make money rather than working a minimum wage job. I was selfish. I'm sorry. I should have gone to school here and I should have stayed with you two until you went to college." Abby sniffled and Kate leaned in close. "You're not an alcoholic."

"I know. And you weren't selfish. I love you, too." Abby leaned over and hugged her. "I'm sorry, too. You deserved the opportunity to go to school. Gran always called you my guardian angel. You were an awesome second mom."

Kate didn't feel like she had been a good second mom at all.

"Abby, sweetheart." Abby pulled away to look at her and Kate gave her a grin. "You sure do *smell* like an alcoholic."

Abby playfully hit her arm and smiled. Sensing the shift in mood, Peyton and Sydney stood up and rushed over for a group hug that nearly toppled them all over the chair.

"Are you making me pancakes?" Abby asked when

she was finally released. Pancakes had always been her favorite breakfast as a child.

"Don't kid yourself, I gave up my mommy years, here's a croissant." Kate tossed a bag from Mrs. Calvert's at her.

Abby opened the bag and was digging inside when she said. "Her baking is better than yours anyway."

All the sisters laughed and Kate was happy to see that the glimmer in Abby's eyes had returned.

***

THE FUNERAL HAD been beautiful with bright, thoughtful bouquets of flowers spilling in every corner and a line up of wonderful people that shared breathtaking stories of how Gran had touched their lives. They'd cried and they'd laughed and when it was all finished, they had hugged one another.

Hours later, the women, accompanied by their father and Haylee, stood in an empty building situated on Main Street. The building saw right across the tiny alley that divided this building from Mrs. Calvert's bakery. They all stared at the run down, two-story mess in front of them. The building hadn't housed a business in years not from lack of interest though, or so the lawyer had informed them.

Apparently, there had been a lot of inquiries about the rental of the building, but Gran had refused to rent. It had been empty for about three years when a "quick summer store", as Abby had described it, couldn't survive. All that remained were lime green, bright yellow, and Caribbean teal splashed on the old, chipping walls.

Kate was pretty sure it had been a hair dresser's salon when she was young. A lot of businesses set up and then left in this town though, so it was hard to keep track.

"She should have rented it out at least to pay the taxes," Sydney said.

Kate supposed that would have been the logical thing to do except the space was totally trashed.

"She would have had to invest quite a bit to get this cleaned up enough to rent out."

"Yeah, but Dad's a handyman," Sydney pointed out. "When did she buy it again?"

Their father was walking around examining the structural parts of the building, the walls, and the fallen off baseboards. He knocked off and picked up tiles from the floor, and shaking his head.

"After this store closed," he said, "I remember when it went up for sale. It was a quick sale and the sign came down, the windows were set up and it was just left here, empty."

The two display windows on each side of the door had little stages where a backdrop hung so people couldn't see into the store, but the windows were all decked up for the holidays. The windows were absolutely beautiful adorned with garland and lights. The door was a large glass door with bunched-up curtains that, again prevented nosey people from seeing the disaster inside.

"And you didn't know it was Gran that bought it?" Kate asked.

He shook his head. "I had no idea."

"She was probably planning on selling it," Kate said. "She must have purchased it at a low cost thinking she could flip it and make a profit. Why else would she buy it?"

"To leave to us," Peyton said, clarifying the obvious.

"With a clause stating we can't sell it for a year," Sydney said, sounding irritated by the clause. "Now we have to pay the taxes," she added.

"This has so much potential," Peyton said. "We could clean it up, paint the walls, add a new floor, and we could open a shop in here."

"I love that idea Peyton," Abby agreed. "There are a lot of businesses we could open for next spring."

Sydney put her arm around Abby's shoulder. "And what type of business? None of us know anything about business."

Peyton crossed her arms and stared at them all with a very serious face. "First of all, Sydney, you've been working at Jake's bar since the accident and you could run that business in your sleep. Second, I am a consummate hair stylist. Third, Abby went to school to be an esthetician and she and Gran were making and selling soap on a small scale. Fourth Kate is an advertising creator and could design all our artwork."

Abby looked up. "You saw my soap?"

"We all bought some. Sydney set us up and we left the cash in an envelope in the cupboard."

"Do you like them?"

"Haven't tried any yet, but they smell wonderful," Kate said.

"I started making little batches for myself and all my friends loved it. Soon their friends and families starting putting in orders, too, so Gran said to start charging. Like, I can't even keep up with the demand. We had just finished tagging those batches before Gran..." Abby paused, her eyes filling with tears.

Sydney squeezed Abby's shoulder and said, "We know sister. It's going to be hard for all of us, especially at the beginning."

"I know." Abby gave her head a little shake.

"See, we could start a little all natural soap store here," Peyton suggested with a gleam of excitement in her eyes. "The demand is high; Abby has already started the clientele."

Sydney leveled her best mom-like glare at her sister. "And you live hours away and Kate lives a flight away so this plan is ridiculous. And Abby, sorry girl, but you can't hold a job."

Abby pulled away from her sister, insulted. "That's because the salons around here are full of a bunch of stuck up snobbish women that I would never be able to a fake smile with all day."

"But we're stuck with this place for a year anyway," Peyton said.

Sydney shook her head against the idea. "Besides all of that, we would need funds Peyton, like serious funds from the hanging electrical up there..." She hiked her thumb to the ceiling and the lights dangling from cut wires. "...to what appears to be a smashed human body through that wall and a staircase that looks like it's going to come crashing down any minute. It's not just a matter of paint and floors, this whole building needs to be gutted and rebuilt."

They all glanced over their shoulders at the broken wall and staircase. Sydney was over exaggerating a little bit. The staircase maybe needed a new railing and the painted wood needed to be stripped, sanded and refinished, but it looked stable.

"Dad?" Sydney called, looking for backup to confirm her opinion that they were standing in a money hole.

"I think you would definitely have to hire an electrician and, by the looks of that ceiling..." He pointed straight up the open staircase to the second floor where tiles were discolored from water damage. "...you might need a whole new roof. The stairs seem fine, but some of the walls are going to need new drywall." He continued checking off a list that only fueled Sydney's argument.

"I think it's more than we all have to invest, don't you?" Sydney asked at the end. "And what if it failed and we lost all our money? It would be thousands of dollars Peyton."

"I think we could figure out a plan," Peyton said.

"Well I think you better come up with a financial plan before we touch a thing in here except for fastening a 'For Sale' sign in that front window when the time comes."

Kate intervened before they had another fighting match. "This has been a long few days, so why don't we all just think about it. We have a year before we have to decide anything permanent."

Everyone agreed, some more reluctantly than others, but the topic was dropped.

"What about that hotel getaway Gran bought for us? When are we taking that? Because I could use it now, so let's drive north," Abby suggested.

At the reading of her will, the family had realized Gran had been full of strange surprises, including an all paid week stay getaway to Crystal Hotel, an eight-hour drive up north with the stipulation that they take a break together as a family.

"With the week I just took off, I think I've used my sick days for the year," Peyton said.

"So scrap paid vacation?" Abby sulked.

"It's a gift certificate thing, you can go anytime," their father said. "But, for now, I have to get going. I'm working the afternoon shift. Are you heading back Kate?"

She nodded. This was her last paid day in the resort, but she didn't plan on boarding an airplane back to her condo. She planned on to stay with Abby until she felt her sister was stable enough to leave. If that meant losing her job...well, so be it. She was working for a genuine ass anyway.

Chapter Ten

"SO IF WE wait until the last song and encourage everyone to the dance floor, in the middle of the song, we'll tear the bag. Fake snow will fall from the ceiling and our guests will have their own inside winter wonderland," Emma announced holding her hands up in the middle of the empty ballroom, pitching her idea to Marc and Violet.

They looked at each other skeptically.

"They can just step outside for a winter wonderland," Marc said. "It's snowing out there."

He heard Violet stifle a laugh.

"And it sounds messy," he added.

Emma dropped her hands and her smile. "That's why we have a cleaning crew."

"They're going to have to chase people down the halls with a vacuum," he said, garnering another partially contained giggle from Violet.

Emma folded her arms across her chest, obviously not pleased with his feedback. Why did they keep asking him for his feedback if they didn't like what he had to say? They always ended up doing whatever they wanted anyway. "It would be magical," she insisted.

"A magical mess. Why don't you use balloons?"

"Balloons Marc? Really? How 1980's of you. Snap

back to the twentieth century. Snow is the balloon of today." Emma said.

He thinned his lips and crossed his own arms, "I don't know." He was only teasing, but she had no idea.

"Well, picture this," she continued holding her hands up to frame the room in front of them. "You're all dressed up and the music is slow and you ask this girl to dance," she paused and a ridiculous smile crossed her lips. "Let's say Melissa."

Let's say Kate.

"And you're moving across the dance floor, in a romantic sway, and suddenly the sky opens mid-song and it's snowing wonderful thick flakes." Emma swayed alone in the ballroom her arms out, twirling like a child.

Marc threw his hands in the air. "Melissa is going to be freaking out. There will be snow stuck all in her hair and all over her dress. She'll end up hitting me in the face and screaming at the staff."

Violet laughed, unable to hold a straight face any longer.

Emma dropped her hands and turned to him, planting her hands on her hips. "That wouldn't happen," she stated firmly. "You're acting all weird. What's wrong with you? A simple yes or no would have sufficed."

"I think it's a lovely idea," Violet said. "I'll look into where to get bulk, fake snow." She glanced at her watch. "Your yoga class starts in fifteen."

Emma looked at her watch and scooted it out of the room, leaving Violet and Marc laughing.

"Oh no, I think one is in my eye Marc," Violet teased, pretending to be Melissa. "Could you just get a little closer?"

Marc rolled his eyes. "Remind me to avoid the Snowflake Ball."

She laughed. "You wish."

Violet started writing notes on her iPad, likely about fake snow.

"So, have you talked to Kate?"

He shook his head.

"Oh, I thought because of that little run in, you two were, I don't know...hitting it off again?"

"Nope, just friends."

"Friends are good." Violet smiled. "I wish I was friends with Joel." She crinkled her nose. "Actually I don't. He's a terrible friend and his friends are the worst."

Violet and Joel's divorce a year ago had been long and messy, especially since he ended up dating one of the women from the resort after it was finalized.

There had been suspicion behind the timing and Marc believed that little home wrecker under his payroll may have been partially responsible for the divorce. But he blamed Joel mostly. He was the one who had shared vows and brought children into the world with Violet. Those two little squirts were the best thing that man ever did.

"My babes will be home any minute. Was there anything else you wanted to discuss about the Snowflake Ball?" Violet asked Marc.

Marc shook his head. "I'll walk you out. I wanted to stop by Dad's study before I stop by the lunch room to find Kent to ask him about a broken sprinkler."

They walked down the long hallway that separated the resort from the living quarters. Their father had built them each a suite centered around an indoor pool.

At the end of the hallway, Marc swiped his access card. Their father's study sat to the right inside the next hall.

"She leaves today." Violet said stopping with him at the study. "It's almost lunchtime so if you go hang near the check-out desk maybe you can have a *friend's* moment."

"That's called stalking."

Marc pulled the door handle to the study. He'd left his suit jacket inside when Emma had passed by earlier, rushing him out before her morning class. It was locked. He turned again. That was strange, the door was never locked. Well, it hadn't been locked since his dad had passed away anyway. When his father had been alive, he'd spent hours behind these locked walls, which was why it had a deadbolt instead of a swipe card like the rest of the resort. His father liked his privacy. Especially in this room.

"It's locked," Marc told Voilet.

Violet reached around him and tried the door herself as though she might have the magic touch. She came up empty handed like Marc.

"That's strange," she said, stepping back.

Marc knocked on the door. "Hello? Is someone in there? Hello?" No reply. He must have accidentally locked it on his way out.

"Don't you have the key?" she asked.

He shook his head.

"You're the only one who goes in there. Who would lock the deadbolt? It doesn't even make sense."

He agreed. "I'll talk to Mom later. I'm going to grab a suit from my suite."

He opened the glass doors stepping into the tropical poolroom. As Violet ducked underneath his arm, they heard the study doors open and turned to look. His uncle walked out of the office looking suspiciously around, probably for whoever was knocking on the door, when he found the siblings staring at him.

He straightened his body, dusted his jacket and greeted them with a smile.

"Uncle Carl, what are you doing in there?" Violet called out, stepping back out of the poolroom. Marc let the door shut.

Their uncle walked towards them with a friendly smile. He shrugged. "Nothing."

"Why was the door locked?" Marc asked, his voice full of his own suspicions.

"The door was locked?" he asked, acting innocent. Of course the door was locked...he just unlocked it to get out Marc had heard the click.

"We were knocking and calling through. Didn't you hear us?" Violet asked.

He shrugged. "I dozed off in there." Marc eyed him skeptically. Something was off. "It's all yours now."

Violet's phone went off and she sighed. "Joel's here. I have to go."

Carl took her arm. "I'll walk you. I missed those little squirts this week," he said, walking her into the pool room.

"It's always so quiet when they're gone," Violet agreed.

The two left Marc and he made his way into the study, and grabbed his jacket off the center of the sofa where Carl had supposedly fallen asleep. Not a wrinkle on it. He looked around the room, wondering why his uncle would lock himself in and then lie about it, but everything seemed in place. Just another oddity to add to his uncle's list of odd behaviors.

Walking through the resort, Marc nodded and smiled as he passed the staff and guests until he reached the staff lunchroom. He pushed the door open and found more staff members then he had ever seen making a ruckus. Noisy enough that they hadn't heard him enter.

He quietly closed the door behind him, wondering what they were all gathered around.

Then he heard her laugh.

"What does that even mean?" someone asked.

Kate laughed again. "It means I design ads for companies to sell their products."

The crowd parted just enough for him to see her. She was dressed in black again, only instead of a dress, she wore tight-fitting black pants that disappeared behind black heeled boots that ran halfway up her calves. A sleek black blazer covered a lace black blouse. She looked slim, sophisticated and gorgeous.

Her hair was down, finally, and longer than he had ever seen it. It cascaded halfway down her back in large curls.

"That sounds like a fancy way of saying you draw for a living," someone else teased, causing everyone to laugh.

Marc chuckled, too. At the sound of his voice, everyone turned, and then split away like scattering ants.

"Oh come on," Kate said, as they took turns giving her hugs and kisses, quickly departing. "Most of you remember when he was in diapers."

Marc hadn't noticed that much of the gathered staff were those who had been employed at the resort for many years.

They chuckled at Kate's teasing, but continued to clear, nodding respectfully as they passed him and out the door.

"See you later sweetheart," Kent said, kissing Kate's cheek and following the rest of the staff out the door behind him, until they were left alone.

Instead of stopping Kent, whom Marc had been looking for, he let him pass and stared at Kate instead.

She frowned at him. "Aren't we intimidating?"

He shrugged. "What can I say?" He leaned forward. "I *am* a Caliendo."

She nodded in agreement and pursed her lips. "The name is a bit terrifying. But I think they would be able to differentiate all that is you from all that was him."

Marc shrugged.

He liked that she knew the name had nothing to do with the person attached to it. "In time. Are you leaving?"

She nodded. "Yes, I am. All packed and ready to head out."

"I'll walk you." He held out his arm, and she linked hers with a quiet, "Thank you."

Abandoning his duties for the moment, Marc walked Kate to her car in the underground parking garage.

She pulled open the door, but didn't climb in right away. He noted that she squeezed in beside the door though, putting a barrier between them.

"The resort looks good. A lot has changed since I was here last," Kate said.

"Thank you."

She nodded and that awkward silence adamant on

scuffling between them returned.

"It was nice seeing you," she said.

"It was nice bumping into you." She flushed as was his intention.

"It was interesting," she said.

He shrugged. "I'm going to stick with nice."

A smile curved her red lips. "Alright, you do that."

He leaned over the top frame of the door and kissed her cheek. "And you take care of your knee," he whispered.

"I will."

Reluctantly, Marc tore away and Kate practically dived into her car.

He waved as she drove away.

Marc didn't like the unsettling feeling deep in his gut, that he was letting her go again. Just like six years ago, she'd made it clear that she didn't want to stay.

Chapter Eleven

THE NEXT MORNING Kate enjoyed the aroma of Abby's soap while sitting alone in the sunroom embracing her first coffee. She was used to spending her mornings alone, so she fit right in with Abby's lazy morning routine which involved staying in bed and calling lunch breakfast.

Her solitude was short lived as she heard the front door open and Sydney's voice yell out, "Kate!"

She looked at her one-third finished coffee and knew the small amount wasn't nearly enough to help her function properly.

She wanted to ignore her sister, but called out, "In here."

Sydney appeared in the doorway looking exceptionally wide-eyed for just past seven a.m..

"I tried calling your cell like a dozen times." Kate had turned it off to avoid texts from Derek. "I tried calling here. Why didn't you answer?" Sydney looked on the edge of a panic attack.

Kate shrugged. "The phone didn't ring. What's going on?"

"It's Abby."

"Abby? Abby's still sleeping."

Sydney crossed her arms in front of her chest. "Really? That's funny since she didn't come home last night."

How would her sister know that? Kate reluctantly set her coffee down instantly missing the heat on her hands and went to bang on Abby's bedroom door. "Abby," she called. No response. She knocked again. "Abby." When there was no reply a second time, Kate opened the door and found an unmade bed, but no Abby.

Oh no.

"She's gone," Sydney said from the end of the hall.

"What do you mean she's gone?"

"Jake called me last night. After she was done with her shift she met up with a wild crowd hanging there. This is not a good crowd. When I got there and went to talk to Abby, the guys started to get a little out of control. Jake stepped in and he got in a fight with one of the guys."

Kate gasped. "Syd, is he alright?"

"Yes, but Abby didn't stick around and ended up leaving with that Riley guy. I'm not sure about him Kate. I mean Jake says he's a nice enough guy, but honestly where did he come from? Who is he? What's he running from? Sorry, but I just don't trust him and Abby right now is kind of all over the place. She goes to work one day, skips the next."

"Why didn't you call me?"

"I assumed he was taking her home."

"But he didn't?"

"Of course not," Sydney practically screamed. Kate realized how Sydney had grown so much, taking on that motherly side. A side Kate wasn't used to seeing in her. "She's not in there. She took off with Riley up to the Crystal Hotel."

"How do you know that's where she is? And that she's even with Riley?"

"Mrs. Calvert, how else?"

Kate found her purse and began rustling around inside for her cell. "Did you call her and try to talk some sense into her?"

"Of course I tried, but she didn't answer and honestly I'm worried. Abby hasn't been herself and who knows what that tattoo biker can persuade her to do. What if he's in a cult and he's been trying to pull some innocent blood in?"

First, Kate didn't think Abby was really *that* innocent. Second, that sounded crazy, just like her sister. Third, this was way too much to deal with first thing in the morning. She needed to talk to Abby and go from there.

"Let's calm down."

"Calm down, oh my gosh, one day this is going to be Haylee with some probably murderous, biker guy and I'm going to be alone chasing her around." Sydney started pacing back and forth in the kitchen getting under Kate's skin.

Kate rolled her eyes. Sydney's daughter was nothing like Abby. Haylee was nothing like any of them. She was sweet, kind, nice, and book smart. She was innocent in all meanings of the term. Her mother, on the other hand, sounded like a crazy lunatic. And her jittery movements were starting to resemble a crazy person's.

"We need to go get her," Sydney said.

"We need to call her."

"You go ahead and call her. Tell me how that goes. In the meantime I'm calling Peyton." She pulled her cell phone out of her back pocket and started dialing. Kate was annoyed she still hadn't found her cell phone. "I'm telling Peyton the situation. Take your week off work Kate because we're going up there, whether you like it or not."

"I'm still going to try calling her first." As soon as she located her cell. She glanced around the kitchen. Where was Gran's phone?

"They're on a bike," Sydney snapped. "They drove down on a *motorcycle*. Do you understand? He is going to kill our sister in this nasty weather. Have you watched the weather up north, huh, have you? There is snow piling up everywhere and you're just going to let our youngest sister die alone with a biker!"

"Sydney, calm down."

"Don't make me call the twin." Because Avery was going to be so much help from whichever town he was strumming a guitar in.

Kate looked up at her sister who was going to have an aneurysm at this rate. She wasn't about to hop on a plane and go home. So what was a snowy drive up north to rescue her youngest sister from the cult grips of a murderous biker?

"Alright, you call Peyton and let's go get Abby."

***

SEVEN HOURS LATER, Kate drank her favorite red wine, enjoying the warm, tingly feeling it created in her body, alleviating the stress of her day.

Kate glanced over at Sydney, who was still texting Haylee about the situation. She then glanced at Peyton who was retelling how she quit her job after Sydney's 911 call that Abby was in trouble. And lastly her eyes settled on Abby and she chuckled to herself.

That kid was sneaky. Purposely terrifying Sydney in order to force a family vacation, even if she wouldn't admit it. Kate could see exactly what had happened. Now Peyton was out of a job and Kate was going to miss a pitch she'd worked months on, but Abby's beautiful laughter almost made it worth it. Almost.

Sitting in the bar, around a tall pub-style table, Kate listened to the music coming from a live band playing at the far end.

"Holla!" Izzy hollered carrying over another round of drinks for everyone. "Pass these around." She'd brought a new glass of wine for everyone.

"You three overreact," Abby said. "I was fine. I just wanted a break and threatened Riley that I was going to drive up on my own." She glanced over her shoulder in the direction Riley had disappeared towards the men's room.

Sydney looked up from her phone. "Are you two a thing?"

Abby laughed. "No! Oh gees, he's not interested in me at all."

"You wish he was," Izzy teased before taking a sip...or rather a gulp...of her wine.

"You're interested in him?" Sydney pressed.

Abby grinned. "He's easy to look at." Laughter broke out between the two friends.

"He's delicious," Izzy said. "I could stroke that beard forever."

Abby laughed at her friend and swatted her. "You're so strange."

Izzy caught her hand mid-air. "Oh don't give me that. I bet you ten bucks you'd like to stroke that beard right now."

Abby laughed. "You are the daughter of a multimillionaire and you bet me ten bucks!"

She shrugged. "I would do it for ten bucks."

All the sisters laughed at that one.

"Oh get out of here!" Abby teased, swatting her again.

Sydney shook her head. "He's not easy to look at."

Abby raised her eyebrows. "Are you kidding me? Jake is tattooed from top to bottom and his mother was actually in a biker gang and he has a bad ass, scary edge to him. This one," she jerked her finger in his direction. "Is harmless."

Kate laughed. That was the perfect description of Jake, now Riley on the other hand, she wasn't so sure was harmless.

Sydney glared at Abby. "First of all, Jake is harmless, and secondly it doesn't matter because I'm not interested in Jake."

Abby sipped her drink before saying, "Sure you aren't."

Sydney's defense walls went up around her like a pop up tent. "I'm not. And we're not talking about me."

Kate smacked her Sydney, to quiet her up when she saw Riley heading their direction.

"Do it, stroke it," Izzy's chanting voice repeated.

"Don't let her play you like a violin," Kate told Sydney. "That's how we ended up here, remember?"

"I didn't plan this," Abby said. "I can't help it you all think I'm crazy."

Peyton rubbed her youngest sister's arm as Riley slid into his seat with his plain cola. "Abby we *know* you're crazy." Peyton said.

Abby yanked her arm away and slapped her sister. "Get away!"

"But we love you unconditionally," Peyton said with a smirk.

Abby slanted a look at Riley. "See what I have to deal with?"

Riley grinned.

"Since I'm officially out of a job I suggest we get that shop up and running," Peyton said.

"I'm in," Kate said. The girls all looked at her to see if she was joking. She wasn't. "I'm serious. I just had a major falling out and I'm quitting my job when I get home, so I'm almost officially out of a job, too."

Peyton's face beamed.

Sydney's face dropped. "Kate, have you thought this through? It's going to be so expensive."

Kate shrugged. "Peyton is the brains behind this operation so don't look at me. Are you in Syd?"

Sydney shook her head. "I don't know."

"Are you in Abby?" Kate asked.

Peyton was nearly bouncing in her chair with excitement.

"It's my soap you plan on reproducing, so hell yes I'm in! I want my cut."

"Woohoo!" Peyton cried. "Sydney, Sydney," she started chanting and the others followed. All except for Riley. Kate noticed he seemed to be the shy, quiet observer and she started to soften towards the man. He seemed to have a soft spot for Abby, too, and she seemed to be completely in control of her own trials of life. He wasn't even drinking.

"Guys, I can't just decide out of the blue like this. You

need to have a plan, an outline...and money."

"Sydney. Sydney."

She rolled her eyes. "What choice do I have? Two out of three of you are unemployed and Abby only works part time."

The table cheered.

Kate held up her glass. "It's official. The McAdams sisters are opening a shop down town in Willow Valley." They all drank to that.

Chapter Twelve

THE NEXT MORNING Kate was climbing out of the shower when a hard knock on her door startled her. Quickly wrapping a towel around herself and fastening it at the top corner, she crossed the room, and glanced at the clock beside the bed. It wasn't even seven yet. What were her sisters doing up so early?

When she pulled open the door, she was surprised to find Marc's Uncle Carl on the other side. He was wearing his usual dress slacks and grey, button up collar shirt, which matched his short wavy hair.

"Carl, what a surprise," she greeted, her eyes automatically glancing past him looking for Marc.

"Can I come in?" he asked.

She moved aside. "Yes, of course. You caught me in the shower. If you don't mind, I'm just going to go change."

He looked around the room with a nod. Kate ducked into the bathroom and threw on the black pencil line dress she was planning to wear for the day, skipping her nylons and raking her fingers through her curls to give them some bounce.

What was he doing at *this* hotel? What were the odds they would both end up here together and how did he know this was her room? She returned slowly to the living area where he was waiting for her with a serious look on his face.

"This is a surprise," she said.

"This is business," he corrected.

Alarms bells went off in Kate's head. "Regarding?"

"Your debt with Robert."

She stilled. So he was aware. She had figured as much.

"I have no outstanding debt with Mr. Caliendo." She would stand her ground, not back down. She wasn't some scared young girl he could walk all over.

Carl walked menacingly around the couch, his hand grazing the top, seeming to contemplate his next words. The tension in the room thickened.

"And yet you showed up at the resort and defied the deal you both had agreed upon."

Her lips thinned and her eyes narrowed. She could feel her jaw tightening. "It didn't seem to bother you at the time."

"In reality. I'm not bothered at all," he said. "I have no quarrels with you. Whatever went on between you and Robert was your business. However you have been trying to pay the money you took for a couple years." He knew a lot more than she presumed. "To no doubt be able to come home, to your family, to the life you left...to my nephew."

She had to muster all her strength not to gasp at his truthful words.

"I will allow you to pay off your debts and walk away from the arrangement you and Robert agreed on with no remaining obligations, rules, terms or threats from any of the Caliendos. Not me, not anyone. You will have the opportunity to do as you please, go where you please, your life will be your own with nothing hanging over your head."

That was very generous of a man who was staring at her with eyes of steel, eyes similar to those of his older brother.

"The agreement will be destroyed like it never happened," Carl said.

Only it had happened. It would never truly be destroyed for her.

"You will be free to pursue whomever you wish, Marcus included, and this will never, ever be spoken of again. I give you my word." Why didn't she believe him? What was the catch? And who even said she wanted to pursue Marc?

"What do you want in return?" She suspected he wouldn't have gone to such dramatics if there wasn't something underlying his offer.

"Marcus is here in this hotel." She hated that her excitement arose at the idea of Marc's presence.

It had been six years since she'd seen him and now there was a chance she would see him twice in two weeks.

A child-like feeling of butterflies began to fill her stomach.

"I need you to distract him after lunch and keep him away from this hotel until tomorrow morning."

Kate eyed Carl suspiciously, trying to mask the giddy girl swirls consuming her body at the thought of spending not only a whole day, but also a night with Marc. They were unrealistic thoughts but wonderfully exciting, none the less.

"What do you propose I do?"

"Be creative. I'm sure you can think of something to entertain the two of you. I see the way you two look at each other."

So she wasn't the only one who saw lust in Marc's recently eyes. She couldn't tell if it had been lust or she hadn't been thinking clearly through her own.

Kate was saddened at his implications, saddened that his thoughts were so similar to Robert's. She had misread him. As wonderful as that sounded, if she and Marcus were ever to be together, it certainly wasn't going to be because Carl blackmailed her.

"I'm not going to sleep with him."

"My dear, I don't think that would be the worst thing you have done."

Kate's calm was wearing thin. "And if I don't?"

Carl shrugged. "Why don't we skip the 'if I don'ts' and prevent me from threatening you. We both know you can distract him. I don't care how you do it."

"And if I don't?" she repeated.

"You already know."

"Say it." She wasn't agreeing to a single thing unless he had the balls to stand up and blackmail her directly.

"I will tell him everything Katherine, and he will never look at you the same. We both know that to be true. Marcus might be forgiving and understanding, it's his trait, but everyone has their limit. So, I'm offering you a chance to be with him or be privy to his hatred."

That's exactly what she thought.

"You're just like your brother."

"I'm nothing like him. If I was, you wouldn't be getting this concession."

This wasn't understanding concession. It was blackmail!

They stood in silence, staring one another down.

What was at this meeting that was so important he wanted Marc to skip out on it? What did it matter anyway?

Regardless, this man had proven his true identity in spades and she would never look at him the same again. He waited for her answer.

"What choice have you left me?"

Carl smiled, but it lacked triumph.

He gave her the details of Marc's breakfast location and time, expecting her to whisk him away immediately and not return until the next morning.

Kate wanted to slam the door when he left. Slam it right against his old, grey-haired ass!

She was so angry she had to squeeze her hands tightly around the wooden doorframe to keep from completing the action.

Years had passed her by with only dreams of again spending the day and evening with Marc, but not like this, not by blackmail. In a simple five-minute conversation, Carl had ripped away any possibility of a future with Marc just like Robert had. He may have promised her a "get out of jail free" card, but how could she ever pursue a future with Marc with Carl mulling around and this hanging over her head?

Kate wasn't a child anymore, she could say no. But really she couldn't. She was trapped like a mouse, foolish enough to latch onto that cheese and the painful trap. A life without Marc was a life she hadn't expected, but a life in Willow Valley with her sisters was a wish granted from a fairy god mother. If Carl and the Caliendos would let her live her life in Willow Valley, she would be able to open a soap shop with her sisters and finally be around the family she had been missing all these years.

Kate had to get to her laptop and figure out a plan to get Marc out of the hotel and stuck somewhere. Somewhere without taking their clothes off.

She groaned. She was going to have to explain this to her sisters, and, as usual, not tell the entire truth. Lies and deceit these seemed to follow her around everywhere. Derek's white manipulative smile flashed in her head. She was no better than him. Now she was sweeping Marc off his feet with even more lies and deception.

She pulled out her laptop. She better get to it, she had less than an hour to finish getting ready and swoop in on her prey with a fool proof plan.

Chapter Thirteen

THE STRUCTURE OF the building was good, an old inn transformed into a sky rise hotel, which was very similar to their resort. The amenities were less: they usually were when compared to the Caliendo Resort. No hotel or resort could actually measure up to the extreme offerings his family had worked hard to create. The Caliendo Resort literally had everything.

The set up in the front foyer here was welcoming, with a long, solid cherry wood desk against a speckled marble floor. The chocolate coloured walls contrasted against the sun that streamed through the front glass wall. The room, especially the suite he had stayed in, was magnificent and bright white with contemporary furniture and a large Jacuzzi centered in the bathroom. His dad and uncle had a real eye for an amazing hotel. He wasn't surprised, his dad had never made a deal unless it benefited him. Unfortunately, if you were on the wrong end of the deal, his father would make you pay...dearly. He had been like a darkening storm that thrashed around at its own pace, showing no mercy, and finishing you off with careless destruction.

Marc smiled and nodded now at a passing employee who did the same with a soft greeting. The staff here had been very welcoming, helpful and kind. It was an exquisite five-star hotel.

He planned on checking out the gym, pool and sauna after breakfast. Sauna. Flashes of Kate and their interaction in the hot steaming room back at his own resort clouded his trail of thoughts.

He shook the vivid images away like an etch-a-sketch, knowing his mind was ready to redraw them at any point.

With his mind still back in the sauna, he rounded a corner and through a set of wide open double French doors a little too quickly, colliding with a tall, slim brunette.

"Oh my goodness, I'm so sorry," she quickly apologized, gripping the front of his shirt, as though the collision was her fault.

His hands caught her bare arms and he found himself dragging her lowered head away from him, annoyed he was hearing *her* voice, knowing it couldn't possibly be her. But he still needed to see. As she pulled back from him, he saw Kate's russet, emerald flecked eyes staring up at him.

"Kate?"

"Marc?"

She laughed. "What are you doing here?"

"Business, and you?"

The surprised smile he had been enjoying dropped. "Abby again. She took off and put Sydney into a panic."

"Is she alright?"

She smiled and nodded slightly. "Yes. And guess who was on board for her little adventure?"

He shrugged, but when she arched her eyebrow at him, he rolled his eyes, suddenly comprehending. "Izzy."

She nodded and smiled.

He could feel the heat from her warm hands through

his button up and smiled, realizing they were standing in the entrance, her gripping his shirt and him holding her arms, their bodies pressed together, having a...moment.

Reluctantly, he let go and stepped back. Realizing their stance, she released her hands too and mimicked him.

"Are you finished with your business for the day?" she asked.

He arched his at her. "I'm not needed now." How was this possible? He felt like he'd etch-a-sketched her into reality, instead of erasing her off the board like he'd tried to do.

Her smile widened. "Do you want to get out of here with me?" *Oh Lord, did he ever.*

"Why? Don't they have everything here?"

She shook her head and gave him a mischievous grin. "They don't have *everything* here. If you're willing to drive I will make it worth it. I promise," she added.

How could he say no to that? He had the whole morning and into the afternoon before the meeting. All gyms, pools and saunas looked the same to him...unless, of course, Kate was with him.

He gave his uncle a quick call on their way to the underground parking lot letting him know he was going to miss breakfast.

"What's up? Is something wrong?" Carl asked.

"No." He glanced at Kate. "Ran into an old friend and we're going out for breakfast." She elbowed his side and mouthed, *old friend.* He grinned.

"Don't worry about it Marcus. I've told you this is a closed deal and this is just the final signing. No need for your presence," his uncle reassured him. And yet, Carl had told him over and over again how he'd wanted him there. His uncle's odd behaviors made him wonder about his stability. Carl insisted Marc not help with certain aspects of the resort and their business deals, but then with others, he was welcoming and encouraging. It confused the hell out of Marc. But it was the deals Carl insisted on managing on his own that alarmed Marc the most.

"No rush back boy," his uncle was saying now. "Maybe you should enjoy yourself today. You have been so deep in work the last few months it might be nice to have a break."

"I'll be there for the deal," Marc confirmed.

"Alright."

Marc said goodbye and slid his cell into his shirt pocket while unlocking the car door. He helped Kate into the passenger side and then ran around to the driver's side.

"Do I get a clue?" he asked, putting his key into the ignition.

She tilted her head, seeming to debate his question. "It's my downfall."

He thought for a second and wondered about the one thing Kate would drag him around for, or maybe sneak into a kitchen for. "Are we on a search for ice cream? In November?"

"I looked up a cute little shop."

He laughed. So he hadn't been off at the funeral home when he tried to distract her. In all the years apart, her soft spot for ice cream hadn't changed.

"What?" she said defensively. "It calms me down and Abby's been stressing me out!"

"I'm sure they have ice cream at the hotel."

"Not the good flavors. Not the *real* flavors."

"But for breakfast?"

"Don't be judgmental and turn left up here."

He obeyed her directions and they pulled up to a quaint little restaurant with an all year round ice cream bar. The restaurant had a fifties edge to it, with a long counter and spinning chrome stools, and booths lining the walls, in old fashioned teal, pink and black. He imagined it was the kind of place Elvis had frequented in his day. And he probably ate ice cream for breakfast all the time.

Every flavor of hard ice cream you could possibly dream of ordering was on the menu. Kate snuck in front of him to peek at the ice cream flavors like a child would with her nose pressed up against the glass. She ordered a large bowl of pralines and cream with extra whipped cream and extra caramel. It was still breakfast time. It made his insides cringe.

While they were scooping out her breakfast, he ordered a special with eggs, bacon and toast, then led her to a small booth in the back corner.

"You're so original," she said as the waitress slipped his plate in front of him. He thanked her as he watched Kate twirl her spoon in her ice cream. She swept the spoon over the whipped cream and into the caramel, sticking a large spoonful in her mouth. His stomach turned and not in a good way. It was much too early for ice cream.

"That's a child's dream order right there in front of you. All you're missing is sprinkles."

She made a face at him. "Those things are disgusting."

He chuckled. "This coming from the girl eating ice

cream before eight in the morning."

"Where's your adventure Caliendo?"

"I think it left with you." He had only been adventurous when she'd been around. Before Kate, he'd been simply content reading books, lots of books. Gallivanting around the hotel having adventures had certainly been inspired by her. During his time in university, with her being so many miles away, he'd had no problem concentrating on his work and acing everything, so there had been no adventures. But knowing she was waiting also pushed him to succeed. He had missed her so much.

She stopped playing in her ice cream and looked up at him with a serious frown. There it was again, that look of regret that he never could figure out. If she regretted leaving, if she'd loved him as much as he'd loved her, why hadn't she come back? Why hadn't she phoned? Maybe she'd been seeking her own adventure...without him.

"That's a shame," she said finally. "Just when you were beginning to come out of your shell."

He shrugged.

Her eyes lit up then like a spark of genius had hit her. "How about you and me go get into some trouble?"

He raised an eyebrow. "Trouble?"

She shook her head. "Alright, let's not call it trouble. How about we call it an adventure?" There was that word again, never far from her thoughts.

"You don't think that," he paused, pointing at the puddle of gooey mess she was consuming in front of her, "is adventurous enough?"

"Oh come on. It will be fun."

"What will?"

"I don't know yet. I just threw the idea out there," she said. Then she grinned at him and teased him with her excited eyes. "Do you want to come on an adventure with me Marcus Caliendo?" He wanted to go to the edge of the world with this woman at one time, but now, after all these years...adventure was still the first thought that popped into his head with her, even against his better judgment.

"Let's see if you still have it in you after all these years," she teased.

His eyebrows rose in response. "Are you calling me old?"

She laughed. "First adventure, open your mouth." She dug her spoon into the ice cream and twirled whipped cream around it, then dipped it into the caramel. She held her creation towards him.

As much as the thought of all that sweetness first thing in the morning mixing in his mouth with the flavor of eggs and bacon appalled him, he didn't even hesitate biting the whole spoonful and tugging the spoon with his teeth. "Conquered," he said with a mouthful. His mother would have gasped, but not Kate.

She laughed and pulled her spoon away. "I'm not sharing the whole thing with you."

He shrugged, resisting the urge to grab the tall glass of ice cold water in front of him and flush the sweetness away so he could continue with his regular morning breakfast. "You never were a good sharer."

"Yes I was."

"Not when it came to sweets."

"Who is?"

He was curious what this woman thought was

adventurous at their age and what she could possibly plan on the spur of the moment for them in the late days of fall with snow covered grounds and white snow continuing to fall.

As they got back into the car, he realized she was apparently she was a pretty quick planner. She used her phone and directed him, using an online site, to an outdoor skating rink. They spent the morning in the park skating as genuine snow fell around them, reminding him of Emma's plan for the Snowflake Ball. As the large white fluffy flakes danced and teased around them as they skated, laughed, slipped and fell on the rink, he found it romantically enticing...just like Emma had been explaining. When they were too exhausted to continue, they stopped in a little coffee shop across the road to warm their fingers.

It was still too early to sit down and eat lunch but he asked, "Do you want something for the ride back?"

"The ride back?" she asked as if the words were foreign to her. "We're not done. Get our hot drinks to go while I run to the ladies room and then we're off." She left him standing in the lineup feeling a pleasure that he had long dismissed...and one that he needed. Sure, he'd dated after she left...a long year after she'd left, but never had any of them boss him around or leaving him with this thrilled feeling in his gut.

He ordered their drinks and waited for her at the door. They couldn't be any longer than two hours. That would give him enough time to drive back, shower and meet with his uncle with minutes to spare before the meeting. He explained his timeline to her while she directed him with the map she'd pulled up on her cell phone, promising him they would be done with lots of time to spare.

"My vehicle does have a GPS," he told her.

"Yes, and then it would tell you where we're going and you wouldn't get the whole effect."

"Is it that scary?"

"It's not scary." She paused. "You know what? I'm going to be truthful with you here Caliendo. We picked a snowy winter day to be adventurous and since I know you are a pro at skiing, it doesn't leave any adventurous things to do that are scary." She tilted her head at him. "Unless you want to get a tattoo?"

"I don't."

"We could get matching ones."

"I'm going to pass."

She shrugged. "That's what I figured, so I opted for this. Turn right up here," she directed, hiking her voice up a notch, hinting to him it was right around the corner. "And..." A big wooden distressed sign appeared around the corner reading, "Collins All Season Cottage & Horse Carriage Rides."

"We're here," she squealed in delight, clapping her hands together.

He sent her a sideways grin as he clicked the signal before turning. "You rented us a cottage in a secluded bush for the weekend?" he teased. "That's *very* adventurous of you."

She slapped his arm playfully. "No. We're going to have a winter wonderland horse drawn carriage ride."

He found *his* adventurous suggestion much more appealing. "And I'll request a short tour and have you back in a couple of hours for your meeting," she promised as he pulled up to the front doors to let her out. She smiled and winked before disappearing into the chalet. He found parking, grabbed his scarf from the back seat and met a thrilled Kate exactly where he had dropped her.

"They said to meet them around the back," she said. He motioned for her to go first and placed his hand on the small of her back guiding her along the shovelled and salted rock pathway that led them around the back where a horse and sleigh awaited them.

"I have never done this before," Kate said. "Have you?"

He shook his head. "Horseback riding would have been much more adventurous," he told her.

She shook her head at him. "You are like Prince Charming on a horse so that would be only adventurous for me, and I'm not getting on a horse."

"I think we found something Katherine McAdams is afraid of."

She glared at him. "You already knew that," she accused.

She was right.

The driver met them at the stairs of the sleigh. He was a scrawny teenager with long hair hanging out from under his hat and a pair of ear buds dangling around the collar of his thick black work coat. He was dressed much better for this ride than the two of them. Marc instinctively took Kate's arm and helped her up into the sleigh before climbing in himself, leaving the driver to shuffle through the deep snow to his position at the head of the sleigh.

A thick, warm antique blanket used from the days of actual horse and carriages welcomed them and Kate immediately wrapped it around her legs and stuck her bare hands underneath with a shiver. He sat beside her and covered his own legs with what was left of the blanket. "You're cold," he said as the buggy started to move. "We didn't come very prepared."

She shrugged. "It'll be worth it." Her eyes gleamed up at him, the exact same she had look whenever she was dragging him into trouble. Before she knocked his brother to his knees all those years ago, he hadn't even known what trouble was.

The blades of the sleigh slashed through an already ridden path that disappeared under the fresh snowfall. They then turned into the darkened bush sheltering them from the nasty wind. Gorgeous ice covered branches glistened as the sun peeked through the snow clouds above.

"This is so beautiful," Kate whispered as another shiver vibrated beside him.

She was freezing.

He wasn't much better.

Marc pulled his scarf off and wrapped it around her neck before moving against her side, pressing their bodies together for combined warmth.

He wrapped his arm around her shoulder and enjoyed her snuggling against him, her head resting against his side.

They settled into the relaxing ride, enjoying the rabbits scattering throughout the bush as they passed. Some stopped to simply stare at them, obvious acquainted with the noise of the sleigh.

Marc liked the idea of horse sleigh rides. He was going to toss the idea around at the next family meeting. They had horses throughout the summer for the guests and if they purchased an antique working cutter sleigh, which he was sure they could find at the Willow Valley Antique Mall in town, they could also offer sleigh rides in the winter. The winter guests would surely enjoy it especially for Christmas work company parties that generally filled all the ballrooms, as well as booked a minimum of thirty rooms per party. If they added sleigh rides they could turn a profit and make the winter wonderland at the Caliendo Resort even more special.

Time seemed to stop around them now, as they, listened to the trot of the horse breaking fresh snow.

Marc hoped Kate had found whatever had dragged her away all those years ago and he hoped it made her happy. He wondered if she missed him like he had missed her. Or if she longed for him as he longed for her? Maybe she was considering a long distance relationship with him...like he was.

Stop that! She had made it crystal clear she didn't want to take this any further.

As the driver guided the horse out of the bush a bump startled the horse into a fussing stop. Marc sat up and watched the driver climb out, giving soothing words to the horse. "Is there a problem?" he called.

"I'm sure it's nothing," the driver called back, waving at them as he stepped around to calm the horse.

Marc tried to sit back, but Kate was also trying to see what was going on and he bumped her.

"Hey look," she said pointing into a snow-covered opening. "Over there."

He followed her finger's direction although he was more curious as to where the driver had disappeared.

Past the bush, about thirty feet in an open area, sat a little log cottage.

"What's he doing?" Kate asked.

Marc shrugged.

"Do you think something's broken?"

"Are you going to get down there and fix it?"

She shook her head. "I'm freezing."

The driver came around to their side. "I'm afraid the ride stops here," he said. "The sleigh needs repairing before it will move so I'm going to ride back to the work shed, grab the supplies and head right back. I should be back in no longer than an hour and a half."

An hour and a half?

The driver was dug in his pocket and pulled out a large ring of keys. He shuffled through them and unclipped a set. "These are for the cottage right over there. You can stay there until I return or, since it hasn't been rented out, and this is an inconvenience, it's on the house for the night."

Inconvenience was putting it lightly.

"We can walk back to the chalet," Marc said. They were on the short tour and it must have been almost an hour up until now so they had to be close to the chalet.

"Sir, it would take you an hour by sled to get back to the chalet." He laughed. "It would take you way longer by foot. And out in this snowstorm, you would get lost."

Surely this young fellow knew how to calculate time on that little contraption hanging out of his pocket. Marc quickly informed the young lad exactly the calculations it would take to get back to the chalet by sled and foot.

He glanced at Kate, then back to Marc. "Sir, you booked the long route. That's a two hour ride, and we're halfway into it. You can't walk back to the chalet from here."

Two hour ride? He was going to miss the meeting.

Marc stood, throwing the blanket aside, noting there was only one horse and three of them.

"Can't you fix it now?" Marc asked.

"With all due respect sir, if I could, I would."

Marc was getting tired of all the "sir" and no answers.

"Phone someone to pick us up."

"I called the office, and they are all out on different trails. None of them are close to us, but I can send one as soon as possible. Or you can have the cabin for the night."

Marc's fists clenched at his side. "I meant by vehicle," he said, through gritted teeth.

The boy shook his head. "This trail isn't permitted for vehicles."

How convenient.

"Can you bring a couple extra horses for us to ride back to the chalet?" Marc suggested, growing tired of all the suggestions on his part.

Kate grabbed his arm. He had completely forgotten she was there until her little fingers gripped his forearm, tightly.

"I'm not riding a horse back," she said.

He wasn't missing this meeting. He turned his head to her. "Think of it as an adventure," he snapped.

Couldn't she very well sit back and let him figure out a solution? Of course it didn't matter that he was frustrated and trying to structure a way out of missing the meeting. She shook her head. "No, I'll take the cabin," she snarled at him and reaching past him to grab the keys. She smiled at the young boy and stuck the keys in the pocket of her wool jacket. She tried to pass Marc but he moved in front of her.

"I'm not leaving you here alone," he said.

"I didn't say you had to."

"I'm not staying."

She smiled. "I'm a big girl."

"Absolutely not."

"I think I might even spend the night." She wriggled beside him and let the driver help her into the deep snow bank. Marc groaned as her short boots disappeared into the bottomless snow. She was walking over thirty feet with snow halfway up her calves.

He growled inwardly, but seeing no other alternative, climbed off the sleigh, his own leather loafers landing just as deep into the white fluff. He was thankful it was fluff and not wet packing snow that would have soaked immediately through their clothes.

She hadn't bothered to wait for him and she was quickly trudging through the snow as though she had no feeling in her legs.

He glared at the little punk that he was sure was not even qualified to be giving these rides, since proper backup was not even on his list. He didn't seem to notice that Marc was furious, his thin brown eyes just staring up at him without even so much as a hint of remorse at the situation at hand.

"I want you to call the cabin as soon as you can pick us up," Marc instructed, barely waiting for his nod of understanding before taking off after Kate.

Kate must have heard him because she didn't bother to even glance over at him as she hollered, "Not double straddling the horse with the driver?"

He ignored her and called for her to stop. She was still quite a distance away but she turned and her eyebrows peeked with curiosity. Evidence of her cold state stained across her porcelain face, mostly pinching her rosy cheeks and nose.

"I will carry you the rest of the way," he called.

Her face squished together, perplexed. "You will what now?"

Had she really not heard him? He repeated himself anyway then added, "So you can either get on my back or I will throw you over my shoulder."

She bit her lower lip as if contemplating her options and crossed her arms in front of her, rubbing her chin as a trembling smile formed across her lips.

"I like this whole..." She paused and waved her finger at him and said, "...muscular man thing you got going on in your old age." He wondered if there was ever a time in this woman's life where her mouth stopped talking long enough to do what needed to be done. They needed to get out of the two feet of snow and into the dry cabin. "I mean back in the day I would have been slinging you over my shoulder."

"Those are your options."

She pursed her lips together as if actually contemplating her choices. But, of course, she wasn't.

"I think I'm going with choice three." She sunk her bare, no doubt freezing, hands into the snow and pulled a handful of snow, creating a ball in her hands. It infuriated him and excited him at the same time.

"You wouldn't dare."

He knew it would only spark her adventurous side.

"Oh I would," she said, before throwing the snowball at him.

Marc dodged it, but she had good aim. He found

himself laughing and forming his own snowball. But she was much quicker and hit him in the arm before he'd even rolled his.

He wasn't afraid to throw one back at her, she was nothing like his sisters who would cower away. He rounded one up and threw it at her hitting her arm. She gasped and laughed looking shocked that he was participating in this little adventure.

"Oh, Caliendo, you are going to pay for that," she threatened, swiping damp hair from her cheek then digging back into the snow for more.

"Only if you can catch me." He darted towards the cabin with ulterior motives. He had to get this silly woman out of the cold even if she thought she wasn't ready. She was going to get frost-bitten feet.

She laughed in delight as she threw a handful of loose snow at him.

"Ouch," he called. "Watch out for that white fluff," he teased.

"Oh *you* watch out for the white fluff."

He wasn't prepared when she jumped on his back, grabbing his shoulders and lifting her body up, wrapping her legs around his waist. They both went tumbling into the snow.

She screamed in surprise as they landed on their sides, separating at the ground and rolling away from each other.

"I have snow everywhere," she cried.

He rolled onto his knees and sat up. She was lying beside him on her back, white fluff across her like a thin blanket. She stared up at him in shock.

"Apparently you still can't hold my weight," she said, raising her hands to the sky to dust the white snow off her sleeves.

"Oh I can hold your weight." He didn't give her a chance to react and grabbed her raised hand and, in one quick motion, pulled her up to her feet and over his shoulder. Against her objections, he carried her straight to the cabin. Unfortunately, he didn't have the key and was forced to drop her to her feet by the door.

"It's freezing out here," she complained, only half-heartedly, while she fished the key out of her pocket doing a little jumping dance to stay warm.

Her hands trembled as she tried to stick the key in so he took it and quickly unlocked the door.

They stepped into the dim cabin. It was a small, old-fashioned one room kitchen/living room combo with a fireplace against the far right wall with a couch facing two overstuffed chairs, each garnished with a knitted afghan folded neatly across the back. The room was pulled together by a large hand weaved, braided rug and an old baggage cart transformed into a coffee table. The kitchen was a little nook with small wooden cupboards that wrapped in a "U" shape. Hand built tall stools, a small log table and matching chairs say in the middle. A door on the far wall likely led to the bedroom.

They quickly tore off their shoes and Marc rolled up the rim of his pants so the wet didn't stick against his leg.

Kate flicked on the lights. "Brrr," she trembled.

"There's the adult in you," he teased.

"I think I need a hot shower." She headed towards the door on the far wall and turned suddenly. "You're not going to leave on me are you?"

"How do you suppose I do that?"

She shrugged, looking reluctant to leave him. "I had fun today Marc." She smiled at him and disappeared behind the door.

He'd had a fun time, too, but it would have been even better if he wasn't missing the meeting.

Marc rubbed his hands together to warm them.

The meeting.

He pulled his cell out of his shirt pocket and dialed his uncle who answered on the first ring. "Marcus, where are you?" Now he sounded a bit exasperated about Marc's absence. The man had been nothing but unreadable.

Marc quickly explained the short version of where he was and his uncle agreed to do the meeting without him. His voice almost sounded relieved.

Relieved?

It didn't make sense. Marc hung up feeling more confused than usual. He was starting to feel as though he would never understand. Was he reading into all the situations differently because of his father's deathbed warning?

Considering the possibilities, weighing the options like a balancing scale in his head, Marc crossed the wooden plank floor to the fireplace.

He formed a teepee of kindling, carefully balancing the wood tips together over the coal bed. He compared the setup to his uncle; both were always on the edge of collapsing. He opened a newspaper from a bucket nearby, crumpled it up and threw it on the teepee sticks. An old tin match holder was tacked above the fireplace filled with little wooden matches. He took one and lit the paper and the flames wrapped around the kindling, sneaky and determined, just like his uncle had been acting about this deal. He tossed some logs on top, shaking his head and deciding he needed a distraction. This game could play in his head all day long and he would be no closer to a solution.

Soon the fire was blazing and he rubbed his hands close by to warm them. This was a nice cozy getaway. It could be a romantic or even a family getaway that would draw a different crowd of people looking for a down to earth, weeklong retreat in the summer or winter instead of an all-inclusive resort. People who were attracted to having quality time, with no television, no computer; he checked his phone; and no Wi-Fi. They could replace technology with the shelf of games on the far wall or a book in the corner nook.

By the front large window, sat two antique parlour chairs angled toward the cream-colored, sheer curtains. Two bookcases met together in the corner holding a large variety of books available to read. It was like his own personal haven. He envisioned holding a mug of coffee and reading a copy of "Uncle Tom's Cabin."

Marc turned towards the games.

They were more Kate's department. Monopoly, Clue, Risk, Scrabble...ahhh Scrabble, that was a game in which he excelled.

He pulled it from the shelf and carried it over to the refinished planks of the baggage cart surface. They were going to be here at least a couple hours while that little teen arranged pickup. When this was sorted, he was going to talk with the manager about this driver. Surely, there should be an easier back up plan than this one. How infuriating. He, as a business owner, would appreciate such details mentioned about his staff and service.

Marc unpacked the contents of the game. He recalled doing the exact same thing before with the woman who now stood naked in the shower.

Whoa.

That thought jarred his insides alive again and he forgot about the negligent driver and their present predicament.

He shook his head. He had to build a strong wall of resistance to erase those while they were together, alone and in this romantic cabin. Kate had made her feelings for him clear at the resort not two weeks ago and, no matter how deep his feelings were for her...or his sexual desire...he had to respect her. They weren't in their late teens anymore sitting about her house, after her mom had died. She might have had a twin the same age that could have shared the responsibility, but Peyton sure had been lacking in motherly instincts. He remembered when the younger twins were sent home with the flu and there was vomit spilling out everywhere.

Peyton had been a mess, freaking out, gagging, so totally out of control that Kate had sent her to stay with Sydney who had been living with Haylee's grandmother. One diaper change later and Peyton was back home hiding in her bedroom. Kate had had all these little young eyes looking up at her for guidance, shouldering a responsibility no sixteen year old should have had to take on. But she had jumped right into the role of dressing and feeding them, making lunches, and cleaning. She'd even watched over her dad and had made sure he was up and dressed for work every day. She'd then sneak over to the resort when one of the staff had called to say he was too drunk to work. That was where Kate's true handiwork showed, when she would show up and sneak around taking on all her dad's duties with the help of staff. They'd hit it so well from his parents so, at the end of the week, he would still get a paycheck to buy groceries.

Kate was never one to sit around but after all that working, and school, she had always curled up with Marc in the family room to play games.

A lot of the times, when her father didn't come home, she would fall asleep in Marc's arms and he would stay with her.

That was the beginning point of his father overstepping into his life. After a lifetime of living with a man who was too busy to give him two seconds of his time, all of a sudden he had an awful lot to say when Marc stopped coming home every night. His mother worried, too, but for an entirely different reason. She worried out of love and for his future. She worried she'd have grandchildren too early, whereas his father worried about his reputation.

But none of their worries stopped him. He had talked with his mom to ease her worries, although he was sure it hadn't and he'd faced his dad for the first time ever. He loved Kate and she had been there throughout his childhood when he needed her. He had fully intended on being there with her when she needed him. And he had every day until after high school when he went off to university. Even then, he was with her as often as he could return home. Until one day she wasn't there.

He heard the bedroom door open now. He'd been sitting on one of the comfortable overstuffed chairs facing the entrance, flipping a scrabble piece between his fingers. He looked up.

Kate was wearing a white robe with, he was sure, nothing underneath. That knowledge brought with it a whole mountain of memories.

Her hair was much longer when it was wet, the water pulling the curls into long wavy strands. She held her wet clothes in a bunch in front of her. "There's another robe in there if you want a hot shower to take the chill off." She smiled. "It feels amazing."

We could have conserved the water.

He shook his head when she turned away and watched her cross the room, her feet hiding behind fluffy white slippers. She draped the clothes by the fireplace then turned and saw the Scrabble game all laid out ready to play. Her face squished together looking disappointed. "You were always better at this than me." She recalled.

"I remember."

She eyed him suspiciously. "So you assume you're going to automatically beat me now?" she questioned.

He shrugged, but gave her a little half grin that told her that was exactly what he was thinking, even if it wasn't true. He liked to watch the spark come alive in her eyes.

She gasped. "You do," she accused, shaking her head. "Well, if you're having a shower get on with it." She shooed her hands at him. "I will see what's in that welcome basket to nibble on and when you get back we'll see who conquers who."

He stood, holding his hand out towards Kate. "I accept that challenge." When she shook his hand, the tender warmth of her tiny fingers wrapped around his own and sent sparks throughout his whole body.

He recalled, as he closed the bedroom door behind him, how difficult it was to play Scrabble when they were teens without tearing off each other's clothes.

How the hell were they going to do it with only robes on?

Maybe he would take a cold shower.

Chapter Fourteen

WHEN KATE HEARD the door to the bedroom shut behind Marc, she breathed out a sigh of relief. She'd wondered whether he would actually be on the other side of that door when she was done with her bath and had considered not even running the water. But her feet were so cold they burned when the water had run over them and she had shivered clean through to the bones until her body had been immersed in the hot bath.

If he'd walked out, they wouldn't have had to face the dark secret she'd kept hidden all these years. Should she tell him now? He wouldn't understand. It seemed selfish but she would keep it hidden for her family, too. Maybe this could be the beginning of a friendship for her and Marc. After all these years she would love to be his friend again. She would actually love to be much more, but that wasn't an option now.

She also hoped this whole plan with Carl did not backfire and expose her. She'd been so nervous sitting in that sleigh wondering if the driver would be able to keep up the charade against Marc's overbearing manner. So far it had worked and the meeting had begun without Marc. And his uncle had promised her a clean slate. Now, as long as Carl stood by his word, her life could possibly move forward.

Kate sat on the stool by the kitchen island that isolated the small kitchen from the rest of the living space.

She pulled the basket she'd had included with the reservation and ripped the plastic away, finding some hot cocoa packets. A little cocoa would make an entire game of excruciating Scrabble more amendable.

But before putting on the kettle, she had to call her sisters and let them know her whereabouts.

Kate phoned her twin's cell first and was greeted with a loud, "Where the hell have you been? You have been ignoring all our texts."

Where to begin? It was such a long story.

"I'm stuck in a cabin with Marc," Kate answered. Basic was good, keep it simple.

The voice on the other end went silent.

"Um, just a sec."

"No. Wait, Peyton." She glanced over her shoulder. Door still closed. "Peyton!" she snarled, in a whisper.

The phone absorbed the background noise and Peyton said, "You're on speakerphone." Her sisters all greeted her. "Can you repeat that?" Peyton asked.

Through clenched teeth, she repeated herself, and was praised with hoots and whistles from the other end.

"Oh stop that. It's not like that." Even though she wished it was like that instead of the situation that had brought them here...lies.

"What do you mean by stuck?" Sydney asked.

She quickly explained the short version, the same version that Marc knew. The real version was strictly between her and Carl and, of course, the driver.

Questions flew from her sisters through the phone demanding a relationship status and curious how far along it was. Was this why she wanted to start a business and come home? Had they been talking since the funeral? And the questions continued.

She shook her head. "I'm not doing this right now. I just wanted to check in with you three so you didn't worry."

"Oh we're fine, just sitting around the pool sipping margaritas."

"You're at the pool?" she asked, horrified. "Take me off speakerphone."

"Oh relax," Abby said. "Oh wait, I bet you are really relaxed."

Laughter filled her ear. Hearing their enjoyment made her heart a little heavy. She might be here in this secluded cabin with her first and only love but it was under entrapment circumstances and it was actually a little awkward. She would much prefer being at the pool with her sisters, under real circumstances, brought together by fate, not by one man's manipulation.

Abby continued. "You get some action since we all know I'm not getting any from my company." She sighed. "I mean look at him over there."

Obviously she was talking to her sisters since Kate was on the other end of the phone and couldn't very well look *over there.*

She could envision the tall, longhaired, unshaven face of Riley though. Probably shirtless, all those tattoos showing...trouble with a capital "T."

"I would tap that," Abby said.

"Abby!" Kate heard Sydney scold but then erupted in laughter. They had all obviously *tapped* into a *lot* of liquid happiness.

"Look at those muscles and tattoos." She listened as

her sisters hummed in agreement with the youngest and drooled over a man who didn't seem to notice how he turned women's heads or that the sad, little permanent scowl moulded on his face silently screaming "try and fix me" dug deep into their souls.

"Hey," Kate hollered into the phone, trying to snap their attention away from the man candy and back to her. "No one is tapping anyone. You hear me?"

"Everyone hears you," Sydney said.

"Take me off speakerphone."

They all laughed.

Abby decided to make her a deal. "How about I tap this, and you tap that, and then we're both tapping something we want."

The longing and desire deep within Kate was a subject all on its own.

"This is not funny. You're not tapping that, and I'm not tapping this..."

From behind her, Marc cleared his throat.

Kate froze.

Her eyes fell shut.

How had she not heard him come out of the bedroom? How had she missed the hum of the shower stop? Because she was on speaker phone, that's why, and the loud background noise made it hard enough to concentrate that she had completely blocked out every other sound in the cabin.

The conversation continued while Kate sat there frozen to the seat.

"I would have to get him really drunk because he has absolutely no interest in me sexually," Abby was saying. "I actually think he might not even like me."

"Oh please," Sydney said. "You think he can resist you in that? What is *that* anyway? It's like nothing. I wish my body looked that good that I could wear next to nothing with such confidence."

"You could wear that," Peyton said.

"What do you know? You've never had a kid so you don't know what this..." There was a pause and Kate envisioned her sister twirling her hands around in the air above her belly. "Looks like."

"Sydney, you're beautiful," Abby complimented. "I will lend you one."

"You have more than one?" Sydney asked.

Kate heard Marc move from behind her and she opened her eyes. He walked around the counter wearing a matching white robe and poked around in the basket. He took the hot cocoa she had fully intended on preparing out and smiled down at her. She nearly sunk into her robe.

"I think I'm going to go," Kate said realizing she was getting nowhere with her sisters except deeper into a hole. They knew she was safe and that was the main reason for the call.

He turned his attention, thank goodness, to shuffling through the cupboards until he found a kettle. Kate couldn't help watching him fill it with water and plug it in the wall, all the while remembering exactly what lay beneath that robe.

"We miss you," Abby said. "And we decided to stay the whole week so we have lots of time when you get back from your stranded *tapping*." They laughed. Kate said goodbye and reluctantly hung up the phone.

How embarrassing.

Marc leaned against the cupboard, crossing his arms

over his chest and staring at her with a smirk across her face.

"How do you even know what that means?" she snapped.

"I wasn't raised in a cave."

Kate slid off the stool and walked over to where the game was waiting for them. She purposely sat in the chair across the table so there was a division between them in case he got any ideas from his eavesdropping. There would be no tapping in this little cabin, especially after Carl's insinuations.

Marc joined her shortly after, setting down a cup of steaming hot cocoa for each of them. He sat across from her on the couch, just as she had planned. He dug into the bag of letters and set them up.

"You can go first," he said. "You'll need the extra points to even get close to my score."

She wrinkled her nose at him but set up her word regardless. Competition hadn't been in his nature. Probably because he was so naturally smart that he generally won with no extra effort. In his younger years he had been very somber. This new Marc instigated her competitive side.

"I'm sorry you missed your meeting."

He shrugged. "My uncle can handle it."

"What was it about? If you don't mind me asking?"

He was switching around pieces on his wood stand, eyes lowered in concentration. She glanced down at her letters and wondered if that was why she always lost because she didn't spend every second of the game trying to create bigger, better words.

"Before my dad passed, he and Uncle Carl had unfinished deals all over the province. One of them was buying the hotel."

"You're going to buy it?" He didn't even seem to notice the surprised tone of her voice. It wasn't every day an ordinary person just bought an entire hotel. But then, the Caliendos weren't ordinary.

"That's the plan."

"Is this the first hotel you've purchased?'

He slanted a quirky look at her. "Yes. I've only been working with my family over the last six months."

"Oh." She didn't know that. "Since your dad passed?"

He nodded.

"You didn't work there before?"

He finally looked up. "After I finished university, I never went back to the resort. Not to work anyway. Of course I returned to visit my family." His eyes darkened. "Sorry, I didn't mean it like that."

Mean it like she was some awful person that didn't come back to visit her family after she left for college? Of course, that's not what he meant at all.

She shrugged, looking down at her tiles, fighting to mask her emotions. She knew he wasn't intentionally being ignorant, but it still hurt...the truth hurt. But after today that would all change. And what perfect timing because she didn't want to work for a boss who had cheated on her, and she didn't want to stay away from her family...or from Marc. After today, her whole life was about to change. And obviously the meeting wasn't as important to Marc as it was to his uncle Carl so what was the harm?

Chapter Fifteen

MARC COULD SEE in her troubled little hazel eyes that his truth had caused her pain. But he couldn't do much more than give her an apology and even then it had been her choice to stay away from her family...from him.

"My father asked me to take over the resort. He wanted me to fix mistakes he had made throughout his life which, I'm not sure how I ever would."

Somewhere hidden like a buried treasure had to be lists of the inexcusable affairs his father was involved in, but how would Marc ever know what they were, or where the files were? And there was that warning signal again, warning him against his uncle. Did he know more than he led on?

"Farmer," Kate announced proudly as she laid her tiles across the board.

Marc looked down at her word and noticed she had missed a good point opportunity. He began picking up her tiles.

"Now, if you had just set them up right here," he said, lining them up against the far side of the board. "Then your last letter would land on this orange square here." He double tapped the board to get her attention...her attention span was like a two year old. "You'd have a triple word score. That's what you look for to earn more points."

"Is that your secret?"

He nodded.

"Do you want to know my secret?"

He nodded.

She leaned closer to him, which was way across the table. "I hate this game."

He mimicked her and said, "That's not a secret."

"I always have."

"I've always suspected as much," he retorted.

"I played because you enjoyed it so much."

"I still do."

"I can see that. It's your turn." She sat back.

He looked back down at his tile sorting the letters in his head and taking in the best point locations on the board.

"That's a strange request," she said. "Your father I mean. Why didn't he just fix his own regrets? That's an awfully big load to leave for someone."

He didn't disagree but how could he say no to his father when after all those years he'd actually opened up and attempted to bond with him. "It is."

"Are you going to do it?"

He shrugged. "I would first have to learn what those mistakes were."

"How would you do that?" That was exactly the question he'd been asking himself in between learning the resort and working it. "With your mom's help?"

He shook his head. "No. I would never burden her with such a high demand."

"And yet your father did with you."

"Yes."

"How will you know what his mistakes were? Does he have them filed away?"

"Not anywhere I've looked." And he had looked. He had searched for hours through all his father's files, books, notes and cabinets. He'd searched for any type of unusual stuff that might lead him to wherever his father's paper-work was filed away. But he'd come up empty handed. Everything was perfectly filed and perfectly legit. Everything was accounted for.

"Did you ever consider that maybe it was his illness talking?"

"You believe my father did no wrong towards people?"

She didn't answer right away and stared down at her tiles instead. "No...But no matter what he has done how would you be able to fix it? I can't possibly understand how he would expect this of you and quite possibly maybe you shouldn't take it so literally."

If he couldn't find anything there would be nothing to fix, but if there were something, somewhere, he had to find it. He had to make sure his dad hadn't in some way wronged people who hadn't deserved it. But why was he pouring his father's last wishes out to Kate? The woman who had abandoned him without a word. But it felt good to tell someone and he could trust with his secrets.

"I'm sorry your dad put that kind of pressure on you."

He shrugged. "We deal with what we are dealt and sometimes parents just aren't aware how their actions affect us." Her father hadn't given her an easy time either.

She looked up at him. "He's been sober for five years," she said proudly.

"That's a good achievement."

"But I haven't," she blew out a deep breath. "All this

talk is dampening our mood. Let me grab that wine I watched you sneak into an ice bucket." She stood. "Do you want a glass? Or two? Or three? This seems like the perfect time to down a few and forget all the expectations that await you at home."

He chuckled. "One glass is fine."

Her slippers scuffed the wood floor to the bucket and back then passed him the wine and a cork screw. He popped the top off and filled the two glasses she held. She crawled onto the couch beside him and bent her legs up in front of her, wrapping her arms around them as if to create a barrier between them.

"Remember the first time I introduced you to alcohol?" she asked.

He chuckled. "I think there were a lot of firsts that night."

"Yes there were."

"It was the first time I picked a lock and broke into a kitchen." She had been a bad influence, but she had dragged him out of his shell.

She nodded, her smile helping him go back in time with her.

"It was the first time you picked a lock," she agreed. "Well kind of. I sort of did it first, and then let you think you did it."

He laughed. "That makes sense why that was the only lock I could ever pick."

She gasped. "You tried again? Without me?" Her lips curved.

"Of course."

"And you couldn't do it?" He sipped his wine,

enjoying the length of her smooth neck as she tossed her head back in laughter. "Not entirely. I can pick an indoor household lock."

"Those are easy."

"But not a kitchen keyed lock." He shook his head.

She sipped her wine and he followed the liquid down her throat staring at the island of skin left uncovered by her robe.

"It wasn't the first time we broke into the kitchen it was just the first time I let you think you did it," Kate said.

"And it wasn't the last."

"It was however the first time you got drunk," she continued reminiscing. "Oh my goodness I could hardly get you out of the kitchen. You just could not hold your alcohol."

That was the first and the last time for a long while that he had drank alcohol. He preferred to be in control of his actions and feelings, not let some bubbly drink define them.

"Then I had to sneak you around the halls," she continued and he leaned back enjoying the story from her perspective. "So we didn't get caught because your father would have killed us both. And we ended up in the library."

They had been inseparable.

"That was a first for you," he interjected.

She pushed his leg with her foot. "Just because not all of us have a mother to build us a private library doesn't mean I didn't read a book." She eyed him. "You do know that I develop and proofread copy ads?"

He stared down at her. He had never thought that she wasn't smart or was lacking whatever she was insinuating. Even before her mother had passed, Kate was the most independent, strong-headed, and hearted, opinionated person he had ever met. He never doubted that she couldn't do more than work with her dad in maintenance. He felt sad at the possibility that somewhere deep down she might have been pushed to college to achieve a degree to be Marc's equal. But it was never about any of that for him.

He moved his arm from its resting location on the back of the couch and slid a loose curl from her face, tucking it behind her ear. "I knew you would take the world into your hands."

A shy smiled crossed her lips and she quickly sobered. "Well, don't get all carried away. I'm not chief director."

A joke to undermine her achievement...too proud. God forbid you ever take a compliment Kate.

"I am actually considering quitting."

Quitting?

Why would she just quit? But, in the next instant, he almost got excited at the idea of her moving home.

Calm down, she hasn't said anything of the sort. "Why?"

"Well, it's still in the works, not official yet, but Gran left us an empty commercial building in town. The one right beside Mrs Calvert's Bakery. It's been empty for years and it has a Christmas themed window display right now. Do you know which one I mean?"

He did.

"It's destroyed inside and needs to be completely gutted and re-built. Peyton was throwing around the idea of opening a business in there."

"What does Peyton do for a living?"

"She's a hair dresser."

There were already a couple of hairdressers in town so there wasn't a high demand for another one. That was the business man in him, the pros and cons popping into his head right away.

"Abby," she continued, "has apparently been making handmade soap with Gran. I guess it was a little side job for them but they have done a marvelous job and Abby has been selling to friends. So then Peyton suggested a spa/soap shop."

"What do you think of her idea?"

"I think it would be expensive and I think she is very impulsive when it comes to serious decisions about her life and she doesn't always think them through."

"But, what do you think of the idea?"

She eyed him. "What do you think of it? You're the businessman going around buying up hotels."

"Why do you need my opinion first? Tell me what you think of it."

She smiled, looking confidant again. "Like I said, I think Peyton is impulsive and she doesn't realize the work behind opening a business from nothing. I believe she would start it with the full intention of completing it only to see something better on the other side of the fence. Then I think I would be left by myself to run everything. But on the other hand, Abby enjoys making soap so much, she would have her own job and I could move home. Maybe she would feel a connection to Gran everyday in a positive way."

"So the reasons behind the shop are pushing you to open it. But what about the actual product?"

"Abby's soap is amazing. It is an all-natural product with no preservatives and essential oils are added which also have benefits. I think there is a big demand for such a product as well as other things, like face creams, oils, salts, shampoos, body cream...anything natural for the body." She smiled at him. "So what do you think? What is your professional opinion? Remember I will respect it highly."

He took a deep breath and put his businessman tie on. "There are two spas in Willow Valley already, not to crush your sister's dream, but that would be stiff competition especially since the population of Willow Valley is left with only one half the population in the winter. However, there are no natural soap stores there. All natural, homemade seems to be on the rise as people are becoming more aware of what they are consuming and using in regards to the ingredients on the label. I definitely feel the all-natural body soap shop would be something worth looking into, worth trying to get the funds to start it. But you would have to look into whether one business in a seasonal town can support the four of you. You have to look at what your gross sales weekly would have to be to write out four paychecks plus pay all the bills. Since you are making the soap yourselves, consider looking into wholesaling it out yourselves. That would be an extra income since you are already producing large batches."

She nodded her head taking in his words. "You have good points I will definitely run that by the girls."

"Does she have a financial plan?"

Peyton wasn't that organized. "No."

"Does she have a business outline?"

"At this point, no."

"Does she know how to make either?"

She shrugged. "I don't even know if she understands what either of those things are."

"Are you sure she's the best person to go into

business with?" he teased.

Her eyes lit up. "When did you become such a joker? You used to be all serious and quiet."

He liked the way her face lit up whenever he teased her. It had all started in the sauna when he had taken his bad day out on her and she had retaliated in a saucy way.

"A little bit of you must have rubbed off on me before you left," Marc said.

Her smile dropped like a kite from the sky with no wind and her eyes landed on her half empty glass of wine. He could tell her absence was a touchy topic for her. It seemed to bother her more than it bothered him and it really damn well bothered him. He let her chew on her lip for a few minutes, lost in her own thoughts, before he reached over and lifted her chin with his fingers.

"Hey," he said quietly.

Her hand moved against his and pressed his palm against her soft, warm cheek. She closed her eyes. He wanted to kiss her eyelids, her cheek, her jaw line, her throat, and down underneath the robe where the rest of her warm, soft skin was hiding. When she looked up he found his own desire reflected in her eyes. He wondered how she left him if she felt the same way towards him as he felt towards her. He would have never left her. What was it out there that she had found that was better than all their feelings at that exact moment?

"Why did you come out with me today?"

He had no idea. Why had he snuck out to meet her in town late at night when they were young? There was something about her that he had never been able to resist. "I can't say no to you."

"You should have." Her hand fell and again her eyes trailed back to her wine glass.

There were things in his life he regretted like not fighting harder when she left, or not bonding with his father earlier in life, but sitting right where he was at that moment didn't even make the list.

"I didn't want to," Marc said. He ran his finger under her chin again and slowly lifted her eyes back to his. "Did you want me to?"

She stared at him long and hard as if bouncing the question around in her head. She finally shook her head and whispered, "No."

"I want to kiss you."

Her lips parted in a quiet gasp. She bit her bottom lip before letting them purse out again.

"I don't want any mixed signals." She had made it clear this was going nowhere two weeks ago, but now he saw in her eyes the same desire he'd seen in that sauna. "I want to kiss you Katherine McAdams. Do you want me to kiss you?"

Time stood still as she contemplated his question. It felt like forever. He knew she wanted this as much as he did. He had been with other women and never was the desire between them this thick or this strong. Every other woman was after his bank account—not his heart. And it hadn't mattered anyway because he had given his heart away a long time ago. When Kate left, she had taken it with her. Now that she was back, he felt his heart racing off the charts for her.

"Yes," she finally breathed.

Marc couldn't have waited another second if he tried, he leaned in and felt her tense body ease under his touch.

He bent down and pressed against the forbidden,

dangerous desire of her taunting lips. Her wine flavoured tongue pressed deeper into his mouth, wanting to explore as much as him. He felt her hand snake around his neck and her legs falling, allowing her knees to sink into the sofa in front of her and propping up her body. She thrust her body against him and his body moved without instruction onto his knees.

Wrapping his arm around her waist, he pulled her body harder against him, hungry to feel her every curve.

The deliciousness of her mouth was the very cause of their separation, when she spilled the glass of wine she'd awkwardly been holding between them and shrieked, pulling away as the liquid began to soak through their robes.

She stared down at the empty glass in her hand and the red stain on the front of her white robe. She looked up at him, horrified, her eyes glazed, before bursting into laughter.

Marc took the half full glass of wine he'd managed not to spill on her and her empty glass and set them on the table.

"I'm so sorry," she said.

"You don't look very sorry."

She covered her mouth. "I am, I swear."

Marc grabbed her robe belt and hauled her body back against his.

"I don't know what we're doing Marc," she said.

He pulled the tie on her robe loose. "I am getting you out of these wet clothes."

She smiled, the moment of reflection lost as she watched her robe part open. "How thoughtful of you."

"It's a very selfish thought," he said and she laughed, snaking her arms around his neck. He balanced one of his feet on the ground and scooped her up into his arms, lifting her up and dropping them both backwards on the couch. She landed directly beneath him, her robe flying open in the process. He eyed her naked body.

"Let me show you how thoughtful I can be," she said reaching down to his robe tie.

He captured her giggle with his mouth and forgot about the meeting at the hotel, the resort, the stress and obligations since his father's death and felt only the desire that had never been extinguished.

Chapter Sixteen

HOURS LATER SITTING they were curled together against a mound of pillows with one blanket wrapped around them as they watched the fire dim.

Kate snuggled her head against his bare chest, trying to ignore the remorse overshadowing her desire. She wanted to relish in the tenderness between them instead.

When he had asked to kiss her, the answer had nothing to do with how they had ended up here, but yet, this guilt gnawed away at her, constantly distracting her from this incredible afternoon.

Marc wanted this, she wanted this, and if they stayed the night, they could have more than just this one afternoon. She wanted to indulge in the future they planned all those years ago.

What if he finds out? What if his uncle isn't as honest as he claims? What if she has to walk away from this...again? From him.

"I'm going to need to put more firewood in the fireplace."

She didn't want him to go anywhere. What if all the "what if's" actually happened? She would never get to feel how perfect she fit against him like two adjoining puzzle pieces, again.

She shook her head. "I don't want you to go."

He kissed her forehead. "You will when the fire dies."

She tilted her head and caught his mouth with her own. "I'm sure we can figure out other ways to warm each other," she said against his already warm, delicious lips.

He chuckled, then his mouth travelled alongside her cheek, tracing her jaw line, and to her neck. She welcomed him, tilting her head back and giving him access to any part of her.

He abandoned her suddenly, just when she thought he was going to trail all the way to her toes. He slipped into his briefs before adding more wood to the fire.

She wrapped the blanket around herself and pouted up at him. With the poker, he stirred the coals around with the same fortitude he stirred her desire. She was doomed. She had intended not to sleep with him, at least not here. She had fully intended being just friends because she was afraid of more, afraid of his uncle. But her heart seemed to dismiss the reality overtaken by his charm.

The phone rang and she jumped. The clock must have read well past mid-afternoon by now, but she wasn't sure exactly what time it was. It felt like time had stopped as he had caressed and kissed her entire body on the sofa, then the floor and...

Lost in her own thoughts, she'd missed her opportunity to pull him down to her and convince him they didn't need to answer that phone. He trailed into the kitchen and picked it up. They were probably offering to send someone out to rescue them.

She heard him say hello, agree, thank you, and agree again with the caller, while her gut tightened like a twisting wrench around a sink pipe. Her breathing wound down like the dimming fire and her body stilled as she analyzed the one-sided conversation. How important was this meeting? More important than this? His uncle was sure putting a big chance on it that it wasn't. But surely Marc would assume they could continue this after the meeting. Only she knew better.

"Kate?"

As she twisted toward him, she modified her anxious face into a seductive grin. Allowing the blanket to completely drop from her shoulders, she leaned her naked arms over the pillow hill, and propped her face down on her hands...trying her hardest to achieve a provocative stance. She arched her eyebrows at him as her reply. She doubted her voice was going to speak without an uneasy tremble.

"They can arrange for someone to pick us up now," he said. He held the phone low, one hand covering the receiver.

She pouted her lips into an over-exaggerated frown. He was across the entire room and she wanted him to see it.

His grin rose. "Do you want to leave?"

Keeping her eyes locked on his like the jaw of a vicious shark latching onto its prey and slowly shook her head.

"Should I leave?"

Was he serious? Get back here and wrestle with me under these blankets. And that had nothing to do with any arrangement.

She shook her head again.

"Should we take advantage of their offer and spend the night?" Then he flashed her a seductive smile and she nearly melted into the blanket like a snowman built beside the roaring fire.

She nodded and her voice produced a weak, "Yes."

He put the phone back to his ear and let them know they would be keeping the cabin for the night.

Thank goodness.

Kate turned, rolling her eyes towards the heavens and thanking cupid for pushing them together rather than apart. She stood on her shaky feet and grabbed one of the smaller afghans, wrapping it around her body.

"Hungry?" he asked.

Famished was a better word for her rumbling stomach. Was it hunger rumbling in her stomach or nerves? It didn't matter either way.

She climbed onto one of the stools as Marc rummaged through the basket again. There was a little bag of pancake mix with a mini bottle of syrup or pasta sauce and noodles. A little "keep them over for the night" basket, just as she'd ordered. Sneaking groceries into the cabin would have looked suspicious and would have been a little difficult to hide.

Marc decided on pasta. Kate sat back while he pulled cooking supplies from the cupboards. She remembered him once rummaging around her kitchen looking for cooking supplies, showing off the amazing skills his mother had taught him.

He stopped in front of her with two wine glasses. "I'm going to mention this idea to my family," he said pouring them each a glass.

"What idea?"

"The sleigh rides they offer here."

"For the resort?"

He nodded, sliding her glass across the counter towards her.

"Thanks," she said before taking a sip.

He began explaining what the benefits of having sleigh rides at the resort would be if they added them. She listened. He was serious as he spoke about his idea, ever the professional businessman, just as he'd transpired earlier giving her pointers on Peyton's business adventure. She was getting excited listening to his idea. It sounded fabulous, just like the ride they had taken. When he was finished she asked, "Do you like working at the resort?"

"I do."

"Are all your siblings working there?"

He shook his head. "Violet runs the wedding planning. Emma runs daily events like yoga, exercise, game tournaments that sort of thing. Anya used to manage the kitchens and was a top chef but she left after dad died and left me scrambling to replace her. Then there's Izzy." He shook his head. "She's not currently employed with us."

"Does she work somewhere else?"

"She doesn't work."

"Oh."

"Exactly my thoughts but currently not shared by the rest of the family, including my mother."

"Maybe she needs some time after your dad. Abby is going through some things with Gran just passing, too. I mean she basically tricked us all into coming here for a free vacation and some quality time."

"Maybe."

"So, what about Melissa?"

"What about her?" Marc asked.

Did he really have to make her ask?

"What does she do at the resort?" Kate asked.

Yeah, that's what you want to know.

He sent her a grin over his shoulder. "She's my secretary."

"*Your* secretary?"

Secretary's generally sleep with their bosses; look at the pretty little blonde in Derek's office. He was definitely banging her.

Marc nodded, looking away again to focus on stirring the sauce he was heating.

"You hired her?"

"Are you jealous?" he asked.

She wasn't jealous. She was curious. There was a huge difference.

"No. Should I be?"

"No. Melissa has worked for my father since she was done her schooling."

Hmm, that wasn't the life she had envisioned for Melissa. That wasn't the life Melissa had led everyone to believe would be hers. Her vision had been more about marrying into a wealthy family worth equal to or more value than her own and never having to actually work. It was an odd trait for a woman so keen on being better than everyone else. That her father, the mayor of Willow Valley, even allowed it, surprised Kate.

"Have you slept with her?" The words were out of her mouth before she could rethink them.

She caught his head shift at her bluntness but if he was shocked or surprised he didn't let it show.

"No."

That was an awfully quick answer, she thought. In ways he reminded her of Derek, who always thought before he spoke but still charmed you into believing anything. He was always sweet and flirtatious, talking his way into her pants and then straight into the maid's.

"Ever?" she pried.

"No."

"Not even right after I left?"

He turned then, crossing his legs in front of him and leaning against the cupboard with his arms crossed over his bare chest still holding the wooden spoon. She wondered when he had grabbed his slacks from by the fire and how she hadn't noticed. "Do you understand the definition of the word no?"

"Depends who's saying it." She thought of Derek and his lies...lies and more lies.

He nodded taking her words in. "Is this an ex you're referring to?"

A very recent ex.

"I would never lie to you," he said in his serious no-nonsense tone. His words struck a chord so deep she could have slipped from the stool and melted into a puddle on the floor. A puddle of lies and deceit that is. It was more like a never-ending ravine. In a way, she was just like Derek because it seemed every time she opened her mouth to Marc it was a lie or a deception to hide other lies and deceptions. She held a one-sided shield of spikes between them. Karma. Maybe she deserved a man like Derek in her life and Marc deserved someone who was honest with him.

She needed to move away from this subject before he asked her for the truth. "I'm going to slip on my robe." She couldn't sneak away faster than a metal slinky slinking down the stairs.

Her robe had landed over the couch, but she moved past it to Marc's button up shirt. Finding it dry, she slipped into it instead and pulled on her underwear. She figured if she was in his shirt, then she would get to stare at that chest all throughout supper. She had to keep it together.

She was tempted to run out that door and out of his life. Let him find an honest happiness she couldn't provide. Being so selfishly close to having her own happiness gave her feet a mind of their own right over back to the kitchen where he was dishing the finished food onto plates.

He glanced over and grinned, looking her up and down with approval. "Better than a robe."

She moved beside him and glanced at the plates of food. "That smells delicious."

"They say you can win a man through his stomach but I believe this is the way to win your heart."

She chuckled and nudged his side. "Oh you think so."

He spun around and wrapped one arm around her waist, picking her partially up and dragging her backwards, her toes sliding across the floor until her rump hit the counter behind.

A low surprised and pleasurable moan escaped her lips as Marc bent down and captured it with his mouth. Her groan grew louder. She loved the taste of his mouth. She couldn't get enough. She trailed her arms around the back of his neck combing her hands through his hair. A mouth she recognized and filled an emptiness inside her that she had tried to ignore all these very long years.

He picked her up and balanced her on the counter.

She encircled his waist with her legs and pulled him against her. His warm hands slipped under her shirt, sliding up her back to her neck where he grasped and lightly pulled her head away.

"Are you hungry?" he asked

"For you."

He groaned and kissed her again deep, hard and so full of a lust that they could flame the deadest coal bed together. He pulled her hands from around his neck and pressed her palms against the counter, then abruptly walked away.

It took Kate a few seconds to open her eyes. Marc walked away, grinning, with their bowls. He passed the kitchen table and headed straight into the living room. How did he do that? Just stop midpoint and move on as though his adrenaline wasn't pumping from head to toe?

"Come on," he said. "We missed lunch, it's almost supper and you had a terrible breakfast."

Almost supper? And she had enjoyed her breakfast, even if it was part of the ploy of getting him out of the hotel.

Kate rested her back against the cupboard regaining her composure with a few very deeply inhaled, needed breaths of air before she slid down and made her way to him. How did he have such composure after *that?*

She glared at him as she playfully slid the bowl across the table and purposely sat on the opposite side of the table.

"That's cruel," he said.

She picked up the bowl and curled herself onto the chair, pulling her bare legs against her chest and blowing on the bowl of warm food. "You're one to talk."

"I wanted to snuggle."

She almost laughed out loud at his term *snuggle* but managed to keep a somewhat straight face. "After that kiss you initiated I want more than snuggling."

He looked like he wanted to laugh, too, but instead said, "You better stay on that side of the table then." He twirled his fork in the pasta and brought it to his mouth. Before he bit down on it he said, "When you're finished eating I'll give you much more than snuggling."

She did laugh then. "Oh promises, promises."

"I never break my promises."

She let the sharp pain that seared through her conscious slide and ate her pasta, pushing the guilt further and further down.

After she'd finished eating she set her bowl on the table but didn't move toward him. He stared at her, his bowl of pasta still half full. She stood up and stretched high, his shirt moving above her thighs.

"I think I'm a little tired now," Kate said. She rubbed her stomach. "All that delicious pasta."

Marc was watching her.

"I think I'm going to go lie in that large queen bed and have an afternoon nap."

He watched her as she began to slowly step away. She unbuttoned the top button.

"But now with all that wood in the fire it's awfully warm." She unbuttoned the next.

He stood.

She grinned.

He slowly walked toward her and she continued taking steps back until his shirt was completely unbuttoned and just resting on her shoulders. Her back was now against the closed bedroom door. Tantalizing brown eyes stared down at her. He stopped inches from her body, not touching, but she could feel him.

He bent down to her ear. She thought he was going to whisper something and she closed her eyes anticipating his deep sexy voice. Instead he kissed her neck. Soft at first, trailing down her collarbone. His hands slid up her stomach and to the middle of her chest, pulling his shirt off her. Then his hands moved down her arms and grasped her hands. He lifted them above her, kissing her.

"Are you ready for more than snuggling?" he finally asked.

She had waited over six years for more than snuggling. He definitely kept his promises. Afterwards, they followed up with a warm shower neither of them needed, but had nothing to do with need. Finally, they did end up snuggling in the warm thick sheets and quilts on the bed, completely exhausted.

Kate closed her eyes, feeling like this was going to be the beginning of a love that had ended much too early previously.

Chapter Seventeen

THEY LEFT EARLY the next morning, but not before a morning play date in bed followed by pancakes and a rendezvous in the shower...again.

To Marc's surprise, a company truck managed their way to the cabin to pick them up. He probably would have questioned them if Kate hadn't been all over him like a lusting teenager.

Back at the hotel in the elevator, they found themselves alone in the four-walled cube. He quickly caught her in his arms for a last kiss. She laughed. Each floor chimed as they passed until, too quickly, the doors opened and they were at her floor.

She pulled away. "Have a safe ride home," she called with a last wave and wink.

Marc slunk back against the elevator wall.

What had just happened?

He hadn't felt so whole in years. Lord, how he had missed her smile, laugh, sense of humor, everything that was her...not to mention her lips, her body.

He shook his head as he sauntered out of the elevator on his floor. He wasn't sure where they stood, or what they were doing, but it felt so good he didn't want to question it. Kate was considering coming home to start a business with her family. They would be in the same town...once again.

Would they have a future together then?

His uncle, showered and dressed in a plain grey suit with a smile across his face, caught him in the hallway. Marc felt underdressed still in his outfit from the day before.

"Good morning," Carl greeted.

"Morning," Marc said, trying to block out the usual suspicions that were beginning to pop up like weeds in his head about his uncle.

"Looks like you had a good night. The car is being pulled around, pack your things and I'll meet you in the lobby." He patted Marc's shoulder as he passed, heading to the elevator.

"Everything went smooth with the deal?"

Alright, so he was a little curious. They hadn't had the lawyers draw up the papers, meet them out here, and drive this whole way for him to dismiss it over one rendezvous with Kate. An amazing rendezvous, but still.

"Oh," his uncle turned half way down the hall as if the thought had just come to him. "The deal fell through." He waved a hand as though it was no big deal.

"What do you mean it fell through?" Marc started making his way back down the hall towards his uncle. How could it fall through? Everything was in that contract from both parties.

"Another day, another deal. Hurry up and pack. We have a long drive home." He turned to leave again dismissing him, as usual, but Marc caught his arm. His uncle turned, sharpness in his eyes.

"What happened?" Marc demanded. Enough of this beating around the bush.

"Nothing out of the ordinary Marc. You'll learn that

sometimes deals don't always go as planned. That's part of buying and selling. You buy some and some you don't. Get used to it."

"I would like to talk to him."

"He just wasn't as interested as they presented. No need to waste either party's time on it. Pack your bags, and meet me downstairs in ten." Carl left no room for discussion, and Marc released his arm, watching him walk toward the elevator. "I'm starving. Maybe we will stop for breakfast on the road."

Back in his room, Marc changed, packed and headed out, against his uncle's warning, to find the owner. He boarded the elevator and set out toward the main lobby.

He'd noted the day before that the offices were beyond the main lobby desk and down a hall off the main lobby.

He left his bags at the front desk with the friendly ladies and headed across the foyer.

He caught sight of his uncle standing by the very hall he needed to pass, conversing with Kate. Those suspicious weeds wouldn't have started growing had their body language not been rigid and bitter. They had matching icy cold stares like the frosted bush he and Kate had trailed through the afternoon before.

Marc stopped dead in his tracks. His uncle held an envelope in his hand that he kept pushing at Kate. She pushed it back, shaking her head. A chill so cold in her eyes made its way through Marc's entire body. There were words exchanged, words he could, but they obviously weren't friendly. Each of them seemed sparked by anger and disagreement.

A realization set off the ticking time bomb quietly resting in his mind, finally reaching the end of its wick. His mind slowly put together the envelope, their *accidental* run-in, the stranded mess in the woods, and the missed meeting that had coincidently fallen through for no reason...all the events suddenly clicked together and sent the bomb exploding. Anger coursed through his body all the way to his clenching fists.

Marc didn't want to talk to either of his betrayers, but they were blocking the hall to the owner's office. He couldn't simply walk by his uncle without prompting more friction between them.

Marc walked right towards the two and took Kate by the arm, planting a kiss on her trembling lips.

"Will you excuse us?" He managed to guide her down the hall and around the corner. When they were out of sight, he let her go.

"Marc, what are you doing?" she asked with a smile forming. "That was awfully blunt right in front of your uncle. We don't even know where this is going." She looked anything but concerned.

"Using you, like you used me." His tone dripped with icy venom.

Gone was the sweetness they'd shared this morning.

"Don't look so shocked Kate. I'm not the fool you seem to think I am. Did Carl pay you to sleep with me?"

Her eyes grew round horrified. "Marcus!"

"Is that a yes in disguise? Whatever is going on between you two probably dates back to my father."

She quietly glared at him.

"I'm not far off am I?"

Her arms crossed slowly in front of her like a rope binding them below her chest. "I refuse to be a part of this Marc. If you have something going on with your uncle, take it up with him. Don't throw accusations at me."

"Accusations I've always suspected." But never wanted to believe. Didn't believe. Until now.

She stood tall and didn't shy away like a scared kitten. "I didn't sleep with you for money from your uncle. If that's your first instinct on a conversation I'm having with your uncle, we should both do ourselves a favor and stop here."

"Consider it stopped."

She nodded. "Watch it Caliendo, your reflection is starting to look a lot like that of your father's. I guess my decision, all those years ago, was the right one." Without a blink, she walked past him, and left him alone in the hall.

The office door was only a few feet down the hall, but confusion muddled his head. He stared after Kate. He hadn't thought any of that conversation through, sounding a lot like an accusing, unfiltered Izzy. But how far from the truth was he?

***

EIGHT SILENT, TENSE hours later, Marc was beyond furious as he parked the vehicle in the underground parking lot at the resort. He popped the trunk for his uncle but refused to get his own luggage, leaving Carl alone in the parking lot.

Marc was at his limit. One second Marc was doing everything right with his uncle and the next, he was being swept under the rug. Marc couldn't figure him out. As usual, when Carl didn't want to go into detail, he had brushed off the detailed conversation he had shared in that office. Marc was giving him the benefit of the doubt. *Come clean; tell me what is going on.* But Carl had said nothing.

Marc didn't know what to think. His father's warning, and then the hotel owner telling him that he and his uncle shared a lack of thirst for power that his father had possessed...what the hell was he supposed to do with that?

If his uncle wouldn't talk to Marc about it then he was going to go to the next best source, Eliza. And if the two of them or either one were undertaking shady deals like his father, he didn't want his name attached to it. He would pack a bag and go back south.

However, now wasn't a good time to face his mother. He was exhausted and angry. In all his life he couldn't remember being this furious, except when Kate had left. Maybe that was what was spawning this reaction that was so unlike him. He felt the need to cool off in his suite until his thoughts could rationalize. He was the spitting image of his mother—level-headed with no temper, but not at the current moment.

Unfortunately, his mother sat stretched out by the pool, her nose buried in a book. He hoped he could sneak past her but she was too observant and glanced up at him with a huge, smiling, delightful greeting asking him about the trip.

"We didn't buy a hotel," he said straightforward, continuing his pace.

"Your uncle already told me."

Marc stopped a few feet away from her. Of course he

had.

She waved her hand at Marc. "Who needs another hotel anyway? Just more responsibility. I want to know how your day was. With Kate," she added.

She wasn't the least bit curious about the reason behind the deal falling through. He suspected because she knew exactly why they didn't get it. Funny, he had no idea.

"I don't want to talk about it."

She frowned. "Oh no Marcus, what happened?"

"Nothing," he snarled, definitely not about to get into Kate details with her.

She sat up straighter, obviously surprised by his attitude. "Marc, what has gotten into you today?" She stared up at him with a puzzled expression.

How could she possibly be puzzled? She knew. He knew she knew.

"Do you really want to know?" he asked.

"Of course I do. Tell me."

That was his mother, always there to listen and guide.

He crossed his arms over his chest. "I'm tired of all the bullshit here."

He heard his sister exclaim, "Marc!"

Marc hadn't even noticed Emma, Violet and her kids across the pool in the shallow end splashing around. He would have never missed a detail like that if he wasn't so distracted.

Violet ushered the kids out of the pool. "Go to your rooms and get changed for bed."

Violet and Emma, neither dressed for swimming, walked their way towards the loud voices.

"What's going on?" Violet asked, crossing her arms.

"I want to know exactly what is going on with Carl and you." He stared at his mother. "I don't want excuses or brush offs. I want the truth Mother and you are going to give it to me."

She looked even more shocked with his abruptness. "Marc, please, where on earth is all this coming from?"

"I am tired of being screwed around. 'Be a part of this Marcus,' 'No, don't worry about that detail Marc,' 'Here's only half the truth,' if it's even the truth." He threw his hands in the air. "You and Carl are taking me this way and that way."

His hands were flying one direction and then the next and he felt like Izzy dramatically trying to get her point across.

"You want me involved, and then you don't," he said. "You want me to take Dad's position, but not all of it. Let's just get all the facts out here so I know where I stand."

He watched the surprise and shock slink away from his mother's face and knowledge and guilt creep in.

"Marc, let's talk about this later," she said. "Maybe once you have calmed down."

He shook his head. He had been all keen for that but now that it was out there he wasn't about to walk away.

"No, I want the answers now."

Eliza looked up at her daughters. "I would prefer to discuss this with Carl present."

"I'm here." His deep voice came from behind them, but Marc didn't turn. He watched his mother glance past him, her eyes speaking to Carl in a language Marc couldn't read. Marc wasn't sure if he wanted his uncle present or not.

She looked at her daughters. "Girls, could you give us

some privacy please?"

Marc held his hand up to stop them from moving. *What difference did it really make if they stayed or went?* They were finished hiding secrets from each other. The truth was for them all, they were a family in this together.

"You two stay." He looked at his mom. "You can explain to all of us why you insisted I come back to take over with praise one second, then dismissal the next. Tell me what Dad was referring to when he said Carl wasn't who he appeared to be. I'm not like Dad if that's what you're trying to recreate. I don't want to be involved in dishonest deals. I didn't come back to hurt people for money."

She slowly rose to her feet, her eyes absorbed with concern. She closed the distance between them. Standing before him, only inches shorter than him, with her shoulders squared she said, "I didn't realize you felt this way Marcus. Why didn't you come and talk to me sooner? You have always talked to me." She touched his hand. "I didn't realize Robert had said anything to you."

"Do you know what he is referring to?"

She nodded.

He hadn't thought differently. "Robert left us with a lot of messes to clean up after he passed. Carl and I have been trying to sort through it quietly without involving any of you children."

Her eyes made contact with everyone, each daughter, Carl and back to him. "Robert was not an honest man. He's hurt people, too, with his actions and we have been trying to repair the damage."

Marc didn't think now was a wise time to mention his father had requested he acquire the responsibilities they'd both taken on.

"Marc, I want you to run a clean resort and I want all the transactions and investments you make to be honest ones. I'm sorry I did not come and talk to you sooner," she looked around again. "I'm sorry I didn't come to all of you and explain our decision."

Marc relaxed, the pent up anger he wasn't used to withholding slowly parted like the fall wind breaking leaves away from the branches. If they had been honest with him, he felt the last months would have gone much smoother. It still didn't explain his father's warnings about his uncle. Marc wanted to glare at his uncle now. He had better not be manipulating his mother. These were her words, but what were his uncle's thoughts?

"Marc you are very much like your father." That was a lie right across her lips. Oh, good Lord, they were not getting anywhere.

"Eliza," a concerned Carl said from behind him. "Maybe now isn't such a good time."

"It will never be a good time," she told him.

What would never be a good time? Why all the secrets?

"Marc, I love you."

He stilled. It wasn't odd for her to profess her love, but the tone told him there was something more to follow. Something not good. He watched his sister's expressions alter. His mother continued.

"Robert was a difficult man who craved power and wealth above all. Above me and above his family. He could be a mean man. But he wasn't always like that."

She breathed a sigh. Marc could sense her mind

travelling back, to a time, to the moments she was sharing.

"There was a time long ago before his father died when he was a good man. But after the passing of his father, he changed. The power and the money he inherited changed him."

Marc realized then, that this was her greatest fear for him and contributed towards manifesting all the secrets between them. She feared Marc might follow in his father's footsteps as his father had followed in his grandfather's. But Marc lacked his father's desire for money and control. He hoped somewhere deep inside his mother would know that he never craved the life his father had led.

"It was the lies and the secrets behind your grandfather's office that changed him and I know your heart is good but so was his, so I feared changing it. Do you understand?"

More than he had before, although he wished she had been upfront and honest with him before this. He couldn't be mad at her about her decision to protect her children.

Marc wrapped his arms around his mother and squeezed. "I understand." Marc turned to his uncle. "I'm sorry I have been short with you lately."

Carl nodded.

"Momma, we can help you in any way," Violet said. "We want to help."

Emma agreed quickly, rubbing their mom's arms. "If we all help, it won't be so much on you both."

Eliza hugged her supporting daughters. "Right now we are tying up some loose ends, such as the deal today. We knew he wouldn't accept the offer but it had to be done in person. They didn't only want us to buy the hotel...they wanted us to provide information your father had agreed upon that would destroy another's life."

So, that was why they didn't want him at the meeting. They were shielding him from the dragon's lair.

She turned to Marc. "There is more. Can we sit please?"

Marc wasn't sure he liked where this was going. They pulled Adirondack chairs into a circle and sat together just as they would from here on in with no secrets between them. Marc remained across from his mother, Carl beside him and a sister on each side of Eliza.

She took a deep breath before she started. "At the beginning, I wanted to help Robert deal with everything that had been given to him. He seemed so lost in that office. Hours upon hours doing...I have no idea what." She lifted her hands into the air and twirled them about. "He learned things, things that made him cold and angry and, as the years passed, he became the man you remember. He became his father."

No one talked about Marc's grandparents. They both had died long before him or any of his siblings had been born. Although their picture hung in the foyer of the suites, and they had built this empire in turn making the Caliendos a wealthy, well-known name, there wasn't much said personally about his grandparents. He knew that his grandfather had bought the property and converted the house into an inn, continually building into the resort they ran today. However, it was never clarified where his grandfather's money came from. Had it been family, money, or illegally grossed money?

His mother continued her story. "At that time, Corbin wasn't even a year old and the hard days turned into years.

Your father had changed so much and whenever I talked to him, he would fume. I felt so alone. So one night I packed a small bag of our things to leave. With a tired three-year-old in tow I wasn't sure what I was going to do, but it had to be better than living alone in fear. Would I say something to set him off? Would Corbin say something to set him off? Would he come home already set off by something at the resort?"

Marc thought about his long lost brother, Corbin, and thought about how strong his mother would have been to try and leave.

Carl continued. "He stopped checking in with staff and customers, and left everything up to me, except his files."

Marc had never seen the files. He'd looked everywhere and found nothing, so he assumed, at some point, his uncle and mother had tucked them all away, more than likely in Carl's suite where Marc wouldn't snoop.

"He caught me trying to leave," his mother continued. "And it wasn't good. It was the worst I had ever seen him."

Marc could see the memories making her tremble. He didn't know exactly what she was about to tell them but he suspected if he had known the next revelation about his father before he passed, they wouldn't have parted on the better terms of their relationship.

She shook her head. "I didn't want to give you more bad memories of Robert. That was not my intention." She paused, her eyes moving to share a moment with Carl that the children all observed but didn't comment on. There was history between them with a man they both loved. His mother inhaled deeply, gathering the strength to continue her story. "It happened more than once. I can't say it ever really ended."

"Momma, what happened?" Violet asked. "Did Dad hit you?"

She nodded, looking ashamed. "He only raised a hand to me once." She wasn't making sense.

"Then what never stopped?" Emma inquired.

"I couldn't leave after that, he wouldn't let me, but I also couldn't stay living the way we were. I needed help and I had no one." His mother lost her family in a fire before she'd met his father. "So, I found Carl and he stood up for me and Corbin. He set Robert right in his place."

Carl took the spotlight. "We were all very young with a lot of responsibility and no family to help guide us. Your father needed guidance even if he didn't think so. There were things I knew that would land Robert in a jail cell so we all came to an understanding."

Marc could never picture his uncle being responsible for sending family to jail. But then, he hadn't pictured his father raising a hand to his mother either.

"It's hard to explain to you so you will understand," his uncle continued. "We were all much younger than you are now and we were all we had. The three of us worked out an arrangement that benefited all of us."

"Marc," his mother said, pulling his eyes away from his uncle. "I say you are like your father because you are soft-hearted and a family man. You stand up for what you believe in and your beliefs are true to your heart. You can define the difference between right and wrong. Robert wasn't that man. He was never that man, but you are. You may have gotten some of that from me, but you got the rest from your father." Her words were conflicting, leaving them all confused.

"I don't understand."

"Carl is that man."

Marc's breathing skipped a beat. He knew the meaning behind that statement faster than it took for his heart to jump back to beat.

His sisters both gasped.

Marc's eyes flew to his uncle...father. It was them, they never ended. There was something between them...love?

"He's also Isabelle's father," she added in a quick breath.

"Mother!" the girls cried in unison.

"Oh my gosh. What about us?" Emma asked.

"You two are Robert's," she quickly clarified.

Marc stood up, but his mother caught his hand. "Marc, say something," she pleaded.

"It seems that Robert wasn't the only deceitful member of this family."

Chapter Eighteen

MARC STARED DOWN at the brightly colored gerbera flower bouquet in his hands. It was the only thing he had purchased.

It had been a week since the big Caliendo breakdown confession show. Izzy had just arrived home yesterday, late afternoon. She'd been exhausted and skipped supper to *rejuvenate herself,* her words, before disappearing into her suite.

It seemed like now that his mother's conscience was freed with three quarters of her children she could hardly wait to tell the last child. He almost understood her desire to keep such secrets to herself as he played out the inevitable scene with Izzy. It caused his stomach to knot with anticipation.

Waiting to watch someone else receive this crazy news, was much harder than receiving it himself had been. And Izzy was one hundred percent more irrational than him, so he figured she was going to go on an all-so-famous Izzy rant. She'd leave everything upturned like a rabbit digging carrots out of a garden and put everyone into a chaotic state. And that was only if it went over well.

His mother was preparing them a meal in her...and Carl's suite. Apparently, although Carl's suite was just next door, Carl had become a regular fixture in his mother's suite since Robert's death. They were continuing their blooming romance, which had been concealed until now. Marc still wasn't sure how he felt about that.

The blue, purple, yellow and pink petals stared up at him bright and bold as if loudly reminding him that bringing flowers to smooth over your sister's paternity revelation was absolutely ridiculous. Would it look odd?

He was one person away from paying when he decided he would present them to his mother instead and prevent any further suspicions before supper even began.

"I would speculate those are for my sister but considering the way you two parted ways, I'm going to assume I'm not accurate." Peyton's voice sliced through his thoughts. "Unless, you're planning an apology. Not that I'm assuming it was your fault because, of course, she didn't tell us anything."

With all the extra family drama and all the women in his life smothering him with concerns, he hadn't had any spare time to think about Kate. Until the lights were turned off and he lay alone in his bed, of course, but even then he was usually so exhausted he passed out in minutes and Kate was only a drifting thought. He couldn't very well tell that to Peyton.

"Didn't go straight home after your trip?"

She smiled and winked those same hazel eyes that Kate had. "I get it, none of my business. And I'm staying in town at my dad's. I have a few appointments lined up at the banks in town." She wrinkled her nose. "I had one this morning that didn't go over as good as I had hoped."

He remembered the empty building Gran had left them. "Your soap shop?"

She beamed. "Kate told you?"

He nodded.

"Hmm, she must have *really* liked the idea then."

He nodded again.

Her smile fell to a frown. "I called in a contractor and got a quote to fix the building up and took it to the bank. Along with the start-up cost of supplies to make the soap and body products on a bigger scale than what Gran and Abby were producing out of their kitchen. It didn't go over so well."

The lady in front of him finished her sale and Marc set the flowers, that would reassure his mother he had forgiven her, on the counter.

He dug one of his business cards out of his pocket and flipped it over, quickly jotting his cell number on the back.

"Here take this. If it doesn't work out with any of your other appointments give me a call and we *will* work something out." He stressed the word "will" to let her know it wasn't negotiable. He *would* help them.

Peyton took his card a bit reluctantly and stared up at him. She seemed surprised. She waited for him to pay and followed him out onto the cold November sidewalk. "Marc, are you serious?"

"I wouldn't have handed you my card otherwise."

She smiled shyly. "That's amazing."

"I'll want to see the business plan, the profit turnover, and the expenses...the whole deal before I hand over a check."

"I have all of it."

He nodded. "So give me a call."

"Thank you."

"Talk to you soon."

***

THREE HOURS LATER his family had all gathered for supper, trading secret glances full of worry between them. Marc had been pulled aside by every member of the family to have a secret conversation.

His mother had wanted to apologize, confirm he was alright and that he had actually forgiven her for all the lies that had unfolded. Even if she didn't come right out and say it.

Carl wanted to verify they were alright and asked for his consent to continue a relationship with his mother, which was completely unnecessary and awkward.

Violet wanted to make sure he was able to discuss the events again with Izzy so soon and make sure he was alright.

Emma ventured over to remind him that Melissa was only a phone call away if he needed someone who wasn't family to talk to.

And Izzy wanted to whack his shoulder a few times and tell him what a dumbass he was for abandoning Kate after they'd been tapping all night. *Tapping?* What was with that term?

He smiled, remembering Kate specifically telling them there would be no tapping hardly an hour before he made her a liar. Kate. They'd exchanged numbers before his accusations, so he was planning on calling her to apologize. He had been way out of line. He wanted to wait until after her trip though and, even then, he knew his words would probably be unacknowledged. He had truly messed up big time and realized it may not be fixable.

His family sat down to a delicious roasted chicken, potatoes and vegetable meal that his mother had been busy preparing all week. Not literally, but the menu had changed a minimum of once a day.

"How was your week?" she asked Izzy.

"Awesome. Those McAdams sisters are crazy. They're all willing to do almost anything, except Sydney, she seems a little more mommy-like and Kate was a little bit..." She looked at Marc. "Distracted. But she busted a mean move on that dance floor. I mean I personally didn't get any action while I was there."

His sisters both sighed in disapproval and said in unison, "Izzy seriously?" and a "Really Izzy, come on, we're eating."

"What? I was just trying to break in that Marc banged Kate in a cabin in the woods where they spent the night together."

Everyone stopped eating and five sets of eyes fell on him. His only went to Izzy's. "What?" she said innocently, then ate a forkful of potatoes before mouthing, *You're welcome.*

"Marc?" his mother asked.

"Long story."

"Where is Kate when you need a good story," Violet teased.

"Well, when she got back to the hotel, she was in quite a mood. She looked like she wanted to drill a fist through the wall," Izzy continued.

They turned to him again. "You do all realize

however many times you glance at me, what happened in that cabin was silly only between me and Kate."

"Have you talked to her since?" Izzy pushed.

"When I saw you two, she was fine," Carl observed. "Did something happen after that?"

"Again, not open for discussion."

"Maybe we should invite Melissa over so you're willing to dish out details to make her uncomfortable," Emma suggested. "Like the whole sauna story," she added.

"I can't help if parts of my life make Melissa uncomfortable. If the two of you would get it through your heads that I'm not interested we wouldn't all have to walk on egg shells."

Emma glared at him. Sometimes the truth hurt...obviously from recent events...and those two needed to move past some teenage dream they were becoming sister-in-laws through him.

"Alright," his mother interjected. "That's enough. If Marc doesn't want to talk about it, let's drop it."

"Until after supper and Mom's all over that," Izzy said. "I call first dibs on the replay."

Eliza shook her head briskly at her daughter complete with a scowl to try quieting her. Izzy retaliated by continuing tales of her fun-filled weekend, throwing in quips about Kate every opportunity she had. They got to hear about Kate's revealing bathing suit, and how she could out drink all of them and still wake up earlier than all of them in the morning with a mouthful of jokes and full of laughter.

Marc didn't comment.

When his sisters started to clear the dishes, his mother ushered everyone into the sitting area. It was time. Before the paternity subject came up,

Eliza eased into the truth about Izzy's paternity by first discussing Corbin.

As his mother spoke, Marc noticed she used "Robert" and not "Carl" not "Dad." She was probably trying to soften the blow.

"Robert was a bad influence on Corbin. He always tried to manipulate Corbin to his own benefit, usually in regards to his family. They spent a lot of time together even against my better judgment and, one night, the night of March eighteenth, when Corbin was only seventeen, he was acting strange."

Marc noticed that her eyes looked so sad as she retold the story.

"I managed to discover he had been instructed to cut the brakes on Carl's car."

Izzy gasped. "That's the night Corbin died," she said. "He had come to you? He told you?"

"Yes, he did tell me and we went to Carl and arranged for the car to crash."

"What?" Izzy looked horrified.

His mother looked exasperated. "Isabelle, let me finish. He never cut the brakes. His car was in the parking garage which is under video surveillance, so we had Corbin fake cutting the brakes, then get in the car and drive away."

"Mother!"

"Corbin didn't die in that crash Isabelle." His mother's unusually frantic voice echoed through the house and finally quieted her daughter.

Izzy sat back in her chair staring wide-eyed at her mother...was she actually speechless?

Marc had to resist pulling his phone out and snapping a picture.

When his mother regained her composure, she ran her hands over her lap and folded her hands on them.

"We whisked him away from the resort and away from Robert. We faked his death to keep him safe."

Izzy's horrified face dropped instantly like a child's and confusion etched its way across her features. "Corbin's not dead?" Izzy looked around. "Why don't any of you look shocked? Do you already know?" Their guilty eyes answered her and her hands flew in the air. "Are you kidding me? You all knew and are just now telling me?"

"No, no," Violet assured her. "We didn't know until this week, but you weren't here."

Izzy laughed suddenly. "Oh my gosh, you all were breaking me into this. I wondered why Momma was cooking. Actually I didn't even know that she could cook, so that's two things I learned today. Oh my goodness, Momma do you know him? What's he like? Does he look like any of us?"

Marc would have liked to have stopped there. Izzy seemed quite content learning about her oldest brother. But his mom continued plainly and told Izzy who her biological father was, quick and fast, like ripping off a Band-Aid.

"I know," Izzy said plainly. Now the puzzled looks crossed everyone's faces.

"You know?" Eliza asked.

She nodded. "Yeah, Dad told me years ago."

Everyone looked at Carl, but he shrugged, just as puzzled as the rest.

"No, Robert told me," Izzy clarified. "He was mad because I didn't want to go to a private school and he was ranting away and it came out."

"And you believed him?" Eliza asked. "Just like that you thought I would have an affair?"

Marc didn't know why she was so shocked...she did have an affair...more than once.

"Of course not, although I wouldn't have blamed you. I thought Dad was just being *Robert*, but then I saw it. The way you and Carl shared glances or would stare at each other when you thought no one was looking. You two laugh together whenever you sneak away into a corner or are alone at a table and I just knew. It was love."

Eliza flushed and Carl turned away.

"Why didn't you come to me?" Eliza asked. "That's a pretty big burden."

Izzy shrugged. "Because it wasn't my place to say."

Marc found that hard to believe. Did she already blank out the entire conversation she initiated at supper about him and Kate? That hadn't been her place to say either.

"More importantly, what are we going to do about Corbin?" Izzy asked. "Do you know where he is Momma? Can we invite him home?"

It was too fast. Marc watched the hurt in his mother's eyes, the concern in his sister's and almost a longing in Carl's as he watched his daughter who didn't seem to care that he was her father. Izzy was so determined to bring everyone back together she didn't even notice the hurt that would need to be healed before they dragged Corbin into this mess. That was if he even wanted to come.

Chapter Nineteen

"CHECKMATE."

His uncle/father Carl, looked up at him and grinned in defeat. "Again. It's ludicrous how good you are at this game."

Marc grinned then, too. "I learned from the best."

Carl stretched out his arms and leaned back in the chair with a grin across his face, enjoying the compliment.

Marc recalled all the games they had played together when Marc was beginning to master the game.

"I suppose you did," Carl agreed.

Marc leaned back in his chair. They had been playing this awkward uncle/nephew to father/son transition game for weeks now and it was exhausting. They were both struggling exceedingly to fill a shoe that neither of them understood how to put on. It left both of them drained.

"You taught me a lot as I was growing up. Chess, tennis, how not to build a stool," Marc teased.

A loud, deep rumble came from Carl. The stool Marc had attempted to build would have been fitting in the "Crooked Man's" house, from the old nursery rhyme.

"No, I taught you how to build a stool. You taught me how not to build a stool." They laughed. "You were not a handy youngster. But you were a good youngster."

"I don't really know how to do what we are trying to

do here," Marc said.

"Me either," Carl quickly agreed, looking almost relieved to get it out there.

"But, I do know that you were the best uncle any of us could have growing up. At times, you were better than *him* at being a father. We have a good relationship here and I don't want it to get muddled because we are trying so hard to adjust to titles."

Carl nodded. "It's remarkable how wise you are. I am very proud of you."

Marc grinned. "I got it from my mom," he teased. Carl laughed again.

"Speaking of which, I was told we're all meeting at Mrs. Calvert's for a late lunch. And, it's getting to be that time."

Marc grinned inwardly.

That was exactly what he had arranged. He had even called ahead and asked Mrs. Calvert to reserve seats for them in the far window facing the McAdams currently inherited building.

"Yes, I'm going to meet you down there. I have a couple errands to run first," Marc said.

When his uncle...father...closed his office door, Marc pulled out his cell and typed a quick text to Peyton. *They're going to be at the edge of Mrs. Calvert's bakery so meet me out front. I will text when closer.*

He snapped his phone shut. This was going to fix all his family problems for a good year.

***

"I THOUGHT THE girls were meeting us here," Kate said, waiting for Peyton to unlock the front door of the shop.

Peyton shrugged. "I told them after lunch. They'll show. Come on, let's look around."

Once inside, Peyton tossed the keys on a nearby desk and started vocally illuminating her vision.

"Everything should be done naturally. The walls a neutral color that will highlight the wood displays Dad is making for us." She stood to the left. "We will have the counter here so we can greet customers as they come in and offer them assistance." She walked to the middle of the floor. "And here we will have a long old harvest table with gift baskets full of our products." She moved to the back wall. "With a huge wooden shelf here as the main focal point with each of our soaps and a card describing their benefits." She glanced over her shoulder at her sister. "Which is where your creativity comes in. We also need you to make us a sign, and logos, and we will need to do advertising."

"I will brainstorm with Abby." The youngest sister was the brains behind the product creativity. During frequent conversations about the shop, the sisters had decided on an all-natural body and face shop carrying not only a wide variety of soaps, but also creams, salts, body washes, face washes and more. Once they sat down and created a list of the exact products they were opening with, Kate would be able to create labels and advertising posters for throughout the shop. She could feel the creativity bubbling through her, anticipating the finished products.

Peyton continued. "Of course we have to run this by all the girls for a final decision. Hey, let's look out back."

Peyton led her through a wide door-less opening

which led to a hall of doors and small rooms. She explained they were built for tanning beds and the contractors would be tearing it all out and opening it up for their soap production area.

Kate envisioned it all with her sister, and almost as excited. It was hard to compete with her dream. Her sister's passion for her own business definitely outweighed Kate's. But her sister had surprised her. She had gotten the loan, and hired a contractor plus researched equipment and products and she had done it all in the span of a few weeks. The excitement of starting this business with her family was amazing. Being home was amazing.

Her goal now was to maintain distance from Marc and all those deceitful Caliendos. The few hour drive from Peyton's condo to Willow Valley had given Peyton time to bring her up to date on the recent events stirring in the Caliendo household. Plus Corbin was not actually dead...thanks to Abby's gossip Kate was well informed. Seriously, that family had problems. She should almost be thankful Robert had sent her away. He had saved her from a life continuously involving unbelievably outlandish situations.

Almost.

Kate inhaled a deep breath for a new start, immediately regretting it when the dust from the boards Peyton was digging through filled her lungs.

Peyton's phone went off, likely one of the girls. She looked up. "Kate, go out to my Escape and grab a measuring tape."

"Why?" She waved her hand in the air to settle the dust away from her.

Peyton turned her eyes wide with excitement. "Look at these old boards." She ran her hands up along a pile of boards strewn in the middle of the back room. "If Dad refinishes these, they would made amazing shelves. Can't you envision it?"

Kate was still choking from the dust her sister was stirring up with her digging. She coughed. "Alright, I will go get it. Where is it?"

"Look for a red bag. It's in the red bag." She turned and moved thin boards into separate piles. "Just bring the whole bag!" she called.

The mild day welcomed Kate and she quickly crossed the street and popped the back door for Peyton's car open.

A mountain of their combined luggage laughed at her. The seats were flipped down and the vehicle packed so full, it was no wonder Peyton sent her out. There was no red bag in sight.

She bent her body far right, and then left, hoping a glimpse of the red bag would pop out. No such luck. A groan and sigh escaped her as she realized she was going to have to dig through the mess. She started yanking suitcases until she caught sight of the red bag deep in the middle.

Deciding not to unpack their entire lives onto the road, she weaved her hands through the other luggage like a snake through long grass. She gripped the edge like the sharp teeth of the snake and let out a sigh of accomplishment. Now she just had to yank like she was pulling a snagged fishing line. As she jerked it free she felt the grip of a strong hand encircle her free arm and spin her around in one swift movement.

An echo of surprise escaped her lips just as another's

dipped down and stole the sound. A warm hand caught the side her face, another arm trapped her arms as she was pulled tightly into a familiar embrace and she knew by the designer cologne it was Marc's lips pressing ever so softly against hers. The softest kiss they had ever shared and he teased from one side to the next in a soft repetitive motion that lacked desire and craving.

Without even dipping past her lips to capture her tongue...why did that leave her disappointed...he lifted his head and stared down at her with those amazing eyes that melted her soul.

Stand your ground Kate. You are finished with all Caliendos.

"You're not Peyton." Those brown eye like chocolate drops of delicious heaven, held a glimpse of distress.

Her thoughts popped. Why the hell was he kissing Peyton like this?

"You cut your hair," Marc said, running his hands through her pinned up hair. "I like it."

Actually Peyton had insisted on styling it that morning, pinning the long locks underneath and letting the short layers disguise the length. Rumor has it that movie stars were sporting this updo and Peyton had been dying to try her fingers at it.

Kate hadn't argued as her sister started fussing with her locks. She'd simply enjoyed her strong black, wake me up coffee and breakfast while listening to Peyton complain about how experimenting with her own hair wasn't possible because it was too short.

Kate had been rather irritated by the bobby pins digging into her scalp the entire ride here.

"I've been calling and texting you and you're not responding to any of them," Marc said.

She'd seen them and every single one left her fingers lingering on the send button, but she had resisted. She was starting a life without him...again. Her heart broke at the thought, but there was so much unresolved history between them. And it was only a matter of time, with all the secrets evolving, that hers would be revealed. Then he wouldn't want to kiss her. He wouldn't even want to look at her. And yet she could stare into those dazzling eyes forever.

Stop it.

But she couldn't get past why he thought he was kissing her sister. And why were his hands still on her face, making her want to reach up and kiss those lips again? And why did his lips always taste so delicious? They were still pressed against one another like in the walkway at the Crystal Hotel. Why did this keep happening? Why did she have all these questions?

"I know." She wasn't ready to face him yet. Although her new plan sounded easy and sensible in her head, she wasn't convinced she was prepared to pursue it thoroughly, especially when he approached her in an intimate hold chasing away Jack Frost with his warm embrace. "Marc, I wasn't ready to talk to you."

His face saddened. "I assumed."

From a distance, Kate heard voices calling them, her eyes glanced across the road in front of Mrs. Calvert's bakery to where Eliza was practically running her tiny heels across the snowy ground. Violet was at her heels. They were running directly towards them.

"Marc," she snarled. "Now your mother is going to

think we're together. How are you going to explain this to her? You should have planned *this* kiss for weeks." Panic arose inside of her. She was cutting him out of her life and now his family would think they were together!

She sent Marc a questioning look–what were they going to do next? Why was he still holding onto her? He stared down at her, looking as annoyed as she felt. That was good at least he could acknowledge he shouldn't go around kissing random people on the street.

I'm not random. Nor am I who he thought he was kissing...Peyton?

"This wasn't how this was supposed to turn out."

"What wasn't?"

He cursed, and it surprised her.

"It's too late to explain," he said. "Play along and hold this out."

He squeezed her hand before turning with a smile and waving at his mother and sister.

Confused, she glanced down where his warm hand had abandoned hers only to find he hadn't left it as bare as it felt–a white gold ring encircled her left ring finger. Not just any ring, a huge princess cushioned rock that screamed engagement.

What was happening?

"Mother, we were going to wait until tonight over supper to make our announcement, but you caught us."

Caught us? Kate was as curious as Mrs. Caliendo to hear Marc's explanation.

"Kate and I are engaged," he announced.

We are what now?

She watched his mother's face light up with joy and

Violet's shade a questioning cast. Kate knew her face mirrored her apparent soon to be sister-in-law's.

Eliza squealed a dozen questions in their direction then pulled Kate into an affectionate hug that lasted forever, her hair smacking the side of her face, and the smell of designer perfume masking Marc's.

"I have so many questions. When did this begin? Oh, I know when this began, in the sauna," Eliza accused with a sly grin. "It must have developed in the cabin." She clasped her hands together. "How romantic. How long have you been engaged for? When did he propose? How did he propose? Oh, let me see the ring."

At that moment, as her future mother-in-law grabbed her hand, she knew exactly where Izzy got her spunk.

Eliza frowned. "Oh, I thought you would have my great grandmother's ring." She smiled, embarrassed then. "But this one is beautiful. Did you pick it out? I know you young brides like to do that nowadays."

"I have heard that." Kate didn't see any reason in pointing out the truth at this moment. It was a little late now, but poor Marc was going to have some explaining to do later.

Marc covered his mother's small dainty hands with his own. His fingertips grazed Kate's hand and she was stuck.

"Mother, you're overwhelming us and we haven't told her sisters, who are arriving any second."

Her sisters weren't the only ones left in the dark.

"Dinner tonight," his mother announced.

"Mother, we're already having dinner tonight," Violet pointed out.

"Yes, I know Violet. But Kate, darling, invite all of your family and we can get all the wonderful details then."

Kate hoped Marc was ready to share all the wonderful details with her first because her version was a jumbled, confused mess.

Marc promised, leaning over and kissing his mother's cheek. She hugged Kate again.

Violet congratulated them, but with a wary eye Kate noticed, and waved as they left. Marc resumed position with his arm around her waist. When they had ducked back into a bakery, Kate looked up at him for an explanation.

He shook his head. "We should go inside and discuss this."

Marc helped her load the luggage back into the vehicle before placing his hand on the small of her back and leading her inside. Peyton was nowhere to be seen. Relieved she didn't have to have this conversation in front of her, Kate considered her possibilities. Either Marc had become so arrogant that he assumed *that* was a marriage proposal or the family crisis he was having at home was taking a toll on him.

Marc paced back and forth, an unusual action for him, which told Kate it might just be the family strain.

"Marc," she began softly. "I can't accept this proposal."

His eyes flew to hers full of confusion.

She felt bad for him. His uncle was his father and his brother wasn't dead, but that didn't change their past. "I can't marry you," she clarified.

He opened his mouth to reply, and then shut it.

"You called me a harlot," she reminded him. "We decided it would be better off if we ended it then, remember?"

"Of course I remember."

"Then why are you assuming I'm going to marry you?" she asked.

"I would never assume that of you. I don't even consider you the marrying type."

The insult irritated her. "You don't know what type I am."

"Your past speaks volumes."

Her mouth dropped open. "You weren't the arrogant type either but look how the tables have turned."

"Arrogant? Look at you. This isn't even about you and right away you're assuming I'm some poor lost puppy."

"Well then who is this about?"

"Your sister."

"Peyton?"

He nodded. "Yes, she agreed to be engaged to me and in return I'm financing this business." He looked around the room.

Engaged? Financing the business? Huh? *Peyton, what did you get us into?*

"You're kidding right?"

He stepped in front of her. "No, I'm not kidding. How would this be comical?" It wouldn't be. "I *need* her."

"You *need* my sister?"

When had this happened? Had it been longer than three weeks? How long had Peyton stayed here and how had they formed a relationship? They were too many unanswered questions.

Her head hurt.

Wasn't there some unwritten law stating you couldn't date a sister's ex? And all those phone calls and texting from him...they were to try and smooth this over? More questions, but only one came out.

"You're engaged to my sister?"

"No," Marc said. "I'm engaged to you."

She looked down at the ring on her finger, still confused. "But you're seeing my sister?"

"No." He looked insulted. "I would never date one of your sisters. Didn't Peyton talk to you?"

She leveled a look at him plainly stating she had no idea what was going on. "But you're planning on being engaged to her?"

"It's a business deal."

"So you gave her money to be your fiancée? Like an escort?"

That word was kinder than the ones that had come to mind: slut, tramp, whore.

"Well," he said moving closer. "In those terms, that would make you my escort."

That's twice in less than a month he had referred to her as such. "Peyton!" Marc jumped back startled by her outburst. "Peyton Grace McAdams where are you?"

She appeared at the top of the stairs. "What are you shouting about?" Then she saw Marc and her eyes lit up. "You're here."

"Yes, I'm here and you are *in* here and you were supposed to be *out* there and now our plan has gone to shambles," Marc accused as she started down the stairs. Kate had never heard Marc talk so quickly, or so loosely.

Peyton sent them both questioning looks. "Why, what happened?" Kate stepped in front of her and held the ring at her eye level.

Peyton gasped. "Why are you wearing that?" Then

grabbed her hand. "Wow, this is gorgeous. This is the price of my condo for a whole year."

"Because you insisted on styling my hair." Kate said using air quotes for the word *styling*. "And now apparently I'm a paid escort."

Marc chimed in at that point, explained the misunderstanding and being caught by his mother and sister.

A smirk crossed Peyton's face.

"This is not funny," Kate said.

This was a disaster. How could her sister agree, let alone formulate this ludicrous plan.

"It's a little funny," her sister said.

"It's really not."

"It's kind of perfect," Peyton said. "I mean you are a way more realistic match than me. No one will question your engagement."

"What engagement?" Kate practically screamed. She paused as a realization formed in her head. "Wait a second, did you plan this?"

"Yes, Marc just told you," she innocently agreed.

Kate shook her head, recognizing that not-so-innocent flicker in her sister's eyes. She turned away. "Unbelievable."

She walked away from her sister to keep from reaching out and strangling her. Everything was coming together—her updo, the tape measure, the texting.

Oh Peyton.

When she felt there was enough distance between them, she turned back to Peyton and Marc, who were both watching her.

"You sent me out there on purpose," Kate accused her

sister. "You made some red bag story to throw me and Marc together."

"I did not."

Liar.

She glanced at Marc. "Didn't she text you minutes before you jumped me?"

He cleared his throat. "I did not jump you." He looked at Peyton. "And, yes she did. She also knew my mother would be watching." He sent her an accusing look.

Peyton threw her hands in the air in defeat. She shrugged her little plan off. "Marc did you actually think anyone would have believed we were a couple?" She waved her hand in the distance between them. "This would have created a mountain of more drama in your family to deal with. With Kate, they're just going to accept her and not think twice because of your history. See, it's perfect."

This was the dumbest plan Kate had ever heard.

Peyton continued as though she were reading an instruction manual. "But we have to mislead Abby and Sydney. They can't know you two aren't actually engaged."

Did she really think this plan was going into action?

"Abby is Izzy's best friend and she would definitely let it slip and Sydney's been hard enough to get on board with this plan that we don't want to give her a reason to back out now," Peyton said.

"This is the most ridiculous thing I have ever heard." Kate looked at Marc. "How did you let her convince you that this was actually a good idea?" Kate was dumbfounded.

Peyton was quick to explain. "When we met up at his office to construct the set up cost and interest, his family was popping in and out of his office interrupting him the entire time and not for business reasons. So I teased and said he needed someone to distract them and he agreed. One thing led to the next and he said he would drop the interest and I said I would distract his family with wedding stuff."

Kate crossed her arms. "Which you were never going to do?"

"Take one for the team."

Kate glared at her sister. "Take one for the team?"

Peyton had no idea what Kate had taken for the team. And, after Marc's accusations, she finally had a clear head on the direction of her life and this wasn't it.

"You take one for the team." Kate's feet overrode her good sense and she crossed the room straight towards her sister. Marc caught her around the waist and lifted her into the air, away from Peyton, setting her down with Marc as a buffer between them.

Peyton stuck her tongue out as the front door flew open and the rest of her family came waltzing in.

"Kate and Marc are engaged!" Peyton announced.

Marc looked at Kate.

"I'm going to skin her," she told him before her sister's screaming excitement overruled and she was pulled away from Marc and into their arms. She should have stopped right there. She should have told them their sister's ridiculous plan. Instead she listened to Peyton go over the business plan and Marc explain the transaction and payment plan.

The women were ecstatic about their new business adventure. Everyone was on board, even Sydney seemed to let down her uncertainties about the shop. They were officially in business...and Marc was shelling out the cash.

A lot of realities had transpired about Marc, one of them the same as his dad: he thought money could buy him anything, including a fiancé.

He made his way across to her. His tone was low. "I like Peyton's plan, you at my side instead of her." He winked at her. "We mesh better."

"Marc, this isn't going to work."

He took her hands in his, rubbing his thumbs along the length of her fingers. "Kate, I'm sorry about what I said at the hotel up north. I was under a lot of stress with my uncle."

"Your father," she softly corrected.

He paused before speaking again. "Yes, my father. I snapped at you and there's absolutely no excuse for my behavior. Maybe lack of sleep," he offered, referring to their time in the cabin. She couldn't muster up a smile. "I'm sorry."

"Did you ask Carl about our conversation?" She already knew the answer, he was still talking to her so he knew nothing.

"I don't need confirmation to know when I've been an ass."

Her lips curved upwards, and then the smile vanished. She couldn't fall for this. She had to put some distance between them and now.

"You should have asked him Marc." Her tone was cold. "Because I'm sure starting your new relationship with him he would have told you that six years ago your father...Robert...offered me money to leave you. And I took it."

The softness in Marc's eyes cleared as his body

stiffened, even the fingers around hers became rigid.

"What?" he said.

She swallowed hard. *Spit it out so he'll end this fake engagement quickly and you can both move on with your lives.*

This is your decision.

"He offered me a large sum of money and all I had to do was stay out of your life." She held her breath, surprised it had all came out as easily as it had, unfortunately it didn't make her conscience any lighter.

That's because it's only half the story.

"And I took it Marc. That's why I left you and didn't say a word. All because your dad offered me a new opportunity."

"How much?" His cold tone and stony stare almost made her crumble.

She hesitated.

"How much was my love worth Kate?"

Your love is priceless, but that's not what this was about.

She closed her eyes as she answered. "Half a million."

He said nothing. She stole a glance through one eye and he glowered down at her. "Where is it?" He looked furious.

"It's gone." After paying for all her sister's schooling and setting up her life, she had never touched it again, and then at the hotel she had written Carl a check for the remainder. He hadn't cashed it yet, but he was in possession of it.

The room closed in around them now. Kate felt like

the air was being sucked away, making it hard to breathe.

"You have no money." It was a statement, not a question, but she shook her head regardless.

"You can't pay for this business."

Her heart jammed. Maybe she had been too rash to fill him in and now her sisters might lose a dream that hadn't formally begun. "No."

"So you *need* my money?"

"We need your investment." Her voice was quiet as she tried to not slink away into the cracks of the walls like a frightened mouse.

"I need a fiancée." No he didn't. He leveled a cold look at her. "Well I guess we're a pretty amazing forgiving couple."

Damn it.

Chapter Twenty

WHO WAS THE fool now? If Marc had ever suspected she had left with a push from Robert, he surely hadn't been ready to hear it from her cold, emotionless lips.

First, Peyton had played him like a fiddle and succeeded. As ridiculous as the plan may have sounded to Kate, her sister had described it as an essential resolution required to eliminate the background noise in his life. He was drowning in the resort. The last few weeks had been a sea of wild emotions and all the Caliendo women were swimming around like piranha's attacking him every second they spotted him. They couldn't find it in themselves to acknowledge and accept that he was fine. He wasn't some little emotional roller coaster that needed checking and oiling before every start up.

He was *fine*.

He had also been fine with the new plan; in fact he had been thrilled since Kate hadn't taken any of his calls. That was until she revealed her true self. She was just like the rest of them—after his money.

Half a million dollars.

What a lifestyle she had lived for six years and now she'd run out. Gone, squandered it away and now he was her ticket back to the lavish lifestyle. After their first run in at the resort she must have known he still loved her.

Loved her? How was that even possible?

That was the reason behind seeking him out at the Crystal Hotel...it had been strategized. The cabin and the intimacy they shared was a means to get into his bank account.

The realization enraged him.

What did she think he was going to do with that confession? Eliminate her part of the arrangement and walk away again leaving her with his money?

Hell no.

She could stick around and play the part he was promised and he was certainly going to make it unpleasant for her.

He was so damn mad he'd hardly been able to drag himself back to the suite to get ready. That's why they were running well over a half hour late for supper with their families. As they reached the restaurant, she slipped her hand around his, for the purpose of this sham, and he felt a pang of cool anger slice through his body.

This was the worst idea ever. His breaking heart wanted to call it off now but retribution seemed to override his heart. He still stole another glance at the mid-length black evening dress that wrapped unlined lace around her arms up and around her neckline, revealing her silky skin and playing peek-a-boo with her cascading curls.

Beautiful.

And she knew he thought so.

Everyone waited in the restaurant as they arrived, his family on the left and her family on the right. There were two seats left for them, smack dab in the middle across from his parents. *His parents.* That was still odd to put into one sentence.

Izzy and Abby made a commotion as Marc and Kate went to their seats.

"Here are the love birds finally," Izzy teased. "What took you two so long?"

"Oh, you know what took them so long," Abby chimed in.

Laughter erupted around the table. It was better they pictured them wrestling in the sheets then the reality.

"Make your announcement already so it's official," Izzy demanded.

Marc, just about to sit down, paused and stood back up. He grabbed Kate's fidgeting hand and pulled her to her feet, wrapping his arm around her waist and noticing her muscles tense under his touch.

"Kate and I bumped into each other in the sauna over a month ago, which I am sure you all remember." He flashed a bashful grin. "The part we left out of the story was that our hearts bumped together again in that small space after all these years of being apart."

The women at the table awed loudly with romance twinkling in their eyes.

"And after our snowstorm stay in the cabin, we rekindled what we both thought was long gone." He paused in case Kate wanted to add anything to the story. She didn't. *That won't look suspicious.* "We couldn't live our lives apart another second so I proposed to Kate and she said yes."

The table erupted with noise, all the Caliendos jumped to their feet and came rushing around the table to hug the bride and groom to be. The McAdams joined with Peyton being the only one playing a role.

"Oh, my gosh," Izzy cried, as if this was the first time she had heard the news. "I knew it. I knew you were still in love with her," she insisted at her turn.

Kate's eyes found his and, beyond that fake smile, he saw a sadness he couldn't explain. He wouldn't let her see his sadness so between his fake smiles he shot her looks filled with the resentment she would understand.

"Thank goodness you didn't listen to me and hide in your office," Izzy continued.

"I'm so happy for you, my pining brother," Violet teased, squeezing his shoulders.

"Congrats son," Carl said, throwing him off a bit with the term but still liking the sound of it.

"I'm very surprised," Emma whispered for only him to hear. "But congrats," she said louder with a smile.

"That means we are getting another Aunt," Violet's kids were saying. He heard them introduce themselves formally and politely to Kate. She smiled and shook each of their tiny little hands until Violet encouraged hugs.

His mother held him the tightest. "There was a click between you two. I figured it was just a matter of time. I'm honestly the happiest mother right now." Her blue eyes brimmed with tears.

Wait until this game was over, the tears would roll like wild dice.

"Kiss, kiss, kiss," Izzy squealed as everyone returned to their seats.

Kate glanced at him looking overwhelmed.

He smiled down at her, a goofy grin for everyone else as he reached with his hand and cupped the side of her face pulling her lips to his. It was short and yet the tiny touch sent heat straight to his groin. How irritating.

Remember she deserted you for money, cold hard cash in her pocket.

"I want to throw the two of you an engagement party," his mother said just as he knew she would. "Immediately." That sounded like a perfect idea to him. "Kate we could start planning with Violet and have this event thrown together in a couple weeks."

"Mom, you're overwhelming her," Violet said. "Why don't us girls just have lunch tomorrow, when I have my schedule book," she shot a glance to her mom. "And we will discuss it." That was also exactly what he had counted on.

"This is girl stuff," his mom clarified being just as she claimed, the happiest mother. He couldn't agree more.

"The McAdams girls have another announcement to make," he said loud enough to catch everyone's attention. "Peyton has all the details." He turned the announcement over to Peyton, who dived into their well-planned business adventure. Now he could breathe without speculating eyes.

***

ANOTHER DINNER PASSED with Marc's family ,but without Marc and Kate was stuck making more pitiful excuses for him.

So it was December, so it was his first year running the resort, he wasn't the only Caliendo working in the resort and they all managed to gather for supper, every single night. His family was becoming wary, not of her presence, but of Marc's absences and what could possibly be the real cause, which, ironically, was her.

It had been over a week since she'd told Marc about the deal she had struck with Robert. He was angry. She knew he would be, that's why she felt it necessary to inform him. His anger was required to keep him at a distance so as not to rationalize the relationship between them. A relationship between them would never work, she could see that now.

Only she hadn't anticipated he would lock himself away from his entire family, after putting *her* in this idiotic situation.

After saying her good-byes for the night to his family, she stormed away from the restaurant in the opposite direction of their laughter. She held a takeout container in her hand, heading directly towards Marc's office.

They were both officially skipping breakfast now, after the second morning when she realized he was choosing not to attend. Kate figured if they were both missing at breakfast his family may presume they were spending the mornings together, alone. When in reality, she wasn't even sure if he was coming back to the suite at all in the evenings. He wasn't there when she went to bed and he wasn't there when she awoke.

Melissa was already gone for the evening and she didn't bother knocking on his office door...who in his family actually did?

He was sitting behind the large carved desk, deep etches on his face matching the grains of the walnut wood. She wondered briefly if she caused those awful lines across his beautiful face. It didn't matter anyway, the truth had been necessary. He looked up, probably expecting to see a member of his family, but gave a surprised look when he saw her instead.

She dropped the round foil container on his desk with a thud. "Supper," she announced.

He glanced down at it then back up to her. "You didn't have to."

She crossed her hands over her chest. "Oh, I know. Trust me, this isn't to make sure you're eating. It's an excuse to come in here and tell you I didn't agree to this charade so you could completely cut yourself off from your family and hideaway all day and night."

He looked back down at his laptop without saying a word.

What was so important on his damn laptop?

She made her way around his desk and leaned over his shoulder to look. The wonderful smell of him drifted around her like caressing hands, and made her own hands want to massage his shoulder before dipping straight down the front of his shirt.

Get it together. Laptop screen.

Pictures of antique cutter sleighs stared at her from the screen.

"Oh, you're back to that idea." He snapped it shut and glared at her. "When were you planning to mention that to your family?" she asked. "After it arrived?"

"Don't be ridiculous, we couldn't incorporate them this year."

She crossed her arms again. "Marc, this has to stop. I'm finished making excuses for you. You can begin attending at least supper every day or I'm going to encourage their curiosity." She knew that would mean he would never get a free moment. "The depression, the distance, anything they say I will push *her*." Kate was referring to his mother and that seemed to agitate him, which was better than the alternative: his solemn pouting.

"It's December," he snapped. "I'm busy. There are overbooked rooms, cancellations, parties and events. You couldn't possibly understand."

"Cut the crap Marc."

He glared at her.

"Everyone's busy," she said. "And everyone can pull away for one meal."

"I don't need this," he grumbled, dismissing her.

"*I* don't need this."

"You don't have a choice now do you?"

Her mouth snapped shut and she swallowed her next words.

Darn it, she hated that she was in his debt. She almost regretted handing Carl that check back, which he still hadn't cashed. She couldn't believe Marc was being so cold to her, so heartless and angry, exactly what they needed to keep them apart.

She softened her voice. "Marc, you can't change the outcome," she told him. "No matter how many times you play it in your head, I will still have left you for money."

"Don't act like you know me because of a young romance. I don't know you, how could you possibly know me?"

She supposed she didn't know the man he was now, just as he didn't know the woman she was.

"You're right. I'm sorry."

His stare was like a scanner, trying to read barcodes, clues in her eyes, her facial expressions or body language.

"Why did you even tell me?" he asked. "Now, after all these years, after we were plopped together and engaged? Why?"

She sighed.

Talk your way out of this one.

"You deserved to know who I am."

"Who you are or who you were?" he asked.

"It's two in the same Marc, and besides, look where I am now and again it's about money."

"So you're a self-centered selfish bitch?" The way he said it was like he was asking her to verify. As if there was the tiniest part in him that still hoped she wasn't that person.

She took a slow breath. "Now that you've labeled me accordingly, let's move on so we can split, on decent terms," she added, hoping it wasn't too much but leaving out the friends forever that he had once promised her. "We're having brunch tomorrow, and then we're going tobogganing with Parker and Sophia. I'm leaving a list on Melissa's desk of your schedule with your family."

He held his hand out. "Give it to me."

She pulled it out of her pocket. She didn't really want Melissa questioning why Marc couldn't remember family events.

"You know your mom is worried about you because she loves you. You're lucky to have her." She wished her mom was still around. "She wants to make sure you're dealing with Carl and Corbin."

"I know." His voice was edgy.

"Maybe you could schedule a lunch with only the two of you. She would enjoy that."

"I didn't pay you to be my therapist. How about you

stick to distracting my family and I won't pull the money away from your sister's business, alright?"

Ouch. The truth hurt.

And the threats were evidence she was doing the right thing. She nodded and quickly left. He was punishing her, making her suffer.

She walked the halls at a quick pace, no matter how logical her reasoning was and how understanding of his feelings she was, the words cut deep and she felt tears forming.

You're doing the right thing.

It didn't feel like the right thing, but what choice did she have now?

Chapter Twenty-One

LARGE, THICK SNOWFLAKES fell from the sky as they trudged through deep, loose and untouched white fluff from the snowmobiles to the bottom of the hill. Marc dropped the old wooden toboggan and snow rider he'd been carrying beside him.

Parker and Sophia started straight up the hill with their crazy carpets. Violet and Emma were right behind them, spouting off rules to avoid accidents.

The resort had a public snow hill where they could have spent the afternoon riding lifts to the top, but the resort didn't give them much privacy so they enjoyed jumping on the sleds and driving across the property instead, through the bush to a private hill.

Since returning home, he had discovered since returning home, although the youngest, Izzy always had better things to do than take the time out to play with her niece and nephew while Emma and Violet had grown closer together.

Kate stopped beside him. "Wow. It looks exactly the same as when we were kids." She pulled her hat down further over her loose curls.

He glanced over. They were dressed more appropriately for the snowy weather than they'd been at the cabin. He was adorned in everything needed from the snowboarding shop they had on site and he suspected, although didn't ask, that the pristine designer white and pink snow pants, jacket and matching hat and gloves she'd picked up were from there as well. Still, her porcelain skin brought about rosy cheeks and nose, but there was that betrayal he felt every time he looked at her that he couldn't shake.

"Some things never change," he said, grabbing the string attached to the rider and walking past her.

He had done as she'd asked, and had brunch with a smile and laughter, treating her like the love of his life. He was even having lunch with just his mother the following day, as she had also suggested. But standing here reminiscing about a life she threw away for money...he didn't want to fake.

He climbed the hill quickly to get to the top at the same time as the rest.

"Momma, don't worry," Parker was saying as he pulled the string from the edge of the ski up to the steering wheel so it wouldn't tangle on the way down. "We've done this before, 'member?" And he was off down the hill, the red pom-pom on his hat bobbing with each groove and bump.

Sophia turned to Marc, still wearing her pink balaclava covering all except the end of her blond hair, blue eyes, rosy nose and mouth. "Come on Uncle Marc!" she yelled, and was off too, laughing in delight as she chased her brother down the hill.

"Alright," Marc said, lining up his rider between his sister's. "The kids might not be allowed to race down at the same time." He slanted his worried sister a glance. He waited as Violet surveyed her children's safe arrival with a motherly stare. When she looked over and wrinkled her nose at him, he said, "But, the three of us should race to the bottom." He glanced at Emma, bundled up in green, looking like a Christmas tree. "Ready?"

She nodded.

Then he glanced to Violet. "Ready?"

She nodded, eagerly leaning forward.

"Ready, set...go!"

The skis sliced through the light snow sending it billowing in the air and across their faces as they bounced up and down without any warning where the bumps and grooves were, finally arriving safely at the bottom of the hill.

Emma jumped off her racer, arriving at the bottom first. "Ah hah! Take that you bunch of slackers. See what happens when you take an office job," she yelled at Marc.

"You guys raced," Parker accused pouting back up the hill. "Not fair."

"You crashed into your sister last time," Violet yelled back at him.

"Not on purpose."

"That's what he claims," she said for only the adults to hear.

They all laughed.

Marc caught Emma walking by Kate, who was still at the bottom of the hill. Emma pulled the sleeve of her jacket. "Come on Kate, let's not race," she said putting up air quotes for the word *not.*

For the first time ever, he watched his sister and Kate share a real smile before starting up the hill.

Violet hit his arm and flashed him a, *what just happened?* Her eyes showed just as much surprised as the rest of them at Emma's hospitality.

"Did you threaten her?" Marc teased Violet, walking beside her up the hill.

Violet laughed. "No. I swear. It must have been your outburst at supper a few weeks ago."

Possibly, but who knew. He was almost glad to see it, but what did it really matter? He and Kate were faking this engagement to the end.

Soon they were all smiling, laughing and teasing as they traveled down the hill. He even let the betrayal feeling slip away here and there as he enjoyed the snow. But it always seemed to creep back, reminding him not to get attached. It was clear after Kate's admission that she had chosen money over him that she'd never truly loved him. She didn't love him like he loved her.

Had loved her...had.

About an hour in, Emma grabbed the old-fashioned wood toboggan and dragged it up the hill. She dropped it at the top and said, "Everyone on."

Marc stared at the size of the long contraption. "We are not all going to fit on that."

"We did when we were young."

"There were less of us and we were also half the size."

Emma was waving everyone on. "Come on, leg over legs," she insisted, positioning the kids at the front folding Parker's legs in front of him then draping Sophia's around him, instructing her to squeeze.

Marc stood back and watched with a grin as they all managed to snuggle close enough and leaving just enough room for him to squeeze on the back...behind Kate.

"Maybe I will catch the next round," Marc said.

Emma whipped around and glanced down the toboggan. "Lots of room, brother. Climb on and grab onto Kate like you do behind closed doors."

"Emma," Violet scolded.

"Oh, I mean like when...you know..." She shrugged. "...I got nothing, just get on."

"Yeah Uncle Marc," Sophia yelled, even though she couldn't turn back to look.

"The train is leaving, all aboard," Parker called in a low manly tone followed by train sounds that everyone copied.

Marc rolled his eyes and climbed on forced to wrap his legs up and around Kate.

"Is everyone ready?" Emma called.

Everyone yelled they were and Marc pushed them off as Kate reached for his arms pulling them around her waist. She didn't resume position around Violet's waist and put all her trust in squeezing Marc's arms. Her head leaned against the side of his shoulder, the curls escaping under her hat tickling the side of his face. Instead of moving away, like he should have, he pressed his lower face against her upper.

"Here we go," he announced, and they were off. The long piece of wood cut through fresh snow, and already trailed snow, marking its long path down. Screams of delight trailed behind them. Halfway down, the death trap hit a bump and turned sideways, first throwing Kate and Marc off then Violet and Emma rolling across the snow together.

They landed on their sides, just as they had at the cabin, laughing and screaming in surprise, but then continued rolling like unravelling mummies.

Marc tried to hold Kate, but she split away, the fluffy

snow grasping at their faces and hair.

Marc dug his hands in the snow and stopped first. Kate hit his side and rolled straight over top of him. He grabbed her and stopped her. Directly on top of him they were stomach against stomach despite padded snow jackets.

Echoes of laughter filled the inches between their faces. She continued laughing until her eyes found him staring at her.

Her face solemned immediately followed by a quick apology from her cold, pink lips. But, neither of them moved.

With one hand, he reached up and pushed the wet hair away from her cheek.

How was he going to survive weeks...months of this torture?

This was why he had stayed away from her all week because no matter what was between them he always found himself wanting to kiss those lips. And now the discovery that she didn't want him was painful too.

"Oh kiss her," Sophia said, as if reading his mind as she passed them on her way back up the hill.

"Gross. Don't do it Uncle Marc. Yuck," Parker said, not far behind.

How long had they been lying there?

Kate sat straight up, straddling him and he groaned.

Because they were out in public and knowing his sisters, especially Emma, would be watching, he sat up and grabbed the front of her jacket pulling her lips against his and unnecessarily dipped in for a taste. He couldn't resist.

Marc heard Parker make a fuss and Sophia cheer him on.

Whenever it came to Kate's lips, he was with Sophia

one-hundred percent.

When he let go, he asked, "Was that convincing enough for everyone?"

Her tongue ran across her lips and she looked at him with that just kissed dazed love look on her face before slowly nodding. "Perfect."

That was the last time he went up that hill when that bloody old contraption was dragged up the hill claiming he was too old. Really, he just feared not being able to help but kiss Kate again.

Chapter Twenty-Two

KATE COULDN'T BELIEVE how much fun she had tobogganing with Marc and his family. Even Emma had warmed up to her.

If she really was Marc's fiancée, today would have been the perfect day; bonding with Parker, Sophia and even Emma. Plus that tongue twisting kiss he had planted on her would have landed them both together tumbling around in the sheets.

If she was really his fiancée.

She'd also observed how wonderful Marc had been with his niece and nephew. He joked, teased and played with them like a fantastic uncle should.

Kate couldn't help but feel a pang of sadness at the realization what a good father he would be. She was sad they never had that opportunity because of her betrayal.

After supper, Marc had gone back to the office. To hide. Big surprise.

When she found herself staring at the ceiling replaying the kiss over and over again, she decided to take a midnight dip.

It was dim in the pool room with soft lights twinkling like stars in the sky lights above. A couple of streetlights shone around the pool, and a soft light glowed alongside the stone edge of the pool reflecting into the water. Each suite had lights outside the entrance and she noticed some of the curtains were drawn and others left open, but all of them remained dark.

She tossed her towel on a lounger and walked toward the shallow end. She was sticking to laps in the pool. No more saunas because they only got her into trouble.

His family was crazy busy with the December bustle and the New Year fast approaching. Not only was the Snowflake Ball a huge event but Violet told her for New Year's Eve they would open the four ballrooms with separate parties and each were already booked to capacity. Most people generally booked the rooms almost a year in advance.

She stepped into the heated pool where rounded stairs descended to the pool floor. She saw a ripple across the water not triggered by her feet and found Marc treading in the shadows.

"Oh, I thought you were in your office." Had he been watching her quietly this whole time?

"I wanted a swim."

So had she. Alone.

She retracted her foot. "I can come back," she said. "I didn't mean to barge in."

He swam to the edge of the pool and grabbed the side, wiping water away from his face as he surfaced. "It's alright. There's lots of room."

She wasn't sure about that, but didn't argue. When her feet touched the floor of the pool, she dove in and swam to the deep end. She pulled herself to the edge not far from him and dunked her head backwards to straighten out her hair.

"Do you sneak in here a lot?" she asked.

"Every night." That distant look was in his eyes, like a lone wolf watching his prey before attacking. It made her shudder.

"I didn't know."

"You're usually asleep by now."

She moved away from the edge treading water and he did the same.

"Wanna race?" The challenge was out of her mouth quicker than a popping bubble. She internally scolded herself. He didn't want to play games with her, he could hardly stand her.

"Alright."

Alright?

The late hour must have him more exhausted then he knew. If he was in his right state of mind he wouldn't have even swam to the side of the pool with her.

"There and back."

He nodded.

Kate counted down and they set off, the heated water splashing against their faces as they dipped their heads into the water then out for a breath. Their arms moved rhythmically, slicing into the calm water and making rippling effects through the pool. Touching the other side, she flipped over and used her feet to push away quickly, but he still beat her to the other side...without gloating.

A small smile crossed his lips and lightened her heart.

He surprised her by asking. "Have you tried the slide?"

She glanced behind her at the towering slide built into the rock hill looking more like a fair ride for kids than something grown adults would use.

She shook her head. "First time in the pool," she confessed.

"You have to try it." He swam past her to the ladder beside the bottom of the slide, and climbed out.

Kate stayed against the wall trying not to notice the way the water stuck to Marc's swim shorts, against his lower body, or that the chest she couldn't resist in the sauna was now dripping wet like a well-oiled yummy pastry.

He looked at her. "Come on," he said.

Reluctantly, she swam to the ladder and he offered her his hand.

Seriously. Back up man before I jump you like an alley cat.

She slipped her hand in his and he practically pulled her out of the water and onto the platform.

This was no better than the sauna. No more evening pool dips for her. At this rate she wouldn't be leaving the suite.

She followed him up to the slide and he hit a button that produced a water flow down the plastic contraption.

He stepped back.

"You first," he insisted.

She glanced down. The slide twirled around and into the rock mountain disappearing before reappearing and ending in the pool.

"Chicken?" he asked.

She sucked in a deep breath. "Of course not." It wasn't going down the slide that was jumbling her nerves, it was him.

"If it's too much adventure for you..."

She pushed him away, immediately regretting the

contact and forgetting they weren't those two same people anymore.

"Don't be ridiculous," she said, casually trying to cover up her discomfort.

Kate climbed on the slide and held the sides to keep from going then glanced back at him. "If anyone was chicken here, it would be you," she added.

He grinned down at her.

Grinned. Those striking eyes lighting up. *At her.* It tickled her insides.

"I didn't tell you how we're going down..."

We?

Before she could ask, he grabbed the rock above them, lifting up from his feet and landing his legs on the outside of hers, leaving her sandwiched twice in one day. She was favoring the second sandwich.

His torso pushed flat against her back, his hands slipped around her waist and he pushed off.

She yelled his name as the water caught them and curved them from side to side like a frying crepe ready to flip over the edge. Her hands gripped his and they flew out the bottom and crashed into the water.

Exhilarated, Kate let her body sink as far as it would go, and then used her hands to guide her to the surface. She broke the water laughing. Marc swam to her and she splashed water at him.

"That was sneaky," she called, then reached for his shoulder to try and dunk him under. He was too strong and she ended up sliding down his side...again...then treading beside him.

"Want to go again?"

Her eyes widened. "Yes."

This time she took off without waiting for him and climbed to the top of the slide.

"Too slow Caliendo," she called, but not too loud to wake his family, before taking off down the slide.

She could hear him calling after her and she was twisting to find him while the slide pulled her into the water. This time she didn't allow herself to sink as deep and raced to the surface just as the water swallowed him causing waves to erupt around her as he disappeared below.

She wiped the hair from her forehead and blinked her eyes.

She felt his fingers around her ankle seconds before he pulled her below, dunking her head back under the water before letting go.

Kate gasped, holding her breath until she reached the surface and caught sight of him.

She smacked him. "Jerk."

He caught her hand. "Who's too slow now?"

She laughed, but it quickly died as the atmosphere around them swallowed them up with desire. Bobbing in the water less than an arm's length away, Marc was still holding her wrist.

"It's like we're back in the sauna." She hadn't realized she'd said it until it was out of her mouth.

They floated close to each other, only one movement from touching body against body.

"Tell me you scraped your knee on the slide." It sounded like a plea from his lips. He wanted her to stop this because if she said it he would. But what if she didn't want to?

"I didn't." It came out in a whisper.

"Kate." A low masculine moan fought its way out of his lips.

She bit her lower lip.

What game was she playing here?

She told him the truth to deter him and the moment he needed her to say the words to end this, she couldn't find them.

"Marc." Her low tone was full of lust and she wrapped her arms around his neck, pulling herself against him.

What was she doing?

She could see his eyes fighting as she felt her own fight wash away into the pool around them.

"I think I scraped me knee." He removed her arms and left her in the middle of the pool, alone.

Alone.

She always ended up alone.

Chapter Twenty-Three

MARC'S FAMILY CLIMBED into the vehicle the night of the beach tree lighting and Kate ended up sandwiched in the back between Parker and Sophia.

"Are you sure you're alright?" Violet asked from her single bucket seat in the middle. Her hair was down but hidden under her knitted black, fur-lined hat.

Eliza occupied the other seat, looking pleasantly cozy in her floor length pea coat, and red knitted scarf wrapped around her neck.

Kate yanked her own wool coat from under Sophia's leg and pulled a handful of hair stuck between Parker's shoulder and her arm.

"One of them can jump in the other vehicle," Violet offered.

Kate looked through the window, watching Izzy, Emma and Melissa climb into the little sports car. It was either suffer with these well-behaved, mini Caliendos or suffer in the company of Melissa.

This isn't permanent.

"I'm fine," she said between the bouncing and wiggling children.

She caught a quick glimpse of Marc grinning at her from the driver's seat, but he quickly shut it down. Just like he did in the pool the evening before.

As they drove to the main strip, Parker and Sophia ranted on about break at the end of the month and the new electronics they wanted for Christmas.

The glow of old-fashioned lantern streetlights on the main strip of Willow Valley appeared. The local businesses that stayed open year around were open late tonight, advertising incredible deals to pull people in.

The streets were filled with people all bundled in their warm winter gear and gathering on the beach where the band stand stage had been cleared off and lit up for the annual lighting of the beach.

Free cocoa and popcorn stands were put on by the local business association and Parker and Sophia screamed delight on either side of her, begging to stop by there first.

They parked both vehicles behind the soap shop in their designated spots, thankful for them with every spot on the main street taken. Her sisters offered to park at Gran's for them. Gran had loved this event, and she had even left the warmth of Mrs. Calvert's bakery each year for the countdown.

Out in front of the shop, she told Marc she was going to pop in for a quick word with Peyton. He nodded understanding, knowing exactly what they needed to talk about.

Kate had been texting and calling but she had wanted to talk to her in person about trapping her in this situation. She no longer wanted to wring her neck like a string mop. Okay, that wasn't entirely true but she knew she could control the urge.

"Kate?" She cringed at the voice calling her name and

was tempted to ignore it and simply slip into the shop and lock the door behind her.

She pushed past the thought and turned to Melissa who was hurrying away from everyone else and towards her.

Melissa was gorgeous, as usual, with her long blonde hair tucked under a tightly knitted hat around her porcelain perfect face, which was not even hazed by the cold December evening. A black and white mixed wool coat hung mid length over her wide legged dress pants that were hemmed perfectly atop her glossy heeled boots.

"You dropped your glove." She held out a black glove.

"That's not mine."

Melissa looked down at it and Kate suspected she already knew it didn't belong to her.

"Oops." She smiled. "Since I have you here, I was just curious, is Marc footing the bill for your new business?"

Kate's insides tightened like a bow and arrow before it released towards its target.

She managed to level an impersonal smile for Melissa. "I don't think what my fiancé is footing concerns you, Melissa," she said, clearly sending the nosey Nancy a warning.

A cheeky smile crossed Melissa's lips as though she had gotten the answer she was seeking.

"It's all a little coincidental that your grandmother dies and leaves you this building the exact same week you start up your romance with Marc and, suddenly, you're opening a business by scratch."

That tightening feeling reached Kate's fists, and she tucked them into her coat pockets.

"I think it's your jealousy creating coincidences that don't exist to try and diminish a love that you can't seem to break through, even after all these years."

"I'm the mayor's daughter," she said in her matter-of-fact tone. Kate recognized it from the snotty teenager she'd once been. "It's not hard for to me to dig into these financial situations and find the truth."

"If you're so sly, why don't you go stand by the man that taught you?" Her father was probably less honest than Robert Caliendo.

"Worried that I'm your fiancés personal secretary? After our entanglement?"

Kate didn't let the floor shifting beneath her show in her face.

"He didn't tell you about that, did he?" Melissa's smirk rose. "How he started the whole encounter by kissing me? Not the other way around Kate. Marc kissed me."

If anyone was telling her about entangling encounters between Melissa and Marc it would be Marc. It should have been Marc.

"If you'll excuse me, there's actually a conversation inside worth my time."

Kate waited for her to walk her sly grin away before she stepped inside the shop. She let out the deep breath she'd been holding.

By the time Peyton appeared, Kate was so angry she'd forgotten she originally sought Peyton out to tear a strip out of her, not the dishonest man mingling in the crowd.

And, here she thought she'd been doing all the lying, but no, there was Marc making out, kissing, having sex with Melissa and not even warning her.

Because Kate who was so distracted, Peyton got off the hook easy. Kate accepted her insincere apology before walking to the beach with her sisters.

She spotted the Caliendos by the main stage where Melissa was laughing with her black gloved hand touching Marc's arm. Fury seared throughout Kate's body like wild lightning.

"Looks like you have some competition," Peyton whispered. "Some people never learn."

She had no idea.

They weaved their way through the crowd and Kate zeroed in on her fiancé.

Her fiancé.

How dare that little tramp flaunt herself around him like Marc wasn't engaged to his childhood sweetheart. She had removed that familiar black glove by the time Kate reached them which was good because Kate was going to tear that home wrecker's arm right out of the socket.

Kate slipped her hand into Marc's, lacing her fingers around his to get his attention.

He smiled down at her and she grabbed the front of his coat, reaching on her toes to kiss him long, and hard. She slipped her tongue inside his mouth to explore, showing Melissa exactly who he belonged to.

When she finished, Abby and Izzy whistled. Those two fed off each other.

Marc gave her a surprised look, and then kissed her forehead affectionately.

Kate grinned back and snuggled against his chest, ignoring Melissa completely.

The ceremony began shortly after the sun dipped

down behind the lake and welcomed darkness for the anticipated lighting.

The mayor stood on the main stage welcoming everyone, cracking jokes that made the crowd chuckle and clap. They were all just pawns on his chess board and one day Kate hoped someone stood up to him and checkmated him right out of the mayoral running.

When Melissa went on stage to assist her dad with the lighting of the trees, Kate ripped her hands away from Marc's. She was so ticked off her energy alone could have lit all the lights that, flickered on around them.

How bloody beautiful, she snickered inwardly.

The local bands would soon start to play and everyone would break into pleasant groups of conversation. She needed to get away from the crowd.

"I'll be back," she snarled.

He caught her arm. "You alright?"

She yanked it back. "What do you care?" she hissed so no one would hear.

Kate weaved back out through the crowd until she was at the road and could breathe.

"Hey." Marc caught up to her. "What's the matter with you?" he asked.

She spun around. "You lied to me," she accused.

He straightened his body immediately into defense mode.

Oh, like he was so damn perfect. Ha! His blood ran thick with Caliendo lies.

When Marc made no attempt to contradict what she was referring to, she informed him. "Melissa just educated me after a long dragged out accusation that I'm using you for your money, that *you* kissed *her*."

Guilt spread across his face like a forest fire.

What had she been expecting? That Melissa was lying? That he would confirm nothing had happened between them...when it so clearly had.

Sucking in the cold air, Kate turned and quickly crossed the road and down the alley. She was heading right for Gran's house. There was no way she could play house with him right now.

"Kate?"

"No." She continued walking and held her hand up to ward him off.

"Kate."

He grabbed her wrist.

She spun around claiming it back. "You lied to me," she yelled.

"Twice," he said solemnly.

Twice? Twice what?

"What?" she asked.

Their shadows were lit in the gloomy alley by a lone light against the side of the building casting a glow not far from them.

He stepped toward her and lowered his voice.

"After you left six years ago...well, it was more than just kissing. And when I returned here this year, it happened again."

Why did it feel like tears were burning the rims of her eyes?

"It was more than kissing?" She couldn't help but ask.

"It only happened the two times. I was confused and she was there so we, I don't know, made out. We didn't have sex Kate. Just like I told you at the cabin."

"Why not? Apparently you can't keep your hands off each other."

Why did it hurt so much?

This was perfect, exactly what they needed to keep them apart just like she wanted.

Marc stepped closer until he backed her against the brick wall.

"Because she's not you," he snarled, sounding frustrated.

He hovered over her and she didn't have a chance for a comeback before he crushed her body against the brick wall, his lips landing hard, angry and hungry against hers, searching, tasting, exploring...*wanting.*

His hands roamed everywhere settling under her rump and partially lifting her up and against him.

Kate gripped the front of his coat, pulling him down harder against her mouth, hungrily kissing him back, searching his mouth for answers she couldn't find.

When he lifted his mouth away they were both panting loudly.

"If you think I want her after this, than you are lying to yourself."

Marc pulled away, leaving her splayed against the wall like a tangled web.

He turned once, glaring at her, before he finally walked away.

Kate watched him cross the road without looking back.

She took a dozen well-needed deep breaths and wondered how, after that, they wouldn't dismiss their history and end up in bed.

Chapter Twenty-Four

MARC MET HIS mother for lunch the next day. They met in the back corner booth of one of the on-site restaurants. As he approached, he saw her waiting for him with a pleasant smile. He kissed her cheek before sliding across from her.

"This was a nice surprise," she said. "Encouraged by Kate I suspect."

He grinned. "It might have come up."

"I don't care how I got you for a whole lunch by myself...I'm just grateful. You've been so busy this week and I wanted to talk to you before the Snowflake Ball."

"I think I'm caught up," he assured her, knowing he was going to have to start attending breakfast and suppers again...per Kate's instructions.

Kate.

The woman was as sensitive as explosive wiring which the previous night's outbursts had confirmed.

"Carl says you both have been adjusting well," his mother said.

Marc nodded.

Marc had told her the same thing he'd told Carl which made a sincere smile of relief cross her face.

"Isabelle hasn't talked to him yet. She's dropped the uncle."

So had he.

"So, I guess that's a start, but she's all over...I can't sit her down," she glanced up. "Like you," she winked.

"Mother, that's Isabelle and she'll come around."

Their lunch was served and they chit chatted until the plates were removed and he thought that was their cue to leave.

"These are three of Robert's files." Eliza lifted a stack of manila files from the seat beside her and set them in front of her. As she opened the first one, she said, "These are locals that needed help." She turned the papers, sliding them across the table in front of him. There was a picture of an older man taken from a distance. "That's Donald Cooper. He lived on a farm outside of town. His farm got into some trouble years back and he borrowed money from Robert. Of course, when Robert's involved there's always a catch. When the banks wouldn't help, Robert would step in. He helped Mr. Cooper pay the debts owed on the farm so his children..." She flipped the page to another family photo with Donald and four young boys and a girl. "These are his children grown. He wanted them to carry on the family business. However interest was never interest with Robert. He always wanted to keep you in his back pocket."

"I don't understand."

"He never named his price right away. Instead, that person went into a 'they owe me in the future' file. Donald Cooper, I don't know if you remember, he died in a barn fire a few years back."

Marc stilled, not sure he wanted to know the rest.

"When Donald refused to do what your father wanted years after the farm was paid off, then Robert had someone else who owed him burn the barn down and unfortunately he was in the barn when it went up in flames."

Marc had to ask. "Was that his intention?"

She shook her head. "I don't believe so Marc. The insurance on the barn had been discontinued, that was Robert's doing and the kids lost their dad and the business in that fire."

That was terrible.

She slid the next file over to him. "This is the man who did it." She flipped it open and tapped on a picture of another older man he didn't recognize. She flipped another page to a picture of a family. "And this is why he did it. This is his family, the family Robert threatened if he didn't do what Robert asked."

"What are you going to do with this?"

Her shoulders dropped. "Right now, nothing. I want to set it all right but, more importantly, I want you to understand why this man..." she reached over, tapping the fire starter's face. "Did what he did and why it, unfortunately, resulted in a death. No doubt he can't handle the regret of this moment."

"I don't think there's any understanding this," Marc said sadly. "He shouldn't have done it."

"I agree with you, he shouldn't have. But, let's take a walk in his shoes. He didn't feel he had an alternative. He was in Robert's books and, after you're in those books, you have no choice. I can't say for sure but I will bet his threat was if he didn't set the fire, someone would set it to his house."

"Mother, that's terrible."

"What would you do in that man's shoes? If you owed a man who threatened your family? What would you do

Marcus? Would you let the man hurt us or start a barn fire?"

Marcus understood. "I would never let anything happen to any of you."

She smiled, relieved.

"So what are your plans?"

"To sit down with all of my children after I figure out a plan. I want to talk to you about Katherine. Before the Snowflake Ball, I want you to understand."

Marc already knew and, now more than ever, he understood what Robert had been capable of and what Kate had been forced into. No doubt that third file belonged to his fiancée.

***

DAYS LATER, AFTER Marc had time to process all that his mother had revealed to him, he walked into the ballroom where the Snowflake Ball staff party would take place in only two days. And when they would announce their engagement to the staff...and whoever else Eliza had invited.

The main lights were off, but the twinkle lights illuminated the room. He spotted a ladder in the middle of the dance floor and made his way over to talk to his future father-in-law to be. Kent's daughter had been playing hide and seek with Marc and he had taken the last few days to think over the file his mother had shown him. Kate's file.

He found Kate, instead for Kent, straddling the top of a seven-foot ladder, her hands working away. Now he understood and he felt the burden and sadness of the secret she held. Helping her dad, some things never change.

"Dad honestly, you need better strength glasses, you didn't even cut this one before you put it up!" She yelled in the direction of the stage. "We'll have to take it down."

Kate was shaking her head but Marc could see a smile on her face until she looked down and spotted him. She drew her lips in and gave him a wave. At least this was under better circumstances. Well, kind of.

"Hey," she said,   flipping a leg over the ladder and making her way down the silver stairs with grace. She wasn't afraid of a towering ladder but there was no way she would sit on a horse.

She skipped the last three steps and hopped off landing in front of him. "How was brunch with your mom?"

"Good."

"Did she get everything off her chest?"

He nodded. She had no idea.

Kate smiled. "Good. She's been taking me aside all week with questions and I thought it best she hear from you."

A slow song flowed from the speakers on low.

Kate chuckled. "That's my dad," she said, stating the obvious.

Knowing Kent was standing somewhere in the shadows watching them, Marc put out his hands. Without asking, she knew and stepped into his arms.

"I don't know when he became such a romantic," she whispered in his ear.

They barely moved, his arm wrapped around her waist and her arm resting against his with her hand clutching his shoulder. Their free hands held each other, close to their side, an intimate embrace.

"In two days we will be standing in this exact room announcing our engagement," he said.

"Thanks to Peyton," she grumbled.

"Kate, I don't want to do this under false pretenses."

She tilted her head to look at him with a quirky grin. "I didn't concoct this plan. You did," she reminded him with a little tease in her eyes.

"I don't want it to be a concocted plan. I want it to be true."

She stopped moving and took a step back. "I don't understand."

He pulled her close. He liked how her body fit snuggly against his, but he was more afraid she would run.

"I have been really angry about your deal with my dad."

She remained silent.

"But you weren't totally honest with me either." She stiffened like a board on the ladder.

He continued to move them slowly, their hips swaying together, their chests rubbing against each other until she was moving in rhythm with him again.

"He threatened you." Marc didn't ask her because he already knew. "He threatened your family. He didn't just offer you money like you claimed, did he Kate?" He needed to hear it from her.

The closest answer he received was a small shake of her head against his chest.

"Even when I was furious with you for taking money from my dad, I didn't want you to go. And before any of that, I accepted Peyton's crazy proposal because you weren't answering my calls." He paused taking a deep breath. "I thought when you discovered our plan, you would object."

He stopped moving and ran his fingers down her arms to grasp her hands in his. She was trembling and slowly her eyes traveled the length of his body and landed on his.

"I love you Katherine McAdams."

He saw her swallow, hard.

"I want to walk into that room with you with intentions to marry you."

The silence escaladed when the song ended, leaving them standing there listening to their breathing.

"I would bend down right now on one knee and properly propose to you, but your father is watching."

A small sound, like a strangled chuckled, escaped her lips and her eyes fell to the floor. He lifted her chin with his hand.

"I don't need an answer now. I want you to know, although I don't feel it's my place to say if you need to hear it from me...I forgive you." He cupped her face. "When you're ready to tell me what happened, I want you to know I will never blame you with a threat like that hanging over your head. Ever. For anything."

Tears were forming in her eyes but he could see she wasn't ready to tell him the story. He leaned down and kissed her softly, lovingly. He knew once she worked up the courage to talk to him about Robert they would be able to move past this together.

"I will forgive you," he said against her lips and walked away.

***

MARC TEXTED KATE that night asking her to meet him in the study. He feared she might sneak away in the night feeling unable to be honest with him. He planned a distraction to ease her mind and what better way to get a smile on her face than to make an ass of himself.

He left the study door open and she walked in, hesitantly. She was already dressed in her night attire, black yoga pants and a loose shirt that hung low down one shoulder.

"Sit," he said, pointing at the couch.

She did as he instructed. "You're not going to propose to me again?" Her tone seemed repulsed.

He shook his head. "No. Can you stop trying to marry me for my money for one second?"

A smile almost touched the corner of her lips.

"It's impossible to stay a bachelor in this place. First Melissa's all over me every down moment I have and now you." He winked at her, but she crossed her arms defensively. "A little much?"

"A little."

"Alright, so close your eyes," he said.

She arched an eyebrow at him.

"Come on," he insisted.

Reluctantly, her eyelashes swept down against her porcelain skin. He grabbed the plaid shirt he'd found in his closet slipping into it. It was a lot snugger than when he was sixteen and the edge of the sleeves lifted up above his wrists. He shrugged into the orange vest that left a little more room. Then he ran his hands through his hair, messing it up. He added his old round glasses as the finishing touch.

On the coffee table in front of her was his laptop with all the "Back to the Future" movie series ready to watch.

"Alright, open them."

Her eyes blinked open, and ran up and down his outfit, then to his hair and glasses.

She smiled rising to her feet. "Where did you get that?" She touched his glasses. "Are these your old glasses?"

He nodded, and grabbed the bottom edge of his vest giving it a tug. "In the back of my closet."

Kate's eyes widened. "You kept it?"

He nodded.

"You know Caliendo, that's a little bit strange."

"You think?" he asked, innocently.

She nodded. "I do."

"Tonight, I'm just that awkward nerdy boy in love and you're just that confident..." He ran his hands through her hair and tousled it.

She caught his hands. "Hey."

He cupped her face. "Wild haired girl not realizing tonight's the night I plan on kissing you."

"I knew you planned it."

"For weeks."

She smiled and reached up and kissed him.

"Had to change the story, didn't you?"

"I'm just more spontaneous than you."

"Come on." They settled together on the couch with popcorn and soda.

"I thought maybe we were breaking into a kitchen."

"I own all the keys so it's kind of lost its appeal." Although he was sure she could make it appealing.

***

MARC AWOKE STRETCHED out on the sofa with Kate curled up beside him, her back pressed against his front. Her head rested on his arm, her hair spilling in every direction and her arms entwined around his.

The blank screen on the laptop was glowing. He reached across and shut it off, then wrapped his arm back around Kate and closed his eyes, but quickly reopened them.

Across the room, edging the bottom of the wall, was light glowing through a crack.

What was that?

He didn't want to move away from the warmth of Kate, but he needed to know what was in there.

Slowly, trying not to wake her, he sat up and climbed over her, sliding off the couch.

He bent down on the floor and examined the thin line of light about four feet wide underneath an ordinary plain paneled wall.

He stood, stepped back and stared. A thought crossed his mind, but there was no way. They weren't living in a castle with secret passages. However, his dad had designed this living area.

Feeling silly and still needing to know, he walked over to the wall and started pushing. He had no idea what he was looking for and nothing moved. He stepped back. This was ridiculous.

He glanced at Kate.

What would she say if she saw him? She would likely push him away and dive into figure it out.

He walked over to the edge of the light, settled his hand on the wall and pulled to see if it would slide open. It didn't. He went to the other side and repeated the action and this time the wall wiggled beneath his hands, but still wouldn't open. He ran his finger up the paneling to a picture. He pulled it down and found a latch behind it. That was it.

This was where Robert's life was, he knew it even before the door opened.

When he pulled the latch the panel slid open. A large wooden desk sat in the middle of a room lined with floor to ceiling cabinets. They must contain the files he'd been seeking.

He found it.

He cautiously walked inside the room as though he was afraid of being caught. He ran his hand along the desk and touched the desk lamp.

He remembered back to the day he'd found the study door locked and Carl had exited claiming a nap had overtaken him inside the room.

Marc almost grinned.

His parents already knew, and this was where his mother had retrieved those three files for their brunch.

He'd barely had time to relish in his find when he heard Kate stirring.

"Marc?"

He turned to her. "I found it. This is everything my father was hiding." He was happy and overwhelmed at the same time, even if his parents already knew about it. He wasn't concerned about the work it was going to be to check out all these files, but he was nervous about what he would find written inside. The three files so far had caused sadness deep within him knowing Robert was responsible for all that heartache.

Kate stepped into the room looking around. He could see exhaustion, surprise and confusion claiming her body all at the same time. He knew how she felt.

"It's probably generations of files," Marc explained.

His father's and grandfather's and if those files today were any indication, there were a lot of ruined lives within these cabinets.

"Wouldn't your uncle know about this?" Her words cut into his thoughts.

He was ready to dive in but he looked over at Kate and saw how exhausted she seemed, but also how incredibly sexy. He would enjoy taking her back to the couch and making love to her. He grabbed her hand shedding the thought. She wasn't ready.

"Come on, let's go back to sleep."

Back on the couch, he pulled a blanket over them. She lie against him, this time her body facing his chest and their feet entwined.

Just as he was beginning to drift off he heard her whisper, "I love you, too, Marc."

Chapter Twenty-Five

MARC HADN'T BEEN able to locate Kate all day. When he'd awoken at five, she'd vanished from the study and wasn't in his suite. She hadn't shown up for breakfast or lunch. He had attended both in case she was there, but nothing. She had just simply vanished. No one had seen her and she wasn't answering her cell. He had texted Peyton who texted the rest of their sisters but they hadn't heard from her all day either.

Maybe she was devising a way to talk to him, needing her space. Maybe she had run away. He hoped the latter was incorrect but it still nagged him all day.

The day hadn't been an office day for him, but Melissa had hounded him with a list of people needing his assistance throughout the resort. From Snowflake Ball details to the sprinkler in the water park to a meeting in the ski wing. It was well into the evening before he had ticked off the last item on the list.

On his way back to his suite, he stepped into Robert's study hoping to see Kate. Hoping she was ready to tell him the truth...the whole truth.

His laptop was sitting on the coffee table where he had left it. As he reached for it, he heard a sound from behind the wall...in Robert's secret room. Normally, he might have shrugged off the noise, more than likely it was one of his parents. They had probably been in that room at other time when he had been in the study.

Marc was planning on telling Eliza and Carl he'd found the room—it wasn't a huge secret anymore—but he'd been too busy to do it today. But as he pushed the hiding wall open he was surprised to find Kate

Kate threw a file she'd been flipping through into a massive pile that she'd strewn across the entire length of the floor. She sat encircled by closed files and opened files spewed around her like petals of a flower with her at the center. She was deep into another file and didn't notice him.

She still wore in her pajamas. Her hair was strewn everywhere, frizzy like she had raked her hands through the locks hundreds of times. Shadowy circles rimmed her eyes; eyes that were bugging out at the amount of papers. She looked exhausted. She looked terrible.

Had she been in here all day?

"Kate?" he said her name softly so as not to startle her.

Her head snapped up so quickly it startled him.

She didn't look surprised by the interruption or guilty for sneaking around in Robert's secret room. She looked strung out, staring at him, but not really seeing him.

"These are coded," she said finally. "They are coded," she spat the words out with distaste. "Did you know they were coded?"

The words came out like an accusation and she didn't wait for him to answer. She stood up, trudged her sockless feet across the strewn papers, not even caring about the mess he'd have to clean later and made her way to one of the many filing cabinets that had doors pulled open, half shut or shut completely. She had made one hell of a mess. He didn't know how they were going to clean this up. He had known they were coded, which meant filing through them now was going to be a massive challenge. He might very well pass this on to Carl after he got Kate out of here.

"Kate, what are you doing?"

She didn't look up at him, but she had heard him. She rambled on without pause. "You won't understand and I'm not dragging you into this. It will make you sad. I'm sad. I'm sad all the time. No matter how much I push it down, it just pops right up. Do you want to be sad?"

He didn't know whether she was being rhetorical or wanted an answer.

"I'm not sure."

"I'm sure. It was the right thing to do. I think about it and think about it and now, now it's worse being here because I look at you and I know you don't know and I know and Carl knows."

Her ramblings were hard to understand but he would be even more confused had he not already read the file she frantically searched for now.

"I think about how different it could have been but I know it could never turn out that way." She stopped and glanced around. "But it's here Marc. The file is here. It's somewhere. I know it is. He wouldn't have thrown it away."

No, he certainly hadn't.

"Kate, talk to me."

"You won't understand."

"Help me to understand."

"No." She shook her head. "You think you can

forgive me, Marc, but you will hate me. I hate me."

He should have looked for her earlier and maybe she wouldn't have ended up so distraught.

"Kate?"

"I just need to know, Marc," she said loudly, firmly. She looked up. "I'm sorry. This will change everything. I know that. I will leave. I promise and I won't come back this time. Not ever."

Leave?

He just asked her to marry him. Why was running her first instinct? Because of Robert, that's why.

He tried to talk but she continued overtaking him. "I know what I'm risking. I know I'm risking my sister's business, I know. But, it's right here at my fingertips. Somewhere." The last word came out exasperated and her hands flew up in the air. "You know I tried on my own, to look it up, but he's good. Your dad was good."

"Kate, my dad...Robert's not here."

"Of course he's not here. If he was here I certainly wouldn't be. He made sure to that."

Marc was beginning to get frustrated talking in circles with her and getting nowhere. She knew, he knew and all she had to do was say it.

He crossed the room and gently touched her arm, stroking slowly to her hands and deftly taking the file away. "Kate." He held both her hands in his, to keep her focused on him. "I will help you find the file you are looking for. We can read it together, but first you have to tell me what happened. I don't want the file version...I want your version."

She stared down at their hands.

"Kate, look at me."

She shook her head.

"Kate."

He saw tears streaming down her cheeks and her hands trembled beneath his touch.

She licked her lips before speaking. "I just want to know what it was." She sounded defeated. "A girl or a boy and I want to make sure he or she is alright." She sucked in a breath. "I need to know your dad didn't lie to me and that the baby was put in a safe home."

There it was—the truth from the file his mom had slipped across the table to him. He'd read it. He knew.

"Our baby," she finally clarified. If he hadn't already read the file the news would have knocked him off his feet. He'd hardly been able to stay in his seat at the restaurant and his mother had gone from sweet and strong to strong and solid, demanding he sit down instead of chasing down Kate.

How could Robert ever do something so cruel to either of them...to Kate? A woman who had done nothing wrong and was dragged through a six year hell because of Marc. It was his family that ripped her from her family and chased her away with threats. He tore away her child. *Their child.*

"The file is not here." The familiar woman's voice came from behind them.

Marc turned to find his parents standing in the wide door he had left open. They both looking guilty.

He felt Kate's hands grip the back of his shirt tightly and he glanced back to find her hiding behind him.

"It's a girl, Kate." His mother's soft voice wafted through the room and whirled around them like a comforting blanket. "Her name is Rosemary and she is safe."

Kate's grip loosened and he felt her forehead lie against his back.

"Robert didn't lie to you. She lives in the Maritimes with an older lady and she calls her Grandma."

He felt dampness through the back of his shirt before he realized Kate was crying.

"Her grandmother is sick and we are in the beginning steps of arranging their both move here."

Kate stilled behind him and then he felt her grip slide.

His mother called, "Marc catch her!"

***

THEY CALLED THE onsite medic to Robert's study after Kate had passed out and they'd informed Marc that she'd had a panic attack. Marc was thankful it was nothing more. When she'd slid down behind him, he'd caught her just as her body hit the floor. It had been one of the scariest moments of his life.

The ruckus in the suites alerted Izzy, who immediately texted Abby, who in return informed all her sisters. And, in exactly a half hour, his suite was filled with every Caliendo and McAdams, concerned about Kate.

Her sisters were in the room with Kate and he gave them space, already knowing the reasons she had passed out.

He stood there through all the commotion thinking about a scared, young pregnant girl forced on the run by Robert. And, not just any girl, his Kate...his girl, his woman. He would have never let anything happen to her or to her family. She must have known that and still she'd left.

He stayed tucked away in the corner of the kitchen by

himself watching his sisters pace and sit, then stand and pace again, worried about Kate and clueless to the events that had taken place in the secret room. He watched his mom cross the distance between them to stand by his side.

"Marc."

He held his hand up. "Not right now."

"Sweetheart..."

"I'm very upset, Mother. This should have never gone this far." He knew she agreed, but he said it anyway. "He should have never been allowed to get away with the things he did and especially not when it came to Kate."

"Marc, I didn't know."

"Did you suspect?"

She nodded.

He pushed himself away from the counter. "Damn it, Mom, I have a daughter," he snarled...obviously a little louder than anticipated because all the women looked over at them and stared.

He rolled his eyes inwardly, shook his head and leaned back against the counter crossing his arms.

"Kate's pregnant?" Of course it would be Izzy to press the issue. "She doesn't look pregnant. How would you know it's a girl so soon? Isn't there like a waiting time before you know and wouldn't she be showing?"

Why did everything in his life have to turn into a dramatic family event? Sometimes he missed the quiet life he'd created living down south where he answered only to himself.

Violet elbowed Izzy. Violet understood.

Izzy rubbed her side and hugged her stomach. "What?"

"We should go," Violet suggested and Izzy sent her a questioning look.

At that point Marc couldn't thank his sister enough until she grabbed Izzy's arm and pulled her reluctantly from the room with Emma lagging behind.

"Filter Izzy, seriously," Violet scolded, leaving him with his mother and Carl.

"I'm sorry, Marc. All I can do is try to fix it," his mother said.

"I hope this can be fixed because she isn't taking it well."

He excused himself and went to his bedroom.

The light from the hallway cast a glow across his bed where the McAdams' sisters had all somehow managed to fit into his bed. Kate was asleep surrounded by her siblings.

He heard his suite door shut and knew his parents had left. He quietly closed the door and made his way back into the living room.

Pulling a blanket from the couch, he laid down and hoped the morning sunlight would bring a new glow to their lives.

Hopefully they could sit down and begin to pick up the pieces Robert had carelessly thrown from a mountain top.

Chapter Twenty-Six

KATE'S HEAD FELT heavy as her eyes fluttered opened. She had a deep, dark feeling inside her that mixed with relief.

Rosemary, she thought with a partial smile.

Marc. Her stomach knotted.

Humiliation, disgust and shame poured through her like running water. She could only imagine what he felt. She knew from the soft sheets and smell of Marc, she was in his bed. He wasn't beside her anymore, but three sisters were. Oh Lord, they would know. She had to leave.

The clock on the nightstand read past three in the morning. She quickly scrambled out of the bed and dressed. Marc would be furious with all the lies and secrets. She didn't want to face his sad eyes.

She didn't turn the lights on. She knew the way to the door and down the hall. As she slipped on her shoes and reached for the door handle, the light above her turned on trapping her like a criminal.

Her stomach tightened.

This could go on of two ways. The person behind her was going to either be his parents assigned to watching her...or Marc.

She would much rather face his parents.

She turned.

It was the latter.

Marc was sitting in the overstuffed chair, wide awake. His eyes weren't sleepy or foggy like her own. He stared at her. Hard. She stared back because she didn't know what else to do. They stared at one another for a long period before he asked, "Are you sneaking out?"

Her eyes fell. That was exactly what she was doing. How could she deny it?

"It's best I do," Kate said.

"Best for who?"

"For you."

"How is that best for me?" Marc asked. "Enlighten me with your rationality on this subject. It certainly isn't best for you. For all you know you could have a concussion."

He sat back awaiting her reply.

"I don't have a concussion."

"How do you know?"

Why were they talking about a concussion?

"I guess I don't, but I don't care either way."

"I care." That's what he always said.

"Why are we talking about this?" She was so frustrated.

"Why wouldn't we?"

"Why do you care?"

"Why wouldn't I?"

"Marc stop!" she yelled.

Why was he sitting in here waiting for her to sneak out and why didn't he just let her go?

"There she is," he said, and his lips curved upwards.

"What are you talking about?" she asked, annoyed

and confused.

"Stop cowering behind your fear. Stop letting the past control your actions today. You were planning on sneaking out of here instead of facing me."

"You don't need me to face you. I'm sure you don't need for me to tell you anything."

He stood up and folded his arms across his chest as if guarding himself from her. That was exactly what he needed to do with her. She was nothing but the enemy.

"Stop telling me what you think I want or need. Stop giving me half-truths that don't allow me to judge fairly. My life is my decision and I want you to tell me the truth. All of it, from beginning to end."

"I'm sure your parents already have."

"I want to hear it from you, Kate. I want you to tell me everything."

Everything?

Had he gone mad, they would be here until the sun rose and set again. "I don't want to."

"Because you're cowering."

"I'm not cowering. I'm accepting what I have done and..."

"Sneaking away."

Yes. Exactly.

"If I stand here and pour out my heart what does it solve? Nothing."

"In the last three days everything in my life has changed and I'm standing here with a woman who left with my baby and got rid of her."

It hurt the way he said it even if he wasn't intending it that way.

"And never told me about her. So now I have to hear it from you." When she didn't speak he rubbed his hands across his face. "Honestly Kate, I'm trying so hard not to lose it here, but don't think I won't."

She stared at him. He was there, only feet away from her. She had longed for this moment since the day she walked out of his life, a confrontation. But as the days had turned into years, that emotion had left and now as she stood here, she wished she could remember just one of the practised scenarios that had played out in her head.

"I hit a guy in the face because you left me and it shattered my hand so my dream of being a surgeon was gone in an instant, as were you." That didn't help. "We both have a lot of secrets. Your turn."

She took a deep breath. "When I came here to tell you I was..." Another deep breath. This was so hard. "...pregnant, I was scared. I was a little excited but mostly I was scared and you hadn't arrived home yet. But Robert greeted me and he knew. I don't know how since I hardly knew." Another deep breath. Her lungs were definitely going to be clear by the end of this, an easy trail for air.

She wanted to race through the rest but if she was going to tell the story, she might as well tell him the entire truth. That was what he thought he wanted.

"He asked me into his study and told me, not suggested, that I was leaving and I would get rid of the baby and never come back. Robert terrified me and at the same time I wasn't about to back down to him." She crossed her hands over her middle. "He threatened my family. All of them. Gran, Dad, Peyton, Sydney, Abby and Avery. Especially my dad. But he said if I left, he would set up trust funds for all my sisters for college as long as I promised never to return or contact you." She looked back up at him. "Your turn."

"I went south and worked at a resort to spite my, at the time, dad. Continue."

That was an easy copout, but who was she to decide which lie or deceit was worse.

"I would have never left if he hadn't threatened my family," Kate said. "But he did, so I felt I had no other alternative. And I couldn't just get rid of the baby, our baby. I was so far away that I thought I could just keep the baby and he would never know. But before the baby was due, he had sent a nurse or doctor, I'm not sure, to my house and when it...she was born, they took her. I didn't even get to see her and I was left there alone with a nurse. No family. Only a full bank account, so I started a new life. Your turn."

Maybe if it had something to do with hurting her or lying or deceiving her that would make her feel less guilty.

"I never stopped loving you."

Was he kidding? That didn't help at all.

"I never stopped loving you," she said back.

"I agreed to your sister's ridiculous plan in hopes to get close to you."

"Your uncle agreed to let me pay off my debt if I could keep you distracted...the day at the cabin."

"You have a lot more secrets."

Her shoulders slumped. "I know."

Marc closed the distance between them and she felt his warm hands wrap around hers. She stared down at the floor unable to look up at him. She didn't understand what was going on between them.

"If Robert were alive now I would put him in the ground, for you," Marc said. "For us. For Rosemary."

Kate looked up.

"Here we stand again in a room full of lies and all I can think about is how to keep you here. I understand all the reasons. It doesn't hurt less inside."

She looked down, again. Of course, she'd hurt him.

He lifted her chin up to look at him. "I'm here Kate. I love you. I am just waiting to see if you want to stay here with me or sneak away."

He loved her so much, she could see it, and she had known all along. But now he loved her through her lies and deception. It was all out on the table like a card game and he was waiting for her to make her next move.

"I never want to sneak away from you again," Kate said.

He kissed her lips, then her forehead and hugged her. She never wanted him to let her go.

"Do you have a picture?" she asked. "In the file? Of her?"

He nodded.

Together on the couch, snuggled beneath a blanket, he passed her a manila file, the same as the ones she had seen in Robert's study.

She looked up at him before opening it. "I never thought this day would come. I never let myself dream of you understanding. Not now after all the years that have passed."

He kissed the side of her head and nudged her to open the file. It wasn't a file anything like the other ones in his office. It was picture after picture of their tiny baby. Pictures of her growing up.

"Rosemary's grandmother has been sending these to my mother for us," he told her. "It's her life."

"I have to tell my sisters. I have to tell them everything."

***

As the sun rose, they looked through hundreds of pictures that summed up the life of their daughter to the present day.

Her sisters emerged from his bedroom together looking like sleep had eluded them during the night. They looked at the pictures and Kate told them everything.

Chapter Twenty-Seven

MARC WOULD HAVE enjoyed skipping the Snowflake Ball to curl up with his fiancée in his suite...alone. But Kate had insisted, with all the bustling excitement throughout the resort, that he was required to make an appearance. He was surprised after everything between them that she didn't want a break from his family, from the resort. He knew he sure did.

He smiled, making his rounds to the staff doing a little chit-chat with everyone, losing sight of Kate, popping in and out of the crowds.

The manager of the ski hill talked about the spike in younger kids with the new bear hill, and that they might need to hire on some extra help the following year. That was always a plus. More people equaled more money.

The twinkle lights draped above the room weaved through sparkling hanging organza with large plastic snowflakes and spinning icicles suspended across the length of the ceiling. The glittering, spinning mirror ball seemed to enlighten and transform the room around him into the magical ball his sister had always intended to create.

He caught sight of his wife-to-be. For the first time, he experienced what the guests must experience when they entered an event planned by Violet.

Kate was beautiful. The long shimmering blue dress hugged her slim body and showed off every curve and he wanted to run his hand along every one. The neckline of her dress dipped low and his eyes couldn't help but travel to the see-through lace that extended across her arms. The dress just graced the floor and flowed elegantly behind her as she walked...directly towards him.

Her magnificent eyes sparkled with specks of green, blue and brown soaked in desire. And love.

After the battle they fought since she had come back to Willow Valley, he had finally uncovered her secret and her love for him.

"You look beautiful."

She smiled. "You don't look too bad yourself."

He touched his designer tux. "Oh, this old thing?" He brushed off the shoulder and she laughed against his lips. He turned serious. "Has it been too much tonight? Should we go?"

His mother and Violet had opened the adjoining ballroom and was sharing the staff party with their engagement party. It had turned out to be a huge gala.

She touched his hand softly. "Dance with me."

His anxious being slowed as he led her across the floor and to where he'd found her straddling the seven-foot ladder only days earlier. Images of them in his suite with her straddling him flashed in his head.

He mentally shook the thoughts away, but not too far away. He fully intended on ending the evening with that scenario.

Marc pulled her close in his arms and began slowly moving her across the dance floor. He'd wanted to attend this party with Kate as his real fiancée and here she was in his arms, forever. He was never letting her go again. There would be no more secrets between them.

"I love you Marcus Caliendo," she whispered. "I never dreamed a day like this could be possible."

He knew another dream she'd kept at bay and he was going to sweep her off her feet and fly her away.

"I love you Katherine McAdams," he whispered back. "I always dreamed a day like this was possible."

She laughed and peered up to look at him. "Thank you, Marc. For understanding."

He cupped her face and pulled her forehead against his. "No more secrets."

She shook her head against him. "I will never hide anything from you again."

"I will never let you go again."

"You will never have to."

He kissed her, loving her warm wine flavored lips as the sky opened up as Emma had promised and white, thick flakes fell from the sky encircling them in a winter wonderland.

Kate smiled and pulled away to look up. "This is amazing."

He caught Emma's eyes across the room and she raised her hands as if saying, *I told you so*, then winked.

He wrapped his arms around Kate's waist, pulling her against him and picking her feet off the floor enough to twirl them.

As the ball was coming to an end, Marc walked Kate toward *their* suite. He liked how that sounded. But before they made it that far he took her to the back door of her favorite restaurant—the only one that had ice cream—and pulled our his card.

"We don't use keys anymore."

She pouted, then snatched the card from him, knowing exactly what was to follow.

As they sat in the kitchen on the floor against the metal fridge sharing a bowl of ice cream, he decided they had shared a lot of good moments in this kitchen and he wanted to add one more before they had to grow up and not act like teenagers.

"I was thinking we should take a couple weeks off and get away."

"After Christmas?"

"I was actually thinking we could start tomorrow."

She glanced up at him surprised. "Tomorrow? The month is just starting."

He nodded. There were a lot of things happening, but he had already sat down and discussed it with his parents. "Yes, we're flying to the Maritimes."

The hand holding a spoonful of ice cream paused mid-air to her mouth. "Are you serious?"

He nodded.

"Tomorrow?"

He nodded.

Her eyes turned into large round olive saucers and her hands flew around his neck, ice cream, spoon and all.

***

KATE SAT HUNCHED down behind the snow fort wall they had built and waited...waited...and then boom! The snowball came flying over the wall and landed at her feet. High pitched hysterical giggles followed from the other side of the wall and she stood up holding her own handful of snow.

"Which one of you was it?" she asked planting a gloved hand on her hip and threatening with her snowball.

Marc's guilty eyes stared back her and even then the little mini them with her brunette curls halfway down her back and matching guilty blue eyes pointed at Marc.

"Hey," he teased, ruffling her hat. She giggled again.

Kate lifted, aimed and threw the snowball at Marc who dodged it, then lifted Rosemary into the air flying her in a circle before calling, "Let's get her."

They were running toward Kate when Rosemary's "grandmother" called them into the house. "Hot cocoa is ready. With mini marshmallows."

Rosemary cheered and started toward the house.

Marc grabbed Kate's hand and gave her cheek a kiss before they followed the tiny footprints in the snow.

It had only been a week since she recalled parking in front of the small farmhouse with her nerves unraveling like a cat rolling a ball of yarn around the house.

"Are you ready?" Marc had asked her.

She had shaken her head. "No, I'm not."

He had waited and she had stared at the little house knowing beyond those walls was the one person that had been in her head like the background noise of a radio. It had happened all so suddenly. She had just found out about Rosemary, finally after all these years, locked and sealed her relationship with Marc and here they were, together. She wasn't alone. She would never be alone now that the truth was out and he had forgiven her. What an amazing man was by her side. But she had been worried before they had knocked on that door.

Would she like them? Would they bond? Would she ever grow to love them?

"Aren't you scared?" she had asked Marc.

"I've never been more scared in my life."

"Me, too."

He squeezed her hand. "I've also never been happier."

She smiled at him. "Me, too."

Now, here they were and it hadn't been nearly as scary as she had first anticipated. Soon they would all be returning to the resort...together. It was amazing what they had accomplished in the short time together...the three of them...as a family.

Rosemary stopped walking and turned her heart-quenching grin at them.

Her grandmother had done an amazing job raising a polite, sweet little angel. Rosemary waited for them to catch up then separated their hands, replacing them with her own for the walk back to the farmhouse.

Kate's heart warmed and she looked up at Marc and almost laughed at his mushy grin. This little girl had him wrapped around her little finger and it was adorable.

THE END

LAKESHORE SECRETS

Next in the Series:

Lakeshore Legends

The McAdams Sisters

Book Two, Peyton McAdams

By The Lake Series

Shannyn Leah

SHANNYN LEAH

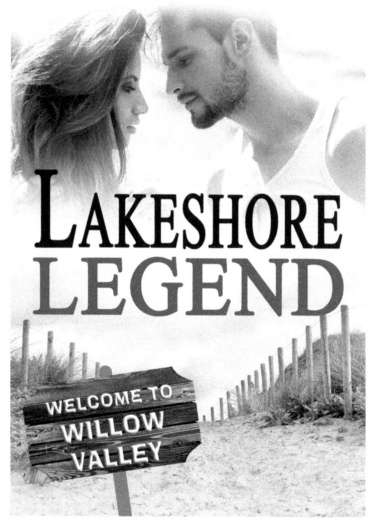

LAKESHORE
LEGEND

WELCOME TO
WILLOW
VALLEY

SHANNYN LEAH

By The Lake Series

The McAdams Sisters:
Lakeshore Secrets (Book One)
Lakeshore Legend (Book Two)
Lakeshore Love (Book Three)
Lakeshore Candy (Book Four)
Lakeshore Lyrics (Book Five)

The Caliendo Series:
Sunset Thunder (Book One)
Sunset Rivalry (Book Two)
Sunset Sail (Book Three)
Sunset Flare (Book Four)
Sunset Shelter (Book Five)

SHANNYN LEAH

Contemporary romance author Shannyn Leah loves olives, lip gloss and reading (and writing) romance novels. Her love of words started at an early age and soon grew until, during her teenage years, she'd started writing her own novels. When her mom pushed to finally publish some of the stories, she quickly amassed two complete romance series (By The Lake and Caliendo Resort series) and, in 2016, released her first Fantasy Romance entitled The Gatekeepers (Part One of the Winters Rising series).

When she's not writing contemporary romance books into the early hours of the morning, Shannyn can be found antiquing with her two favorite people, her momma and sister, in their picturesque London, Ontario hometown.

Shannyn would love to get to know her readers as you get to know her (just don't send her any carrots!)Join her mailing list to be notified when new books are released, exclusive excerpts and prizes:

www.shannynleah.com/contact.php

Connect with Her

Visit her webpage for extras:

www.shannynleah.com

Please join Shannyn Leah on her facebook page if you enjoy her books here:

www.facebook.com/pages/Shannyn-Leah/ 418700801622719

If you wish to get in contact with Shannyn, please email her at

Shannynleah@gmail.com

CPSIA information can be obtained
at www.ICGtesting.com
Printed in the USA
LVHW091957221118
597947LV00001B/105/P

9 781366 027696